P9-DGZ-642

*

ALPHABET of DREAMS

ALSO BY SUSAN FLETCHER

THE DRAGON CHRONICLES
Dragon's Milk
Flight of the Dragon Kyn
Sign of the Dove

✳

The Stuttgart Nanny Mafia

✳

Shadow Spinner

✳

Walk Across the Sea

ALPHABET of DREAMS

*

SUSAN FLETCHER

ginee seo books
ATHENEUM BOOKS FOR YOUNG READERS
New York ✷ London ✷ Toronto ✷ Sydney

Atheneum Books for Young Readers
An imprint of Simon & Schuster Children's Publishing Division
1230 Avenue of the Americas, New York, New York 10020
Book design by Krista Vossen
Map illustration on pages vi–vii by Rick Britton
The text for this book is set in New Baskerville.
Manufactured in the United States of America
First Edition
2 4 6 8 10 9 7 5 3 1
Library of Congress Cataloging-in-Publication Data
Fletcher, Susan, 1951–
Alphabet of dreams / Susan Fletcher.—1st ed.
p. cm.
"Ginee Seo Books."
Summary: Fourteen-year-old Mitra, of royal Persian lineage, and her five-year-old brother
Babak, whose dreams foretell the future, flee for their lives in the company of the magus
Melchoir and two other Zoroastrian priests, traveling through Persia as they follow star
signs leading to a newly-born king in Bethlehem. Includes historical notes.
ISBN-13: 978-0-689-85042-4
ISBN-10: 0-689-85042-5
1. Iran—History—To 640—Juvenile fiction. [1. Iran—History—To 640—Fiction.
2. Princesses—Fiction. 3. Brothers and sisters—Fiction. 4. Dreams—Fiction.
5. Zoroastrianism—Fiction. 6. Jesus Christ—Nativity—Fiction.] I. Title.
PZ7.F6356Alp 2006
[Fic]—dc22
2005036264

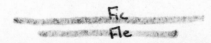

To my sister, Laura

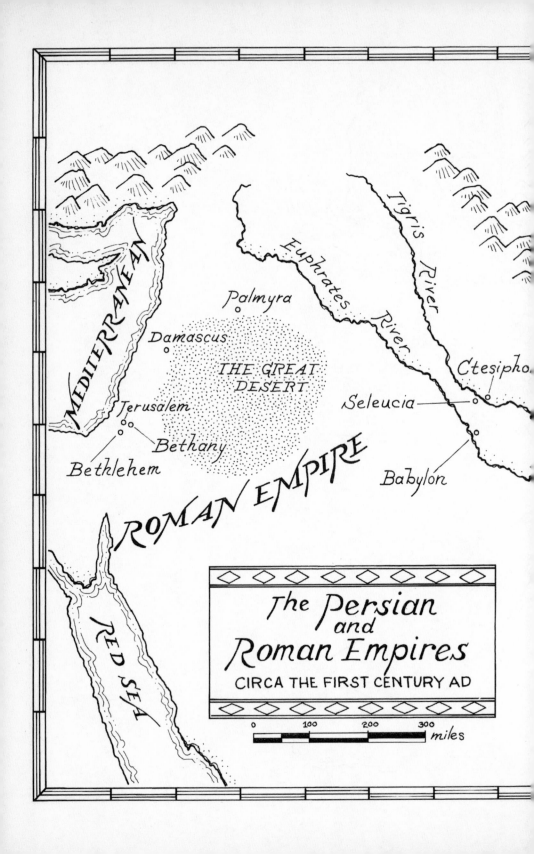

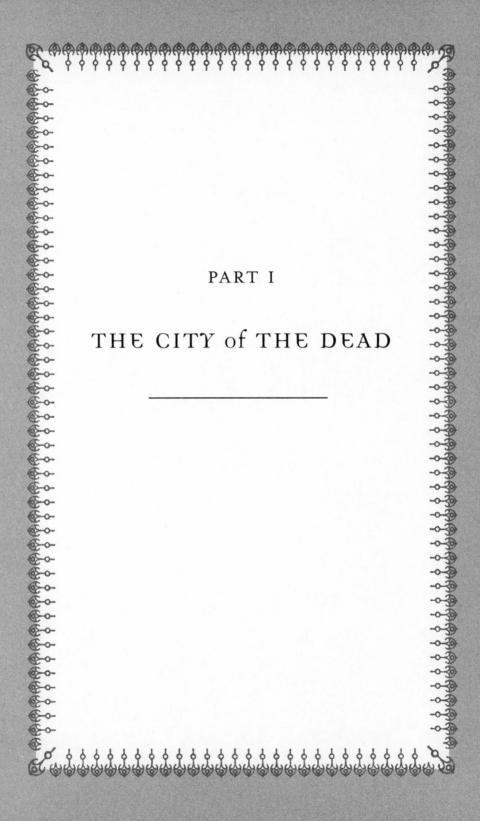

PART I

THE CITY of THE DEAD

CHAPTER 1

BABAK'S DREAM

When we lived in the City of the Dead, my brother dreamed mostly of food. Banquets he would have there, curled up on the stone floor among the ossuaries—melons and olives, chickpeas and dates, lentils and bread. Even noble folks' food was not too fine for his dreams—honeyed lemon peel and almonds, saffron-roasted flesh of lamb.

How did he know of such food, I used to wonder. Was it seeing it in the marketplace? Or does one's true nature bubble up and show itself in dreams? We'd ceased eating as nobles do three years before, when Babak was scarcely two.

Still, this dream food seemed to satisfy him someway. He did not wake weak and peevish with hunger, as I did. There was a kind of glow upon him while the aftertaste of nocturnal feasts suffused his face with joy.

"Sister!" he would say to me. "Such a dream I had. Roasted chickpeas! I ate till I nearly burst! And oranges, all peeled for me and sprinkled with leaves of mint. And warm rounds of bread with sesame seeds!"

But this talk of feasting only made me hungrier, crankier. "Move your feet, Babak," I would snap at last. I would drag him through the honeycombed cave passageways and out toward the gates of Rhagae. "You can't eat dreams," I would say.

But I was wrong about that. Dreams *can* feed you, can send you on journeys to places beyond imagining.

I know this, because it happened to us.

"This way, Babak! Come!"

I snatched his hand and pulled him along the street as he veered toward a broken-winged pigeon that foundered in the dust, then yanked him away from some sobbing beggar woman he was drawn to, drying his tears, because of course he must cry too.

"She's nothing to you, Babak. Remember who you are!" We arrived at the head of the caravan as the first horseman passed the carpet weaver's market. "Look for Suren," I said, though now Babak had no need of instruction. His eyes, fastened on the passing travelers, were hungry with hope.

The swaying tassels, tinkling bells, and bright-woven saddlebags lent the caravan a festive air. Seemed to presage a celebration. A songbird trilled from its gilded cage, and a net filled with cooking pots clanked merrily. A camel-riding musician struck up a tune on a double-pipe; another shook a tambourine, filling the air with its gay, rhythmic jingle. Though I tried to fend it off, I too felt hope seeping into the chambers of my heart. I breathed it in with the dust that bloomed up from the animals' feet, with the smells of sweat, dung, and spices. A Magus, resplendent in his white cloak and tall cap, rode by astride a magnificent stallion. A lesser priest came behind, swinging a silver thurible that perfumed the air with smoke; another bore aloft the coals of the sacred fire in a brazier of hammered copper. I studied the others' faces as they passed—the horse-archers; the attendants and servants; the camel drovers and donkey drovers; the musicians and entertainers; the pilgrims and merchants and grooms. I willed our brother Suren to be among them, to have attached himself to this caravan and returned to us.

But the last of the travelers passed, and no Suren.

I was reaching for Babak's hand to lead him away—not wanting to look at him, not wanting to see what was gone from his eyes—when I noticed a jostling up ahead, by the fruit seller's market. There was shouting, and cursing, and an exchange of blows—a circumstance made in heaven for us.

"Move your feet, Babak!" I said. In a trice I had slipped three pomegranates beneath the folds of my tunic and stripped a sack of dates from a fair-haired Scythian nomad with blue tattoos. The fracas suddenly veered in our direction; the Scythian stumbled, fell, flattened Babak beneath him.

It was then, I now realize—when Babak was pinned beneath the Scythian, when I was kicking the Scythian's back to get him to move—that the man's fur cap fell off. Babak must have tucked it into his sash.

That night, back in the City of the Dead, Babak pillowed his head on lynx fur and dreamed—not of food, but of a birth. A happy occasion. A boy. He recognized the Scythian in the dream. Someone bringing him the baby, settling it in his arms. Someone saying, "Father." Babak dreamed the dream, he told me, as if the Scythian himself were dreaming it.

By chance, we caught sight of the man near the rope makers' market the next day and, before I could stop him, Babak sang out, "A boy! It will be a boy! A healthy boy!"

"Hsst!" I said, and snatched up Babak's hand, and ducked behind a donkey, behind a spice merchant, behind a crumbling wall, and tried to lose ourselves in the crowd before the Scythian could catch us.

But he did.

As it happened, the Scythian didn't recognize Babak from the day before. As it happened, the stolen cap and dates were the last things on his mind. As it happened, he was hoping for tidings—though not from a marketplace waif.

As it happened, his wife was expecting a child.

This dream of my brother's was a good omen, he said, when he had pried it from us. Then he handed Babak a copper. With which we *bought* food—something I had never done in all the fourteen years of my life.

✳

CHAPTER 2

HOPE

"This . . . dream," I asked Babak later, squatting on the rough floor of our cavern, licking the last sweet drops of melon juice from my fingers, "have you been visited by other such? Dreams of Suren, maybe? Dreams of things to come?"

A draft stirred the lamp flame; shadows swam across the cave walls, then settled back round the edges of the chamber. In the distance I could hear the nighttime sounds of these old caves: a leper's bells, an echoing cry, and the constant soft shufflings and murmurings from near and from deep. High up, where the cave opened to air, glimmered a small patch of stars.

"I don't know," Babak said.

He wiped sticky fingers on his tunic. Pomegranate juice ringed his mouth. He reached for a chunk of goat cheese.

"How can you not know a thing like that?"

Babak shrugged his thin shoulders. He held out a crumble of cheese to the kitten he had smuggled into our chamber without my seeing, a kitten with one eye scarred shut.

"Don't feed it!" I said. "We've nothing to spare. There's vermin aplenty; let it catch its own."

"But it's hungry!"

Of course it was hungry. All of the miserable souls who lived in these caves were hungry. And the ones who survived were those who took care of themselves—not every wretch and stray that came along.

"Have you ever dreamed of Suren?" I persisted. "Of when

he will come for us? Of where he is? Of what he has found?"

Our older brother had left forty-two days before, accord-ing to the scratches I'd made on the wall. I'd pressed him to find work in a caravan bound for Susa, where we used to live. Suren knew where our father had buried caskets of gold coins. All he had to do was dig them up and return to us. Surely he could manage that! Then we could all book passage on a caravan to Palmyra, where, we had heard, our kinsmen had fled.

"I dream of you sometimes, Sister," Babak said now. "Of eating food with you. Sometimes Suren is there. I used to dream of Mother. . . ."

Mother.

Women screaming, soldiers through the gate. The flash of sun on swords. Mother calling, "Suren, come!"

I closed my eyes, pushed it away. You would think, after all this time, that the edge would have dulled, or at least that you'd be ready for it—not pierced, capsized, and sinking every time.

"How did you dream of her?" I asked. "Of where she is now? Was it Palmyra you dreamed of? Or only—"

"Only as she was," he answered, "before, in Susa. When she was with us."

Babak was looking up at me, his eyes huge and grave in the flickering lamplight. I willed the worry from my counte-nance so that he would not absorb it into himself.

I didn't know much about dreams, hadn't been visited with one in years. But I had heard that they can come from different places. That some of them foretell things and some do not. That some of them come from the Wise God. Or other gods—I had heard that as well. These foretelling dreams did not visit everyone, but only a few. Might Babak be one of them?

Something stirred inside me. How to find out?

Old Zoya knew about dreams. But the mere thought of asking her pricked my pride. Besides, she'd exact a price.

"Babak. This is important. Have you had any other dreams of things to come—even about strangers?"

"I don't *know*." Babak hunched over the kitten, turning his back to me. I had pressed too hard. He scratched the kitten behind its ragged, flea-bitten ears. It began to purr, still licking his cheese finger with its tiny pink tongue.

I sighed. If Babak didn't want to tell me now, I couldn't drag it out of him. Muleheadedness ran raging through our family like a river in spring flood. Even Babak—the most tenderhearted boy alive—was not exempt.

And yet this dream, this dream of the baby. Perhaps we might put it to good use. Perhaps I might turn dream into coin another time and perhaps scrape together passage. Then, when Suren returned—whether or not he had found the hidden gold—we could go there.

Palmyra.

I breathed in deep and felt it stir again, warming the cold, empty spaces:

Hope.

✳

CHAPTER 3

PALTRY GIFT

Later that night, when Babak and the kitten were asleep, I counted out the last of the dates, hesitated, put four back, then tucked the rest into my sash. I crept backward, lamp in hand, down the dark, narrow tunnel that led from our chamber. It was a snug fit.

I had discovered the passage when, after fleeing Susa, we first came into Rhagae and needed a place to go to ground. I had crept up and found the small room, which opened to air high up on the cliff, too high to be reached from outside. Suren was too big to squeeze through the tunnel. "But I can find another cavern to sleep in," he had said. "What matters is that you and Babak will be safe."

Much of the time it *was* fairly safe in these caves, known as the City of the Dead because of the bones left here in ossuaries long ago. Still, you had to keep your wits about you. Strangers did venture in from time to time. But no one came here anymore to honor the bones of their dead. Even the descendants of these dead—were dead. Most beggars preferred to dwell within the walls of Rhagae, in some abandoned hovel or in the ruins of an old palace. The air was fresher there, not stale and full of death. There were no bones from crumbled ossuaries rolling about loose and rattling beneath your feet.

Only those who must hide from other beggars—unprotected women, the sick or crippled, the very young or very old—lived in these ancient caves.

At the end of our tunnel I paused, listened, then made my way in the flickering gloom through a chain of tall caverns and narrow passageways to an ancient stairway hewn into the rock at the edge of a chasm. I held the lamp carefully as I climbed, clinging to protuberances in the wall with my other hand and nudging bones off the steps with my bare toes—a hip bone, a thighbone, a skull. I heard them ricochet off the sides of the chasm, then clatter, echoing, below. I lofted skyward a prayer against contamination—though little good it might do me. It was well that my grandmother couldn't see me now. I moved through more rooms, more passages, more stairs, until a breath of fresh evening air touched my face.

Old Zoya occupied a spacious cavern that, like ours, opened high on the side of the cliff. But her opening reached clear down to the cave floor and was nearly as wide as the front door of our home in Susa. I peered in and saw her sitting in the moonlight on the lip of the opening, conferring with the youth who often attended upon her, a young man with slanted eyes under a broad, low forehead: thick of tongue and slow of thought. In a dark corner, the coals from her brazier glowed. I blew out my lamp flame, knowing I could relight it before I left, and stepped into the chamber.

"Eh! Who's there?" she cried at the sound of my footsteps. She jumped up, snatching her walking stick, and brandished it at me.

"It's I," I said, edging into the moonlight to show myself. "With a gift. And a favor to ask."

She lowered the stick and peered at me. After a moment she flicked a hand at the youth; he scuttled away.

"Mitra? With a gift? Huh! That's something new."

"Shh! Don't call me Mitra. It's Ramin!"

Old Zoya was one of the few people who knew I was a girl, and I wanted to keep it that way. I had disguised myself as a boy shortly after we came to this place nearly two years before, discarding my ankle-length gown and cloak for a ragged tunic, trousers, and a coat of coarse weave; cropping my hair to my shoulders; and affecting my father's straight-as-a-bowstring stance and chin-forward gait. Suren had chosen the name *Ramin*, after his best friend in Susa. It was safer to be a boy. Besides, a girl couldn't roam the streets freely, as I did. As I must, especially now that Suren was away.

Babak called me *Sister* when we were alone. I couldn't break him of that. I feared he would let it slip before others. But it was something he seemed to understand, a private name. Nevertheless, Zoya had guessed my secret and pried *Mitra*—my true name—from Suren.

"Well, what's this gift?" she asked now.

I pulled the dates from my sash and held them out. Old Zoya squinted, peered, jabbed at them with a skinny finger. She looked back at me in disbelief.

"Three . . . measly . . . dates?"

"It's three more than you had before! Do you think we're made of food? I've got to feed Babak; he's a growing boy."

"Pah! Paltry gift! Suren would've been bounteous. Pinch fisted as ever, *you* are. Pleading poor when all the world knows you come into a fortune today. Traipsing through the market-place like fine folk, laying out coin for cheese and melon and roasted chickpeas . . ."

I should have known. Old Zoya's leathery ears were fine-tuned to the hum of gossip. Some of the cave dwellers spied for her—sniffing out which goods were scarce, which plentiful, and which approaching in the next caravan. Discovering who was feuding with whom and what information would bring something in trade. "It wasn't a fortune," I protested. "It was one copper. And the food's nearly gone now; we were hungry."

"And I s'pose this is the last of the dates?"

"Ah, well . . . there are four left. Only four. Do you want Babak and me to starve?"

"Four more and there'd be seven." She turned to the opening in the wall, seemed to address the stars. "Such a good, stout number, seven. Seven royal families. Seven

9

Spentas. Seven days in a week. One date every morning'd be such a pleasurement for an old woman. But no one cares, no one cares."

"If three plump dates mean nothing to you, I can take them back—"

"No call for that." She whirled round and clamped on to my wrist with surprising speed. I considered yanking back the dates until she told me what I wanted, but I had said *gift*, and now I must live with it.

She stuffed them all together into her mouth, slurping, mashing them between toothless gums. One date each day, indeed! If I'd given her seven, they'd have been gone as quickly as three. I wondered if Zoya's manners had been so coarse back in the days when she midwifed to the sisters of a satrap, before an infant strangled on its belly cord and Zoya went into hiding. You would never think she'd been part of a noble household to see her now: filthy rags hung loose on a bone-thin frame, topped by a hooked nose and a tangled gray mat of hair. Still, she surprised me with her knowledge at times, and highborn words and phrases often peppered her crude speech.

At last, smacking her lips, she swiped the back of her hand across the stream of juice that trickled down her chin. "Pah! Wouldn't satisfy a gnat, and now my tongue's set for dates." She glared at me, then snatched up her stick and hobbled toward the far, dim threshold of her chamber.

"The favor?" I demanded.

She paused, no doubt wanting to make me sweat. But I knew her better than that. Curiosity would win over her desire to cheat me. "Well, out with it," she grumbled at last, turning back.

"Can you tell me something about dreams?"

"Dreams! Why do you want to know?"

"Babak has had . . . a strange one."

"Well? Tell me!"

I related what had happened with the Scythian. Zoya drew

near as I spoke, then motioned me to sit with her on the ledge. Below I could see the town walls and part of Rhagae itself, its mudbrick houses slumbering in the light of a bright wedge of moon.

"Did it come true?" Old Zoya asked now. "Is there a child?"

"I don't know. He spoke of Babak's dream only as an omen. A good one."

"And Babak never saw the man before?"

"I don't think so."

"Hmm." Old Zoya pursed her lips, scratching at the long, sparse hairs on her chin. "Well, there are wishing dreams, having naught to do with the world as 'tis but solely with the wishes of the dreamer. This one—this dream—seems not so."

No. Babak's dreams of food were likely wishing dreams. But not the one about the Scythian.

"There are remembering dreams, where one thing's fused together with another, unfitting thing, appearing in a strange light—backward or twisted, like. Transmogrified. To parse them you've need of a skilled diviner—such as myself. These dreams oft tell not of what's to come, but shed light on what's past but not yet fathomed by the dreamer. Dreams of revelation, like. But Babak's dream, no. It appears to make perfect sense."

I nodded.

"Other dreams are of the prophesying sort, told in symbologies and sent by one god or another, or mayhap the Wise God, himself. But from what you're saying . . . My mother's sister—Babak oft puts me in mind of her—was visited time to time with other folks' dreams. They'd come to her—noble ladies—with some fribble of a garment they'd worn. She'd sleep with it and dream. For good dreams they'd reward her well." Old Zoya favored me with a wry smile. "I won't say she didn't twist a dream or two to make it seem auspicious. But, with the future, truth will out. That's one peril in being visited by such dreams."

"One peril?"

"Well, how if this Scythian's wife gives birth to a girl? Or if the baby dies? Or the wife dies? I'll wager the Scythian's next meeting with Babak won't be so profitable."

I swallowed. I had thought of this, of course. "I don't think Babak is lying," I said.

She shrugged. "With dreams an honest err can be as deadly as a lie. And Babak's gift for dreaming may be weak. Too chancy to be trusted. Another paltry gift." She fixed me with a baleful eye, then sighed and scratched her chin. "Yet still." She turned from me, gazed out at the stars. "Yet still, this isn't the gravest peril, for Babak."

I drew in breath, hugged my arms to my chest. "What do you mean?"

For a moment her face seemed to soften. "The gravest peril for Babak," she said at last, "is if the dream works out to be true."

*

CHAPTER 4

THE MAN with BLUE TATTOOS

It was with much on my mind that I found my way back to our chamber. Old Zoya had been right, had thought through to something that had not occurred to me. Which was troublesome. *I* was supposed to think of such things. *I* was the one who could parse the movements in the marketplace to read danger or opportunity before they broke the surface calm. With Suren gone, Babak and I must live by my wits alone, and I had missed something so clear. . . .

I stumbled, nearly dropped the lamp. What a fool I was! Like Babak, not minding where I walked.

More carefully now I crept up the tunnel to our cave. I could barely see Babak—the lamplight had dimmed—but I lay a hand on his belly, felt his body move in the rhythms of sleep. I tucked his threadbare coat more securely about him; we had turned the corner into autumn, and the cave grew chill at night. I swept a lock of hair off his damp forehead, my fingers tracing the ridge of the scar that cleaved one eyebrow. He had been dawdling about, transfixed by one daydream or another, when he fell and split his brow open. Now he pulled up one knee, scratched it, made a little moaning sound. The kitten, nestled against Babak's chest, yawned, stretched, then melted back into a shape that accommodated Babak's knee. I nuzzled the back of my brother's neck—he smelled faintly of melon and of dust and of the palm fronds on which he lay. Then, regretfully, I leaned back and blew out the lamp.

Babak wouldn't miss it. Like a small, furry animal, he

reveled in darkness. He wrapped it about himself, comforting as a cloak.

But I was profligate with light. I could navigate from our cavern through the dark passages leading to outside without it; even now I could see dimly in the milky radiance that leaked in from above. Seldom did I need light. But I craved it. I begged longer in the marketplace in order to replenish my precious store of lamp oil; I stole for it; at times I sacrificed food for it.

Now, breathing in the last smoky traces of lamplight, I found a faint patch of moonglow on the floor and sat there to think.

If the dream was true.

Yes. People would come seeking us. Not just the Scythian— coming in anger if the dream was false. But many, coming with hope, looking to Babak to dream for them. Some would pay us, certainly. I had thought of that. It wouldn't be much. Nobility would hardly have dealings with the likes of us—not as we were now. And Zoya was right: There would be some devious men sniffing round, seeking to use Babak and his gift without our consent.

But I would be careful. And just think! We wouldn't have to come by all our food by theft. Though I had acquired skill at stealing, it was chancy, dangerous. All too often we went hungry. All too often our store of lamp oil ran dry.

And maybe . . . maybe we could even save enough . . . I let my mind touch it now: *Palmyra.*

Many Persian exiles had gone to live there, I had heard. In Palmyra the family of Vardan would stand tall. Would be served and honored according to our rightful station. Suren seemed able to tolerate the miserable existence we now had, but I could not. Would not! I couldn't bear to think that we would stay like this, eking out a miserable life among the rabble, forever!

I sighed, wrapped my thin coat around me, and lay down on the floor beside Babak. But I did not go right to sleep.

✳

*There was a broom in my mind that I used to sweep across the distant
lands, with little seeking straws that could find my family. I began in
Palmyra—beyond the edge of Persia. The broom swept up my aunts
and my uncles and my cousins, and my mother—she had found her
way there as well. Then it swept them over the deserts and high
plateaus, across the rivers and valleys, until it found my brother
Suren, and it swept him along too. Then the little seeking straws, they
probed at the crevices in the land until they teased out the place where
my father, Vardan, was, even though I had heard that he was dead.
But this was my broom, and it did what I wanted it to, and it found
him, too—alive—and brought them all to Babak and me. Then it
swept us across the high plateau back to Susa, back to our fine old
home in the hills above Susa, where we were sated with good food,
and attended upon by many servants, and esteemed according to our
high station, and safe, and loved. My pony was still there; now he
came galloping through the green pastures and nudged my hands for
treats and gave that whicker that I used to know so well, that whicker
that said, Oh, where have you been? I'm so glad you have returned.*

*I did this, with the broom, nearly every night. It was a waking
dream, not a sleeping one. Not a dream that came to visit, for, since
Susa, dreams had shunned my slumber. No, this was a dream I conjured for myself.*

And then, after I had made the dream, I could sleep.

The next morning, as we neared the bottom of the twisting
path that led down the rocky slope to Rhagae, I saw him right
away. The Scythian. Round of belly, bow slung over a shoulder. Wild yellow hair, blue-tattooed face. He was gazing round
just outside the city gates, accosting one man, then another.
Asking questions, I surmised, because each man shook his
head in response, then walked away.

"Get down," I said to Babak. "Here." We crouched behind
an outcropping of boulders. I peered over the top of it,
watched the Scythian. He approached a spice merchant and

laid his hand flat on the air at about Babak's height. Then he moved his hand up to where, had I been standing there, it would have rested on my head. My scalp, feeling the ghost of his touch, prickled.

"Sister?" Babak whispered. "What's amiss?"

"Don't worry," I said. But of course he would. So long as he felt my worry, *he* would worry. I looked again, tried to see if the Scythian seemed angry. But I couldn't tell. "Let's go."

All that day we stayed within the City of the Dead. Babak did not understand why, and I didn't want to tell him. "It's nothing," I said. "I'll tell you presently," I said. "It doesn't concern you," I said. Lies and lies and lies. But a child's ceaseless questions can drive you to madness. I told him again of our old home in Susa, of the fountain courtyard, paved in bright blue tiles and sweet with the scent of lilies; of the flowering trees hung with cages of singing birds; of the gold-inlaid wine cups and water ewers of pure chased silver. I told him again of the princes and satraps who came to visit our father. "Remember who you are," I told him, echoing my grandmother. "Never forget."

When Babak wearied of my stories, we played games with almond shells. Setting a pebble under one shell and mixing it in with others, then asking him to guess where the pebble lay. Tapping a shell hard on one edge to make it jump, and setting up a contest to see whose shells would fly farther. To a child Babak's age, shells can be fleets of ships in battle or cups for fairy wine or hats for pebble creatures.

We shared with the kitten our last scrap of cheese, then I pulled a long thread from the hem of my tunic and dangled it before the little creature.

"Brave kitten," Babak said, as it pounced upon the string and pulled it from between my fingers. Babak threw back his head and roared. "It's a lion!" he said. "Grroar!" The lion caught sight of its own tail and lunged for it, then bounced round and round in dizzy pursuit. Babak bubbled with happy laughter, as I hadn't seen him do in so long. . . .

But the lion soon curled up to sleep, and Babak grew restless. I struck a light with my flints and ventured with him deeper into the caves, where the walls grew damp and cold, where the air tasted old, of death. We crept through the black passageways to the haunts of his "friends"—he considered nearly everyone his friend—but only the ones I knew to be safe: The pockmarked woman who conversed all day with a husband who wasn't there. The head-twitching youth who claimed to be the emperor of Rome. The one-armed beggarman who told stories of India and Egypt, Greece and Rome. The old woman with a withered leg and a hump on her back.

Our visits pleased Babak because I usually tried to keep him away from these friends of his. They were rough of tongue and manner—baseborn, despite a few grandiose claims. Grandmother would have shuddered to see us mixing with such people. But for now they kept Babak distracted from the worry he must feel radiating from me.

We went to see Zoya, but she was not in her chamber. Thanks be to heaven we hadn't given all our food to her. There remained yet two dates apiece, a pomegranate, and a few handfuls of chickpeas and almonds.

But I couldn't hide much longer. I had to know soon how the land lay, and then decide what to do.

From time to time I ventured to an opening in the caves and peered out. We were too far for me to recognize faces there below, though I could see streams of men issuing forth from the direction of the caravansary near the eastern gates, no doubt supplying the Magus's party as he bathed in the healing waters nearby.

I wondered: Was the Scythian angry with us because things had not gone as Babak had foretold?

Or had Babak's dream come true?

✳

CHAPTER 5

PANDORA'S BOX

Old Zoya called up to me when we were napping in the heat of the day. I could see her lamplight flickering at the end of our tunnel. I checked Babak—sound asleep with the kitten—then crept down to meet her.

Zoya had perched atop a heap of fallen boulders in a lightless chamber near our room. "Did you eat all of those dates?" she asked.

"We finished them earlier."

She heaved her skinny shoulders in a disappointed sigh—a bit overdone, I thought. "Well, I'll give you this for free," she said. "That Scythian is looking for your brother and you."

"I know that. Why do you think we stayed in the caves all day?"

"Eh! You know so much, s'pose I needn't tell you about the baby."

I would have loved to have said *no* and turned my back on her, climbed right back up to our chamber. I didn't want to give her the satisfaction of lording over us whatever she had to tell. But I had to know.

"What about the baby?"

"Oh, so you haven't heard? And I thought you knew everything!"

"Tell me." I moved toward her, but she brandished her walking stick at me. I stopped where I was. "Tell me about the baby."

The light from the lamp she had set beside her bled

yellow across her ravaged face. She lifted an eyebrow, tugged at a long black hair on her chin. Her walking stick went *tap, tap, tap* upon the stone.

"Please."

She shrugged. *Tap. Tap.*

"What do you want?" I sighed. "I beg of you."

"That's what I like to hear." Her face crumpled into a toothless smile, mouth and eyes disappearing in a sea of wrinkles. "Seems like Babak's dream came true. The Scythian's wife bore him a healthy boy."

A healthy boy. The words struck me in the spine, sent shivers arcing up my back. Little Babak could do this? I could scarce believe it, and yet . . . He was a strange child. I had known that always. He someway couldn't separate himself from others. If you were sad, he was sad. If you stubbed your toe, his toe ached. Wounded birds, homeless cats, cripples, lepers . . . if they were hungry, he was hungry.

But *this*—

"How do you know?" I demanded.

"I have my ways."

Of course. Her spies.

"Here's the nub of it," Zoya said now, scooting down to the next boulder. "The Scythian isn't talking about the dream. Only craves to find Babak."

"So?"

"So a thousand bloodsucking fortune hunters won't come slavering after your brother!"

"Just one. The Scythian."

"Maybe. Or maybe he only wants to reward Babak. But it's likely he craves more dreams. Anyway, we can treat with him."

"*We?*"

"Seems like you"—she jabbed her stick in my direction—"need a go-between. A body that's wise in the ways of the world. A body that can . . . make arrangements, like, without letting on where you live. That can make sure you get your due in solid copper."

"Seems to me Babak and I could just make ourselves scarce for a while until he forgets about us or moves on."

"Forget, he won't. You don't forget a thing like that, a first-born son. He lives here in Rhagae, the Scythian does. Not just passing through."

He lived in Rhagae. We could be confined inside the caves for a very long time. And if the Scythian couldn't find us, he might begin talking. He'd likely talk in time, no matter what. As for Old Zoya, if she didn't get her way, she might talk as well. True, she'd told no one I was a girl, but there was no gain for her in telling that.

If only Babak had never had that dream! If only he'd kept his mouth shut!

"Here's what I'll do." Old Zoya picked up her lamp and clambered down from the heap of rocks to stand before me. "I'll go to the Scythian, tell him I have knowledge he seeks. Fetch me his cap, and I'll return it to him, as a token, like, of good faith. I'll find out what he wants and convey it to you."

"And you'll make no promises until I know what he wants. Until I say you can."

She looked at me as if astonished I'd think she'd do such a thing.

"And how if the Scythian follows you?" I asked.

"I have my ways. Slow I am, but sly."

This was true. I had seen her slip in and out among the stalls of the marketplace. If you looked away for a moment, *poof!* She was gone.

"So how do *you* profit from this?" She always profited from her acts of kindness, one way or another. A gift of food when you were starving would cost you a portion of what you begged or stole for weeks to come. An herbal draught when you were sick could bind you to her as one of her spies.

"I? Profit?" The lamp flame wavered from the force of her breath, sending shadows leaping up the cave walls. She was performing again, her face open wide with incredulity. "It's only little Babak I'm thinking of."

"Let me put it to you this way: *If* the Scythian is willing to pay for dreams, and *if* I were to allow it, what would be your share?"

"Two portions out of three seems fair."

"Two of three? Babak would be doing the dreaming; you're just—"

"Eh, half then."

"No. Too much."

"So, one of three. Three of us there are in this, sharing the risk. If Babak's dream was only happenstance and he can nevermore do it again, we'll all have the Scythian after us." She chuckled.

"I see no humor in it! If we do this, and if the dream doesn't come true, we'll return the coin. Babak and I can't keep on hiding; that would be—"

Old Zoya patted my arm, suddenly solicitous. "Of course! Of course! Truly, the risk is very small."

I brushed her hand off my sleeve. I didn't trust her. Suren had; he had even liked her, but not I. "I'm surprised you're so smitten with this plan," I said, "when yesterday you were full of dire warnings. 'The gravest peril for Babak,' you said."

"I've had time to think on it. Think, Mitra—"

"*Ramin.*"

"As you wish. But think. Never again to beg for food nor lamp oil. You could buy yourself a fine wool gown. I might even find you a husband. . . ." She squinted, eyeing me critically. "Though 'twould take some doing."

"I don't want any husband *you* could find me!"

"Hmmph. You're no beauty, oh high-and-mighty one. You think you're better'n the rest of us, but that noble blood of yours means nothing here."

Royal, I corrected her silently. *Not just noble. Royal.*

"But now," Zoya said, "where was it Suren looked to take you? Palmyra, was it?"

Palmyra. To sweep up my aunts and my uncles, and then . . .

"This could fall out well for all of us," Zoya said.

Perhaps. But I doubted it. Zoya would cheat us, that was certain. And if Babak did have prophetic dreams, word would get out in time. And then our lives would take some form I could scarcely imagine.

All at once I recalled a tale that Suren's Greek tutor had told him. A tale about a girl named . . . what was it? Pandora? She had opened a forbidden box and let out all the woes and evils of the world.

It's far easier to let things out of boxes, I reflected as I crept up the tunnel to fetch the cap, than to pack them back in again.

✳

CHAPTER 6

SHAGGY BEASTIES

The next night, after Babak had gone to sleep, Old Zoya called again up the passageway. She summoned me to follow to her chamber, then held out a length of cloth. In the swathe of moonlight that spilled into the room, I could see that the fabric was of a yellowish hue. Some shade of ocher, or maybe, in sunlight, saffron.

"What is this?" I asked.

"What do you think? A headcloth, belonging to the Scythian's wife. She craves one of Babak's dreams."

I folded my arms in front of me, refusing to touch the thing. I'd known it was a mistake to confide in Zoya. "You told me you'd convey a message, nothing more. I never said Babak would dream for them. What did you promise those Scythians? Why did you bring me this?"

"Eh, don't have a palsy. I promised nothing. But if you decide you want Babak to dream for the woman"—she shrugged—"he can begin this very day."

"And how did they know you speak for him? They've never seen you with him; you're not our kin."

"They believed me when I told them! Not everyone's as slit eyed and suspicious as you, oh high-and-mighty one. Besides, I gave him back his cap, remember? And I described Babak . . . and his ugly older brother, *you*." She cackled at her pitiful joke; I ignored her. "The proof'll be," she went on at last, "in the dream. You should thank me. This way they need never meet with Babak again." She thrust the headcloth at me. "Take it."

Reluctantly I unclasped my arms and took the thing between two fingers. It was much softer than the coarse-grained cloth I now wore, though not nearly so fine as the linen of my gowns in Susa. My hands, of their own accord, gathered the headcloth between them, brought it to my face. It smelled nothing like the garments from home, which had wicked up the perfumed oils on our bodies. Still, this smelled of something . . . not unpleasant. Of cloves, maybe. Of a woman's skin.

"I'll talk to Babak about this," I said, "tomorrow."

"Don't. You might plant the idea for him to dream of this woman, and we'd never know whence the dream truly arose. We'd best know," Zoya said, "if the other dream was happenstance. If not, they'll pay us well. We can take their money this once and never treat with them again."

It would not be so simple. I knew that. And yet . . .

Something was stirring in me. A restlessness. A hunger. *Palmyra.* We could save for passage to Palmyra. So even if Suren returned empty handed, we could leave these wretched caves forever. We could find our kin and the life we were meant to live.

Back in our chamber, I squatted down beside Babak. My lamp-light dimly showed the shape of him—his belly moving in sleep breathing, the crescents of his lashes, the sleep-slack curves of his mouth. The kitten, curled up beside him, stretched, opening its one good eye, then curled up again.

What was Babak dreaming? I wondered. Could other people's dreams seep in through that skin of his, as their feelings seemed to?

A scratchy, scuttling sound—rats. Then came a laugh—or a cry—from far back in the caves. I watched Babak for a time, watched him breathe, watched him kick suddenly and roll onto his back, watched him mumble some garbled word, then smile.

But I could not divine his dreams.

I took the headcloth from my girdle, reached toward him, then pulled back. Slipping this cloth next to his flesh seemed like sin somehow. Infecting him with something unknown, without his knowledge or permission.

How if he had nightmares? How if he saw something so terrible, it poisoned his waking life too? Dreams can be dangerous things.

Yet still. I closed my eyes and *home* came flooding in. The cool, shaded courtyard, the soft folds of linen against my skin, the smell of incense and jasmine blossoms, the mingled murmurings of running water and of women's voices.

Mother.

Women screaming, soldiers through the gate. The flash of sun on swords, a seething crush of men inside the courtyard—soldiers and my kinsmen. Blood spilling on the cobblestones, bloodbeat roaring in my ears, a din of metal-clash and bellow. Mother calling, "Suren, come! Come take them, flee!"

I wrenched my thoughts away, nudged Mother backward through the procession of days and nights and days to when the courtyard was peaceful and safe. I tried to will the contours of her face into my mind, but she shimmered and blurred. Each time I tried, she came hazier, fainter. I could still see the silver bracelets on her wrists, twinkling with gems and glass; I could still see the pale green silk of her gown; I could still see the sweep of her dark hair, sleek and gleaming as a raven's wing. But her face had disappeared.

Palmyra. Surely she would have found her way there. Surely she would be waiting for us when we arrived.

I let out a deep breath, let the old, sickening grief crash against me.

This is not just for me, I pleaded silently with Babak. This could mean a life for you as well.

And still I hesitated. Suren, what would he do?

Don't, I imagined him saying. *It's too much to risk.* Suren had grown listless and morose of late, seemed no longer to care that we—the children of Vardan, seed of Mithradates—had been reduced to living in a cave among outcasts and rabble. When I'd pressed him to go to Susa, he'd protested that the Eyes and Ears of the king—Phraates' secret spies—might still be seeking us and it was best to lie low. But it had been three years! If they were going to find us, they'd have done so well before now. King Phraates' enemies were legion; surely the Eyes and Ears had bigger fish to fry.

Sometimes you had to risk! You couldn't just fritter your life away in fear—afraid to take a chance, afraid to act—as Suren seemed content to do before I persuaded him to leave.

Quickly I drew aside Babak's tunic, slipped the headcloth next to his skin.

There. It was done.

When he awoke the next morning, Babak said nothing of his dreams. I had eased the headcloth from beneath his tunic at the first signs of his waking; I'd tucked it furtively into my sash. Now I searched Babak's countenance for signs. Signs of . . . what? Of nightmares? Of demon possession? Of worry? Of sickness? When I asked him how he felt, he sleepily rubbed his eyes and mumbled that he was well. I set my hand upon his forehead, checking for fever, but nothing seemed amiss, except that now he was annoyed with me. He brushed my hand away. "I am *well.*"

He did seem well enough. I breathed out a silent sigh, felt myself unclench. But there remained an itching in my mind. Had he dreamed at all? Or did he just not want to tell? I decided not to push him. To wait.

But for how long? We were desperately low on food, and my precious store of lamp oil wouldn't hold out much longer. And I dared not go to the marketplace. The Scythian would doubtless be there. He would demand to know.

I divided our last pomegranate, feeling the restlessness stirring within me, trying to squeeze it down. If Babak guessed how eager I was to hear of a dream, he might conjure up a false one just to please me. Or he might balk, retreat within himself, and refuse to talk at all.

"Is there more?" Babak asked. "I'm hungry!"

Hungry. So, most likely he had not had one of his food dreams, for they seemed to satisfy his hunger. For a time.

"Just these." I poured what remained of the chickpeas into his hands. He offered one to the kitten; it sniffed and turned away in disdain.

Babak leveled his thick-lashed gaze upon me. His eyes turned slightly down at the outer edges, giving him a look of sadness, never entirely dispelled, even when a smile lit up his face. "Sister, can we go to the marketplace today? Can we buy more melons?"

Only if you tell me what you dreamed!

But I couldn't say it aloud.

"We'll see," I replied.

I was relieved when Zoya called up through our passage not long after. I wanted to meet her alone, but Babak was eager to come with me, and I couldn't think of a convincing reason why he shouldn't. Zoya greeted Babak, then held her lamp aloft and, over his head, shot me an inquiring look.

I shrugged, turned up the palms of my hands. "Babak's hungry," I said pointedly. "We haven't been to the market-place these past two days."

"Eh, such a lazy one, your Ramin!" she said to Babak, chucking him on the chin. "Won't bestir himself to feed you!" She wagged a finger at me. "Shame on you, Ramin. Babak, come with me."

She flashed me a wicked grin, reached for Babak's hand. He made her wait while he picked up the kitten and clutched it to his chest, murmuring, "Roar! Roar!" Then he bravely offered his free hand to Zoya and commenced to regale her with accounts of the kitten's antics as they wended through the maze of dark passages to Zoya's chamber.

Fuming, I followed.

The slow-witted boy was there; Zoya blew out her lamp and told him to give Babak a round of bread and some cheese. There was a gentleness to the boy's manner that I had not remarked before. He broke the tough bread into pieces and handed them to Babak one at a time.

"Did you have food today?" Babak asked him.

The slow-witted boy nodded.

Impatient, Zoya motioned him to leave. The boy set down the bread and cheese on a flat rock. Backing slowly out of the chamber, he smiled at Babak, pantomiming for him to eat.

"Go!" Zoya barked; he turned round and fled.

Babak settled in a shaft of morning sunshine at the opening of the cave. As the kitten licked crumbles of cheese from his fingers, Zoya, speaking low, pressed me to probe Babak about his dreams. Asking him *after* he'd dreamed couldn't hurt, she said. The Scythians would be impatient, she said. If I didn't want to ask, she'd be happy to, she said.

"No!"

It came out louder than I'd intended. Babak turned to look at me, worried. I smiled at him, tried to let the vexation seep out of me so that he wouldn't sense it. He turned back toward the sunshine again.

Truth to tell, I ached to ask, but Zoya's pushing made me dig in my heels. "He wouldn't tell you anyway," I whispered. "If he doesn't want to do a thing, no amount of badgering will persuade him."

Zoya leaned back, crossed her arms, regarded me with one eyebrow raised. "Who does that remind me of?" she muttered.

So hard I was straining to rein in my ire at Zoya, lest it disturb Babak, that I didn't notice what he was about until Zoya set a hand on my sleeve. She jerked her head toward him.

He was scratching at the dirt on the floor with a stick and mumbling something over and over in a singsongy sort of voice.

It sounded like: "Shaggy beasties, shaggy beasts."

Something went still within me. I turned to Zoya; our glances snagged. I set a finger to my lips, then got up and moved toward Babak.

I could see that he was drawing in the dirt, but I couldn't tell what.

"What's that, Babak?" I asked, pointing down at it.

"Shaggy beasties, shaggy beasts."

"What kind of beasties? Lions?"

He shook his head.

"Camels?"

He shook his head.

"Donkeys?"

"No!" He frowned up at me.

I had insulted him. Now I held my tongue. He was scratching little lines all over some roundish shapes—the fur of the shaggy beasties, I supposed. They looked like nothing so much as long-haired rats. I watched for a little longer. Must be careful. Mustn't seem too eager.

"Have you . . . seen . . . these shaggy beasties?" I asked at last.

Babak nodded. "I dreamed them," he said.

Dreamed them.

"A whole great herd. I rode on one. It took me home . . ."

Home. Susa, coming home to Susa . . .

"High in some pointy mountains. There was snow. We had a little round house, with straw on its roof."

I felt myself slump. Not Susa.

"Where was this, Babak? Do you know?"

"No," he said, and by his tone I knew he would tell me no more.

I looked over at Zoya, who was listening intently. She nodded, smiled, rose to leave.

Shaggy beasties? Whatever could that mean?

✳

CHAPTER 7

TO STEAL A DREAM

"Yaks," Zoya said later that day, counting the coppers into my hand:

One.

Two.

Three.

Four.

She leaned back against the wall of her cave and grinned her toothless grin. Babak was napping with the kitten in our chamber; Zoya and I were alone. "Did you ever see a yak?" she asked.

I shook my head. "What are they?"

"Shaggy beasties indeed! Great, lolloping critters"—she held her arms wide—"with freakish, curling horns. I saw one many years since. A trader bought it—as a curiosity, like." She pointed to the coppers. "See, even with me taking my share you're better off than before. I know how to strike a deal."

Oh, yes. Of that I was certain. But I would have wagered all of our coppers that she'd received more than two. Still, nothing to be done about it. And four coppers. I tilted my hand, watched the afternoon sunlight glide across the surfaces of them. One for food and lamp oil. Three for passage to Palmyra.

"So the dream meant something to this man?" I asked. "The pointy mountains? The shaggy beasties, er, yaks?"

"The Scythian's wife is not of his tribe. She's of the high mountain peoples, somewhere to the north and east of

Bactria. She's been craving to journey to her father's home. She takes this as an omen."

"Like the dream about the baby. But we don't know if this will come true—"

"What matter if it's true or not? It's what she wants to be true. Besides, Babak's dream never said when. It's a safer dream than the one about the baby. Harder to disprove. And it didn't pass without notice that we couldn't have known she was of the high mountain peoples. I'd met only her Scythian husband, and he didn't say."

Now Zoya cleared her throat. "So. He craves to meet him."

"Who?" I looked at her in alarm. "The Scythian? Meet Babak?"

She nodded.

"No."

"He's a kindly man. I can sense these things."

"*No.*"

"As you wish." She bowed mockingly. "I'll bide by your wishes, oh high-and-mighty one. But I could squeeze more coppers from him if he met Babak."

I could see where this was headed. "I should never have trusted you," I said.

Something flared in her eyes; they went hard. "Don't worry. I'll say no. Meantimes . . ." She pulled a length of brown linen from her tunic. "His brother'd like a dream too."

His brother, and his sister, and his sister's husband, and his sister's husband's mother. All wanted Babak to dream for them. I had to tell him. No, I had to ask him. It is not right to steal a person's dreams without his permission. Even if it is for his own good.

So, after he woke from his nap, I came to sit beside him, in the narrow shaft of light that slanted down from the opening above. He leaned against me, the kitten in his lap. "Shirak," he called him now. *Little lion.* I combed my fingers through Babak's tangled mop of hair and asked him, "Do you remember that dream you had, the one about the baby? The Scythian baby?"

"Yes," he said.

"Well, it came true."

He wiggled his tooth with his tongue.

"Did you know it would?"

"It was a true dream."

I drew away from him, looked down into his face, half in shadow, half in light. "How? How did you know?"

He shrugged. "I just knew."

I wanted to ask him more, ask again if he'd been visited with other dreams like this. But I'd tried before, and my questions had only annoyed him. Likely, he didn't understand these dreams any better than I. "Babak," I said, "does it trouble you to dream like this? Like the dream about the baby? Like the dream about the mountains and the shaggy beasts? Does it . . . cause you pain?"

"No," he said. "They were good dreams."

"But if they had been bad dreams . . ."

"I don't like bad dreams," he said.

For a full year after we had fled Susa with Suren, Babak had had nightmares whenever he slept. Many a time we had huddled at the side of some road or other—hungry, cold, exhausted—trying to wake Babak as he screamed in terror, trying to comfort him afterward. Many a time I had wanted to curse my father for bringing down this misery upon us.

King Phraates was an evil man. I knew that. But still . . .

The wreck of our lives these past three years. Hiding. Begging. Stealing. Seeking in vain for kinsmen or friends. At last coming to this loathsome place, the City of the Dead.

"Babak," I said, snuggling against him again, "if you sleep with this next to your skin"—I showed him the brown cloth—"you might have a dream about the man who owns it. And if you do, he will give us some coppers."

"Like the man with the baby?"

"Yes, like him."

"And we can buy melons? Those round melons with the yellow meat, and the big green ones, and—"

He *would* fix on melons; their size and shape made them difficult to steal.

"And," I broke in, "we can save the coins for passage to Palmyra, where we might find—"

His face fell. "I don't care about Palmyra!"

"Yes you do!" I said. "In Palmyra—"

"*I don't care.*"

I sighed. I had spoken so much about Palmyra that he'd wearied of hearing of it, especially since Palmyra had caused Suren to go away. There was no purpose in arguing with him now. No purpose in bringing up aunts and uncles he likely didn't remember. No purpose in raising his hopes about our mother.

Still, he deserved something for this dreamwork. "Very well. But you will have to tell me your dreams, Babak. You will have to tell them right away."

"And you will buy melons?"

I nodded.

"Two kinds, the green meat and the yellow meat?"

"Yes, Babak."

"And dates? And roasted chickpeas?"

He drove a hard bargain, this one. "If I can't steal them, I'll buy them," I said. "After you've told me your dreams and after someone has paid us for them."

He smiled that luminous smile of his, so full of joy.

"Babak. If you ever want to stop, just tell me. Do you promise? I don't want you doing this if it hurts you in any way."

His eyes, large and black and soft, seemed to search my face.

"We don't have to get money for Palmyra with your dreams. We'll find another way. I don't mind."

"Yes you do," he said.

I sighed. I could hide some things from him, but not what

I felt deeply. "I would mind it more if the dreaming hurt you in some way. Do you understand?"

He nodded. But I knew he wanted to please me. Would do nearly anything to please me—once he got over being stubborn—no matter the harm to himself.

This still felt like sin, someway.

But I would watch him very carefully. I would protect him. From Zoya. From the Scythians.

Palmyra. Our old life.

It stirred again within me—familiar now, and dark. I squeezed Babak's shoulders, then leaped to my feet, startling the kitten, who hissed fiercely and arched his back. I paced back and forth across the chamber.

Restless, restless.

Hunger. More powerful than before. Hunger for the life we had lost; hunger that fed on hope. Hunger so strong, I yearned to sweep all else aside to satisfy it.

*

CHAPTER 8

SLIT-NOSE

After that, they kept him dreaming. Twice a day—once during the afternoon rest in the heat of the day, and once at night. There was an uncle, too, who wanted a dream, and cousins, and the cousins' wives and husbands, and their cousins; and some of them, after they'd had one dream, wanted another. Babak dreamed of a profitable trade of salt. Of a bride at a wedding party. Of a winning toss of dice. Of an old man's recovery from a rash of painful boils. He dreamed of feasts and betrothals and more babies. He dreamed again of travel to this other land.

The first Scythian requested more dreams for himself; we tried using the lynx-fur hat from before, but no dream came. So Zoya came back with his sash and then his undertunic and then his cloak, all of which gave rise to new dreams. Only once did Babak have a nightmare, a dream of revenge and blood. Zoya took word to the Scythian that Babak would never again dream for that person. If he had another nightmare, she said, the dreams would cease.

Babak took the garments willingly enough. Except for the one nightmare, he didn't seem to mind the dreaming. He seemed to relish, once he was in a mood to tell, the attention he received. He doled out wedges of melon like a bountiful lord and took pride in being of use.

Over the following weeks some of the dreams came true. The salt trade, for one, and the winning toss of dice. The old man's boils began to heal. Others did not come true—

weddings, babies, journeys. "These are deeper into the future," Zoya said. "The Scythians know this. They believe."

"But why?" I asked. "Why do they believe the dreams of a child? How long are they willing to wait for the dreams to come true?"

Zoya tugged at a hair on her chin. "A wine merchant, when he craves to sell his wares, pours out a taste for his buyers. If the taste is good, the buyer takes on faith that the rest'll be so as well. So it is with Babak's dreams. Some have come to pass—a taste—and that'll do for now. With dreams, even more than with wine, folks want to believe."

But there was something else, I knew. All of Babak's dreams were true in this one sense: They expressed truly the wishes of the dream buyers—wishes the Scythians had not revealed to Zoya. To divine the deep desires of a person's heart . . . well, this, too, was a wonder. Sufficient, as Zoya had said, for a time.

We ventured into the marketplace again. The Scythians, Zoya assured us, would not accost us. She would meet only with the one for whom Babak had had the first dream, and he would neither describe us to others nor point us out. She told him that if he, or any of his clan, approached us, the dreams would cease.

It was different in Rhagae since the Magus and his entourage had come. More crowded—even after some of the merchants of the original caravan, impatient with the long stopover, formed a smaller caravan and continued east. The marketplace now bustled with servants running to and fro, snapping up the finest food and goods. They were full of themselves, these servants. They would ignore you unless you got in their way, then they would peer down their noses at you, as if you were lower than a centipede. Flute and horn and tambour blared from the street corners; the city teemed with musicians, some from the Magus's caravan and more who hoped to join it. A juggler flung an arc of bright leather balls overhead, and a conjurer produced baby birds from his mouth.

Rumor had it this Magus was staying here for a time to enjoy the healing waters before resuming his way east to his home in Margiana.

I would have thought that the hubbub would make it easier to be inconspicuous, and yet somehow this was not true. Merchants looked at us more closely now that we were buying food. Remembered us, in a way they had not when we were just part of the ever-present flow of beggars and thieves. This made it difficult to steal, where it's best to be as unremarkable as a flea. We had been invisible so long—we had survived by being invisible—that being noticed set wrong with me.

The back of my neck was forever prickling. I felt watched— even when I could see no one watching. I tried to tell myself that I was just on edge about the dreams, about Babak, but my sense of unease buzzed about me like a meddlesome fly. There were so many more strangers in the city now, and some of them seemed . . . alert . . . in a way I'd never marked before. Once, as I was bargaining for a melon, Babak startled and looked up quickly. Following the direction of his gaze, I saw a horse-archer with a creased, weathered face and a cropped beard streaked with gray. He had watchful eyes that missed nothing— and a slit through one nostril. The man shot Babak a sharp glance. I broke off with haggling and hustled Babak away. When I looked back, the man's keen gaze had swept round to another quarter.

"Why did you jump, Babak?" I asked.

He shrugged, and that was all I could get out of him.

I'd seen this man before, giving orders to the Magus's servants. Still, he did not look rich and pampered, like many of the Magus's men. Though a dagger hung from a fine scabbard at his waist, his leather boots were worn and scuffed, his gray wool tunic unadorned but for thin felt bands at the neck and wrists.

Another day, two weeks after the dream about the shaggy

beasts, I caught a Scythian staring at us, bold as you please. Not *the* Scythian. This one was much leaner, with only a single tattoo that I could see.

A plague on that first Scythian! Clearly his tongue had been flapping! We ducked into an alley, then another, then climbed through a portion of the old palace ruins and took a circuitous way home. When I confronted Zoya, she patted my cheek as if I were Babak's age. "You fret overmuch, Mitra."

"*Ramin!*"

"Eh, yes, of course. But think you: Why would the Scythian tell? He wants the dreams to go on. I'll wager he's collected a purseful of copper for them from friends and kin. Why would he give away the source?"

Even so—though we had to be more careful, though we were *seen* now in a way we had not been before—our bellies were fuller. I could think more clearly. Care for us better. As for Babak . . .

Well. There was more meat on his ribs. His arms and legs looked less like skin-covered bones. But, though his face had filled out too, I had noticed something troubling of late: Dark circles had appeared beneath his eyes. And something else, even more disturbing. At times he would stare off into space, humming or singing softly to himself. When I asked what was amiss, he seemed to come back from a far place. He told me that all was well.

I didn't—quite—believe him.

But our cache of coppers grew—four for each dream. I bought a small pouch for them, and when it grew heavy, I exchanged some of the copper for silver. I took them out one night, the silver coins, after Babak was asleep. I shifted them from hand to hand, reveled in the weight of them. When Suren returned . . .

A pang of uneasiness seized me as I remembered how I had pushed him to go. My hands stilled.

Where was he? Why hadn't he returned?

I tried to stifle the voice inside that whispered that Suren had been gone too long, that the dreaming for coin couldn't last, that word of it would get out, that something ill was happening to Babak.

It didn't have to last, I told the voice. Not for long. Only long enough to amass passage to Palmyra. When we had it—Suren or no Suren—we would go.

This dreaming, I told myself firmly, was all to the good.

Some days after the incident with the thin Scythian I caught sight of him again, standing beside the man with the slit in his nose. I made to slip behind a heavy-laden porter, but too late. "There," the Scythian said, loud enough for me to hear. "There they are."

May he go to the dogs! I snatched Babak's hand and darted down an alley. Looking back, I saw that we were followed—not by the Scythian, but by Slit-Nose. I made for the palace ruins. He was new to the city; he was not as nimble as we; surely we would lose him there. But he was fast. "Wait!" he called. I cut round a water carrier, startling him into dropping his metal cup, then dodged between a portly merchant and a wood-carver. Babak tripped and stumbled headlong into the legs of a juggler; leather balls went flying in all directions. "Babak!" I gasped. The juggler let fly with a hail of curses, his voice high and reedy. I picked up my brother and ran through what remained of the old stone colonnade. I dodged the beggars encamped in the main hall, then set Babak down and pulled him over a heap of shattered stone, then down a tottery stairwell, then zigged and zagged with him through the dark stone underpassageways and came at last to squat inside a small storage chamber.

There. Slit-Nose would never find us now. "Sister, why are we hiding?" Babak asked.

"Shh!"

We huddled together, our bodies heaving with breath—

but we both knew how to breathe hard without sound.

Footsteps, coming down the stairs. They stopped, started again, moved closer, stopped.

No. He could not have followed us so far!

Then a voice, deep and measured: "I'll not harm you. I crave only to talk."

Bloodbeat pounded in my ears so loud I feared he could hear it too.

"The Magus has heard of your brother's dreams. He wishes to speak with you—both of you. Not to compel you— nay. But he'll reward you well."

In the dim light I could make out a man's shape—a darker dark just outside the chamber where we crouched. I set a hand on Babak's chest. *Quiet. Don't move.*

A pebble skittered across the floor, came to rest near my foot. Clutching Babak's hand, I bolted from our hiding place, bounced off of something—Slit-Nose. He scooped up Babak in his arms; Babak was screaming, kicking. I grabbed the man's arm with both hands, sank my teeth deep into the flesh of it, tasted blood, saw Babak poke a bony elbow into the man's eye. He roared out a curse; Babak slipped from his grasp; I shoved him into a crumbling tunnel formed by a heap of fallen stone and timbers. I followed Babak, squeezing between rock and wood, until we found a way out on the other side. I could hear the man above, clambering over the rubble, but it was a large, misshapen heap; it had slowed him down. Just ahead, another stairway, and beyond, the light of day. We were almost there. . . .

"Wait!" Slit-Nose called from somewhere behind us. "I'll not harm you! Wait!"

We burst out from under the rubble. Up the stairs, into the crowded streets, down one alley and then another, over a crumbling wall and through a neglected garden. Another alley. Another street. Through the city gates:

Away.

✳

CHAPTER 9

PEBBLES and STONES

As we left Rhagae and headed up the rocky slope to the City of the Dead, I began to seethe. That loose-lipped, double-dealing Scythian! He had agreed that no one was to approach us in the marketplace. His entire family was getting dreams from Babak—at no small profit to him, most like. And now this! I would tell Zoya there would be no more dreams. No more!

"Wait, slow down!" I turned back to see Babak stumbling up the hill behind me. I halted, trying to stopper down my rage for his sake, but it steamed up through the cracks and fogged my head. "What does he think he's doing?" I demanded of Babak. "Pointing us out to the Magus's man! There'll be no more dreams for them—that I promise."

Babak stepped back, stared up at me with huge, scared eyes. Scared of *me*, I realized. I took in a sharp breath, held it, then tried to breathe out what was in me that was frightening him. "Don't fret," I said, pulling him against me, rubbing his back. So bony he was, and light. Cricket light. "Tsk, little one. No need to fear."

And perhaps, I thought, that was true. Perhaps there was no need to fear. The Magus's man had made no move to follow us, so far as I could tell. And, "Not to compel you," he had said. Besides, the Magi abhorred a lie . . . so our grandmother had ever told me.

By the time the City of the Dead loomed before us, Babak had settled a bit—and so had I.

Not for long.

Chink.

A pebble hit not a forearm's length in front of us. I looked round, trying to find the source of it.

Chink. Smack.

Another pebble, then a larger stone, one to the right of us, the other, left. Babak sheltered himself behind me; I squinted up at the caves, against the glare of the sun. Three people—four, perhaps—stood at the lip of a chamber that opened to air above us.

"Go 'way!" someone said.

Smack.

Chink slap.

Chink.

"Get off with you. Go!" This one, a woman.

They were throwing stones . . . at *us?*

"Rudabeh?" Babak stepped forward. "Why are you throwing stones? You could hurt somebody. You could—"

I snatched his hand, yanked him back, kept moving away from the caves. Rudabeh—the woman with the hump and the withered leg. Once, Babak had found a large, thick-soled boot lying in the street and had offered it to her. She had cut away the sole and affixed it to the bottom of one of her sandals, to extend her shorter leg. In return she had finger-knit a cap for Babak out of some string she had found.

"Babak, 'tisn't safe for you," she called, and her voice seemed less harsh now. Seemed sad. "'Tisn't safe for us, with you here. The Eyes and Ears of the king . . ."

I stumbled, caught myself, turned back to stare. What about the Eyes and Ears of the king?

More people appeared in ones and twos and threes in the openings that pocked the cliff. Usually these caves were silent, with lonely, shuffling figures, few of whom wanted to draw notice, except those whose minds had come unmoored. Never before had I seen a congregation—a mob.

Another *smack*, and another—this one hit my foot.

"Ouch!"

Then a hail of them, all at once—bigger stones and chunks of hardened mudbrick—striking my shin, my knee, my shoulder. Babak cried out; I picked him up, spun round and, hunching my back against the volley, began to flee.

"Cease with that!"

It was Zoya, hobbling up the road from Rhagae. She must not have been far behind us. Now she brandished her walking stick up at the mob. "Shame on you! It's little Babak you're stoning. Leave off!"

The *chink* sounds of rock-against-dirt dwindled. Out of range, I turned round, tried to make out who the other stone throwers were. Some had slunk back into the blue-blackness inside the caves; the others shimmered in the glare of the sun. The one-armed storyteller? The woman who conversed with a husband who wasn't there? The emperor of Rome?

"They've drawn the king's spies, them two," protested a querulous voice. "This is our last safe place, and they've spoilt it."

Spies. *The Eyes and Ears of the king,* Rudabeh had said. Here?

"I told you, nothing's spoilt," Zoya said. "I'll see to the Eyes and Ears. By the morrow you'll have nothing to fear."

Then, "Go," she commanded under her breath, giving me a shove. "Quick—before the wind shifts again. To my chamber—not yours."

✳

CHAPTER 10

THE EYES and EARS of THE KING

Zoya clucked and fussed over Babak, checking him for bruises by the light that seeped into her cavern. "My brave little man," she said.

They were stoning me as well, lest you didn't notice, I wanted to remind her. But even more, I needed to know about the Eyes and Ears.

As I bandaged my cut leg with Babak's dreaming cloth from the night before, Zoya explained that two men dressed as merchants had come earlier to the City of the Dead, asking to know about a small boy named Babak and an older brother or sister. "But they didn't fool me," Zoya said. "How often do you see a merchant with a bow case on his saddle or a bow ring on his thumb? And I've never seen a merchant with eyes that hard."

The Eyes and Ears of the king. I had been so certain they were through with us!

Once, not long after we fled Susa, I had seen them. Suren had motioned us to crouch behind a heap of baskets in a crowded marketplace and told me to watch two riders who were passing on the street. The Eyes and Ears usually traveled in pairs, I had heard, and often dressed as these were—as prosperous merchants. But these merchants moved with a muscular grace, like soldiers. Daggers flashed at their belts, and their eyes, as they swept through the crowd, were searching and pitiless.

"Are they looking for us?" I'd whispered to Suren.

He had shrugged. "Might be."

"But why? We're not a threat to Phraates—we're only—"

"You know better than that. The children of Phraates' enemies . . . tend to disappear."

I had said, "Surely he wouldn't send his spies across the country to search us out," and Suren had just looked at me.

"Sister?" Now Babak scooted next to me, looked up at me with eyes gone wide with worry. I tucked him under an arm.

"I never thought to see *you* short of words, Mitra. Ramin," Zoya amended, with more gentleness than was her wont. She shook her head, made a little *hunh!* sound in her throat. "Eh, you must be noble. Very noble, to prick the interest of the Eyes and Ears."

"Did one of them have a slit in one nostril?"

"No," Zoya said. She shot me a sharp, searching look, one I could not interpret. "Why do you ask?"

I shrugged. Her *no* had seemed startled but had had the ring of truth.

"Did you tell them where we were? Did the others?"

"Eh, the others all slunk away, too scared to say a word. I told the spies that I recollected you but hadn't seen you for weeks. I told them you must have found another place to live. Then, once they'd left, I went to find you, to warn you."

Another favor. What would this one cost, I wondered.

"Tell me," Zoya said. "Who are you, in truth? What happened to you and your kin? Suren told me some, but . . . why do the king's Eyes and Ears want Babak?"

Because of Father. Because he had plotted to overthrow Phraates, to take the crown for himself.

But it had been three years!

"Ramin? I asked you, why?"

"Why should I tell you? So you can betray us?"

"Don't be a thick-wit! I'm your friend. Your *only* friend. If I weren't, I'd have betrayed you long since."

True, she had kept some secrets. About our noble birth. About my sex.

"Maybe the Eyes and Ears heard something about Babak's dreams," I said. "That Scythian who stared at us, the one I told you about—he's been flapping his tongue. I saw him! He pointed at Babak, and then another man chased us."

"Chased you? Who?"

I described Slit-Nose vaguely—leaving out that he was a servant of the Magus. I didn't want her running to the caravansary, selling Babak's dreams. The Magus had power, and power did as power pleased. He could force us to go east to Margiana with him, take us yet farther from Palmyra.

Zoya frowned. "A scar, you say? A slit in one nostril?"

I nodded.

"Well," she said thoughtfully. "Be that as it may. Folks here don't want the Eyes and Ears sniffing round. We all have secrets, Ramin—and none of us craves the notice of the king's spies. No. You can't stay."

"But they didn't find us. They don't know we're here. We could lie low for a while, until Suren—"

"Suren is not here!" Babak flinched and stiffened under my arm. Zoya continued less harshly, but her eyes were fierce. "You don't know when he'll return. The Eyes and Ears of the king have come looking for Babak—here, to these very caves! They're a different breed of steed from the Scythian that searched for you before, Ramin. They *will* find you if you stay. They'll lace folks' palms with silver till they find their way back here. It's only a matter of time till they return."

"But . . ."

Where could we go? Although I'd been planning to leave—eager for it—the prospect now felt like stepping off a precipice. Nothing to catch on to. Nowhere safe to land. I didn't know another place, know the ways of it. Snug places to hide. The best spots to beg or steal or scavenge. And Suren. How would he find us? I clutched at something Zoya had said earlier. "But you promised you'd take care of the Eyes and Ears. By tomorrow, you said, we wouldn't have to worry."

"*They* needn't worry. *You* must. Listen. Have you put by passage to Palmyra?"

I shook my head. I wasn't sure how much it would take, but Suren had spoken of quantities of gold—not just silver and copper.

"But you've put by some. I'll take you to the Magus, ask for protection."

"No."

"Don't be a fool, Mitra. He's all but made of gold. He could keep you safe."

"And we would be forced to go where he is going—not where we need to go. We would live at his pleasure; he would command us. We couldn't book passage for Palmyra, we couldn't slip away—"

"Mitra, you misjudge your peril. The Eyes and Ears—"

"No. Not with the Magus."

Zoya opened her mouth, seeming about to reply, then shut it. "Eh, well. As you wish." She bowed down before me, mocking. "But you'll need to hide somewhere till nightfall. I know a place for it. Then we'll see."

"And we're not leaving Rhagae. Not until Suren returns."

I knew I was being mulish. I knew we had to leave—and soon—but I didn't want to, and I didn't want to go with the Magus, and I didn't want to have to be *grateful* to Zoya, and I didn't want to be pushed.

Zoya was shaking her head. "Mitra," she said gently. "Why do you think the king's Eyes and Ears thought to ask for Babak *here?*"

"The Scythian! I told you, he's been talking!"

"To this city, Ramin. Why would they come here?"

"I . . . I don't know. They've likely been to many cities, they—"

"They said they had—*to come to this city*—traveled far." Zoya waited a moment, waited for the word to come to me.

"*Suren.*" It came out in a whisper, like breath.

"Mmm." She nodded. "And why now, after all this time?

And," she said, holding up a hand to hush me, "if they asked for Babak by name, why didn't they ask for Suren as well? You—you're a girl. Not like to come avenging your kinsmen one day. But Suren . . . how long is it he's been gone?"

"A little more than two months."

"Well." She shrugged. "It's my guess . . . Suren's been captured."

✳

CHAPTER 11

CAPTURED

Captured.

The word rang in my ears as Zoya pushed aside a tall basket set against a far, dark corner of her chamber, revealing a low opening. *Suren—captured.*

Something was wrong with my mind; it was like polished marble, with no soft, porous places for *captured* to seep in and penetrate. There was only the light of Zoya's lamp, moving before us through the dank and airless passage, and the feel of Babak's small hand in mine. There was the smooth, hard rock against my feet, and baskets of dried fruit and nuts along the walls.

Captured. Try as I might, I couldn't imagine it. I could see him only as he had been years ago in Susa—the older brother I had adored, had followed like a puppy. I could see the lock of hair that fell across his eyes as he bent to untangle a halter rope knot I had botched. I could feel his strong hands lifting me out of an olive oil jar where I had hidden and become stuck. I could hear his patient voice defending me to my mother after I had committed some offense—lost my temper, perhaps, or stayed out too long riding, or ruined yet another gown.

A whiff of fresh air restored me to the present. A little way ahead, a different kind of radiance: an opening. Drawing near, I saw that a boulder stood a short distance outside the cave mouth, blocking the entrance from prying eyes.

So this was where Zoya stored her cache. This was how she managed to get in and out without anyone's seeing.

"Sit down now," she said. "We'll bide here till dark."

"And then?"

"And then we'll see."

"We'll see? Don't treat me like a child; I want to know. Perhaps Babak and I will find our own way."

It was dim in the faint sunlight that leaked into this place. Still, I caught her look of scorn. "Your own way. And I wonder what that might be. Listen: I've a friend, not two hours' walk from here. I . . . did her a favor once. She owes me."

Of course she did. But, "Two hours' walk. There is no city, nor even a village within two hours."

"Her husband's of the marsh folk."

The marsh folk. I had heard tell of them. It troubled me, though, to put our fate in Zoya's hands. For so long I had trusted no one but Suren and myself.

Captured.

Could we trust Zoya?

She didn't wish us ill, I didn't think. Though desire for her own gain pulled her hard, she did seem fond of Babak. *Her brave little man.* And she truly could have betrayed us before now.

"When can we go home?" Babak asked.

I flashed Zoya a silencing look. "In a while," I lied. I rubbed his back, as my mother used to rub mine. To Babak, *home* was a tiny cavern in the City of the Dead. And now he was denied that as well.

Zoya stayed with us for a time. She leaned against a wall and began to snore so loud, I was certain we would be discovered. I poked her to make her stop; she grunted and thrashed at me with her stick. Babak curled up against me, and soon I felt his body breathing in the slow cadences of sleep. Dreaming? What would it be like, to dream? To escape this life and dwell, for a time, in another? It had been so long, I could scarcely remember. I closed my eyes for a moment or two but opened them when I heard a soft rustling. Zoya was tucking something beneath Babak's tunic.

"You'll need coin for the journey," she explained. "Once you're gone, there'll be no more from the Scythians. Here." She pressed four coppers into my hand. "Your portion, and Babak's. I'll collect for the whole after you're safe away."

I took the coins. I found it oddly comforting that Zoya was trying to squeeze out one last bit of profit from Babak's dreams. It made me less wary of her kindness. And we would have need of coins. Of that I had no doubt.

Soon, Zoya told me she was going out to seed the rumor that Babak and I had gone east with the earlier caravan—through the Caspian Gates to Margiana. "With luck," she said, "the Eyes and Ears'll fall for it."

"Why would they?" I demanded.

She regarded me with an expression I could not quite fathom. Pity, perhaps, but with a flinty bite of judgment. "Suren told me what you would not hear—you were so intent upon his going. He told me he feared the Eyes and Ears—"

"He told *me* he feared them!"

"Feared they would force him, by means of . . . pain, to tell where you and Babak lived. And so, when not in pain, he would also tell them you had gone to Margiana. Which they might believe if, once here, they also heard rumors to that effect." With that she hobbled outside.

I slumped against the cave wall, feeling a chill wrap itself around my heart.

By means of pain.

Oh, Suren!

He had not wanted to go. I had quarreled with him, cajoled him, pressed him without mercy. I had accused him of being soft, of settling for the brutish life of the City of the Dead, of growing content with the companionship of the caves' lowborn dwellers. *If you care nothing for yourself,* I had flung at him, *think of Babak. Think of his birthright.*

My birthright. Thought, but never said. How could I survive without hope, without dreams of reclaiming our old life?

Once, Suren had been strong. He had rescued us in Susa, had gathered us up and hidden us from the soldiers in a secret chamber beneath the house. He had led us away at night, through many nights, through many weeks, through many months. But in time, it seemed, something vital had leaked out of him. He would spend all day in the City of the Dead, sleeping, wandering through the passages, gossiping with this pathetic old beggar, listening to the woes of that one. It was I who stole or scavenged all our food, I who kept our lamp in oil.

You can't have your old life back, he would say to me. *It's over. Done.*

But I had shamed him into leaving.

And despite that, he had laid plans to protect us?

Something was drifting apart within me, like a tattered old spiderweb, snapping one thin strand at a time—some false hope that kept me strung together so long as I pretended to believe in it. That Suren would go to Susa, find the gold, lead us all back to Palmyra, as he had led us here. That he would reunite us with our kin and the life we were meant to live.

Now we were alone, with no one to care about us—only those who would shun us, or use us one way or another, or . . .

Captured.

A shudder passed through me.

And what the Eyes and Ears of the king wanted with Babak, I did not care to think.

✳

CHAPTER 12

STAR DANCE

At last, when the light from outside had faded, I heard a scraping sound. A faint glow of lamplight seeped into the passage to Zoya's chamber. I sat taut and coiled—wondering if I ought to wake Babak, wondering if we ought to flee—but soon my ears recognized Zoya's shuffling footsteps, and soon after, my eyes found the shape of her stooped form.

She came to squat beside me. "The seeds are planted," she said. "Let's hope they bear fruit." She reached into her sash and pulled out Shirak, who opened his one eye wide and let out a protesting mew. "See what I found."

I groaned but took the kitten. I had forgotten all about him.

Zoya reached into Babak's tunic for the cloth she had put there and secreted it into her sash so quickly I caught only a flash of white. She held up her lamp to illuminate his face. "Has he dreamed?"

"I don't know. He was peaceful all this time."

"Best wake him now. Time to go."

"Babak," I said, gently shaking his shoulders. "Wake up." His eyes blinked open, then shut. "We have to go now, Babak. Look."

I set Shirak beside him; the kitten purred and butted his head against Babak's belly.

"Ask him about his dream," Zoya murmured in my ear. "Ask him."

"No," I whispered. "He'll balk."

"Babak," Zoya said, ignoring me, "did you dream?"

He rubbed his eyes and frowned. "I don't know."

"Think, my brave little man," she said, flinching as I poked her but continuing nonetheless. "Those dreams you had for others. Did you wake from one just now?"

He gathered up Shirak, clambered into my lap, and hid his face against my chest. "He'll tell you when he's ready," I said.

Zoya made an impatient noise in the back of her throat. "Babak—"

"No!" he said.

Zoya cursed softly and turned away from us.

"What is the matter with you? You'll have to sell the dream later; there isn't time now."

By the lamplight I could see her shoulders fall, as with a sigh. She looked up. "You're right," she said. "You can't stay here." She blew out the lamp; suddenly, it was dark. "Come."

We stayed off the roads as much as possible. Like me, Zoya knew many roundabout ways. Before long the moon rose, large and round, washing the landscape with a milky radiance that made it easier to see where to place our feet—and would surely reveal us to any who might come looking. The sight of a shepherd in the distance or the unexpected rustling of a clump of brush or the clattering of rocks on the path sent my heart into my throat. Once, we heard the clopping of a horse's hooves. We dived behind an outcropping of rock and huddled in a hollow of darkness, breathing dust, holding ourselves still. Babak shivered convulsively against me; the nighttime air of early autumn had begun to bare its teeth. I held him tight, praying that his silent movement would not vibrate the air and make us known.

I thought of Suren. Captured.

But when, in a moment, horse and rider passed, I suddenly wondered: How did we know this was so? Perhaps someone had recognized Suren in Rhagae or had overheard him talking and reported it to the king's Eyes and Ears. And even if he had been captured, he might escape. Yes, surely he would! Father had escaped capture once, long ago, and Suren was quick; he could ride like the wind. We had no cause to think the worst.

Babak shivered again. Looking down, I saw that his feet had begun to bleed. I ripped in half what remained of a dream cloth I had secreted in my sash, and bundled up each of his feet. Shirak, also in my sash, poked out his head to watch.

We set off again.

For a stooped old crone who leaned upon a walking stick, Zoya set a rapid pace. Perhaps her back and knees were bad, but the rest of her seemed spry enough. We clattered up heaps of broken rock, skidded down brushy defiles, trudged across long expanses of gravelly sand. Babak tripped and fell. His knees now bled through his trousers, and his feet dripped blood as well. My grandmother's voice said *contamination* in my ears, but I told her there was nothing to be done. I carried Babak on my back for as long as I could, then set him down to walk.

In time the reek of *marsh* began to drift in to me: damp, and rot, and green, growing things. Soon we were threading through a forest of reeds; the ground grew soft and wet, sucked at my bare feet, squished between my toes. And soon again the water rose to my ankles, then halfway to my knees. It felt cold at first, but before long it seemed warmer than the air. Babak began to whimper. I stooped down to let him clamber up on my back. A bullfrog croaked, hoarse and low; I slapped at buzzing insects that alighted on my arms and stung. It was darker in the marsh, especially once the moon had set. I didn't want to think what was in the water, but visions of wriggling snakes and leeches and sharp-clawed, scuttling things began to creep into my thoughts.

"Are you sure you know where you're going?" I asked Zoya. She grunted.

"What is the favor you did for this woman?"

"If you must know, I helped her escape when I midwifed for a princess. She was a slave—a foreigner—and . . . well, 'tis a tale for another time."

Helped a foreign slave escape? This woman's past was full of secrets and intrigues.

On we slogged. My legs began to feel leaden, and my back throbbed with pain. In a while Babak tipped back his head, throwing me off balance. "Babak! Don't do that."

"Stars," he said.

"Hmph." I was of no mind to prattle about stars.

"Like my dream," he said, pointing at the sky.

My feet, of their own accord, ceased walking. "You dreamed of stars?"

And now Zoya had stopped too. She turned around, swished through the shallow water toward us.

"Star dance," Babak said. "Two stars. Near, apart. Near, apart. Three times near and apart."

"When . . ." Zoya looked at me, then back over my shoulder at Babak. "When did you dream this?"

"Today," Babak said. "When we were hiding."

She blinked and shook her head, turned to me. "He said he didn't dream."

"Because you pressed too hard. Didn't I tell you?"

"Stars." Zoya scratched her chin, gazed up at the sky. The night was clear. Stars clustered thick and bright.

"Two stars," she mused. "Dancing." At once Zoya leaned in, thrusting her face right next to Babak's. "Tell me more about this new dream of yours."

I twisted away, putting distance between her and Babak. *"Don't . . . push."*

She glared at me.

Something did not feel right. True, Zoya was ever captivated by Babak's dreams, but now there was a sort of fever about her that I had not seen before. For the first time I wondered what she dreamed of, hoped for. Was her fiefdom in the City of the Dead enough for her? Or did she dream of regaining her old station and hobnobbing with nobility?

"Whose cloth was that?" I asked. "The one you gave to Babak today?"

"They don't always tell me," she answered lightly. Then, "Eh, look!"

I sighted along the line of her pointing finger. Dimly ahead, in the marsh, I could make out a faint sprinkling of lights among the reeds. I hesitated, feeling a cold shiver of unease between my shoulder blades, then shook it off. I was too weary to flee, and there was nowhere else to go. Besides, Zoya wouldn't do harm to Babak.

Surely she would not.

PEOPLE of THE MARSH

It was a small settlement of huts, all huddled together on a dry, hummocky island in the middle of the marsh. Reed huts, they must be, for the lights we saw now appeared to be inside the dwellings, screened fine by woven walls. As we approached, three or four moving, brighter lights appeared. Torches.

"Who goes there?" a man called. Zoya shouted back her name; the torches drew near. Soon I could make out the shapes of six or seven men.

"Wait here," Zoya said, and she sloshed on alone. I set down Babak. Skinny though he was, my back ached from carrying him. His hand sought mine; I clasped it.

"When can we go home?" he asked.

"Hush."

A disputation arose. "Thief," one man said, pointing a finger at Zoya; another man cried out, "Hoaxer!" It seemed Zoya hadn't told me the whole story about her doings with these people.

She spoke to them, low and intent. "One night's all," I heard her say, and "donkey" and "your reward."

The squabbling swelled around her. At last she began to fumble with something, then held out an open hand to one of the men. A glimmering in the torchlight.

Silver coins.

The man hesitated, then took them. Zoya motioned to Babak and me. "Come!"

The hut was close and dim, furnished with a lamp; a scattering of cushions; a few earthenware dishes, pots, and jars; and some reed mats on the floor. Far less than we'd had in Susa, but opulence beyond imagining compared with the City of the Dead. Zoya spoke softly to her old friend while the husband stood just outside in convocation with the other men. The woman listened with quick, frightened glances at Babak and me from time to time. She did not ask our names, and we did not offer them. At last she set out a platter of flatbread and soft cheese, while Zoya fussed over some cups and a jar of wine. I tried to catch her eye. I wanted to know what had transpired back there in the marsh, and hadn't had a chance to ask. Zoya glanced at the woman, then shook her head at me as if to say, *Not now.*

"Here, Ramin," she said, "some wine."

The wine was bitter, the bread stale, and the cheese had begun to grow mold. I didn't care. They slaked the thirst and filled the belly.

It had been a long, long day. The drowsiness that for hours had lapped at me in ripples now engulfed me in swelling waves. Babak took Shirak from my sash and fed him some of his cheese.

"Brave Shirak," he said. "Roar!"

I leaned back on a cushion, allowed my eyelids to shut.

Drifting. Drifting down into a deep, deep place. I could still hear Babak's voice—talking to Shirak, telling him not to be afraid. I listened to the melody of it for a while, little uplifts and downturns, patterning rhythms. Lulling me.

It was just before I went under, before I was entirely drowned in sleep, that I saw Babak's face above me. Worried. I forced a smile, started to rise, but then Zoya was there, taking him away. "Don't pester him," I heard her say. "Weary . . . needs to sleep."

Sleep. Needs to sleep.

I slept.

★

When I awoke, my body was damp with sweat. There was a hard, pulsating knot inside my head, my belly churned, and something smelled odd: of mud and decay, and lush, new sprouting growth. Long, thin shafts of light pierced the walls of the cavern. . . .

Walls. Not stone, but mats of plaited reeds. I sat up, but the room swayed and my insides sloshed. I lay back down again, reached for Babak.

Not there.

I remembered then: Zoya. The hut in the marsh. Eyes and Ears of the king.

A fly droned in sleepy circles round the room. I watched it for a while, then sat up again—slowly this time, so as not to knock loose the painful knot in my head—and looked about. Shirak, curled up beside me. Jars for water and oil. Pots for cooking. Rolls of reed mats. Atop the mats, a folded length of cloth, white as the face of the moon.

No Babak.

But now another sound: children's voices. Laughter, outside the hut. Babak must be there.

I stood—the room swayed gently back and forth before subsiding—and stumbled to the open doorway. There was a stretch of hard-packed earth and then the marsh, reaching out as far as I could see. The sun stood high in the sky. Most of the morning had gone.

How long had I slept?

We had arrived, I guessed, toward the end of the evening watch. I had slept the rest of the night . . . and most of the next morning as well?

There they were, the children, a ragged flock of them—darting in and out among the huts, playing a "catch me" game. I shifted my gaze from child to child, searching for Babak. Suddenly one of them caught sight of me, stopped, pointed. "He wakes!" she shouted.

"He wakes!"

"He wakes!"

They all ran laughing and shrieking into the marsh, disappeared one by one among the reeds.

"Wait!" I cried. "Where's Babak?"

I followed them into the shallow water, but my legs wobbled
strangely and the marsh mud sucked at my bare feet. I could
not keep up.

Drugged. The word floated into my mind. *The wine was
drugged.*

But why?

A sick feeling of dread rose in my belly.

"Babak!" I called.

I heard them still—the shrill voices—but fainter now, farther. In the distance too I could hear men's voices, and chop-
ping sounds, and rustlings of reeds. The mournful croak of a
bullfrog. Another, higher, answering.

My feet slowed, then dragged to a stop. The sweet, rich
reek of marsh rot seeped into the throbbings of my head, the
roilings of my gut.

*I'll take you to the Magus. . . . Don't be a fool, Mitra. . . . He
could keep you safe.*

The white cloth. White, as Magi wore.

Ask him about his dream. Ask him.

Star dance. . . . Near, apart. . . . Three times near and apart.

Here, Ramin, some wine.

Sunlight flickered between the rushes. A dragonfly
buzzed past, a quick flash of brilliant blue green. A *ploink* as
some small creature dived into the water nearby. I slapped at
a stinging insect. Welts, all over my arms.

My knees caved in. I knelt in the dark water, cupped my
face in my hands. The sickness lurched up from my belly; I let
it out.

A swishing of water. A rattling of reeds. All at once a man
appeared before me; children clustered round.

I wiped my sleeve across my mouth. "Where is my
brother?" I demanded.

No one answered, but I knew.

✳

H E L L   H A G

I turned away and plowed back through the marsh water. I would find him. I would find him and steal him back. My head pained me, my legs did not work right, and my mind felt numb and cloudy. I had no idea how I would do it, but I would find him. I would.

"Wait!" A man's voice.

I looked back. More men now, their reed-cutting knives at their sides. The urchins stared at me, whispering and pointing. One of the men drew near, and I recognized him by his long jaw and bristly eyebrows that went up at the ends: the husband of Zoya's friend. "Babak," he said. "The boy that came with you and the old woman. He's your brother?"

"Yes! What did she tell you?"

The men exchanged glances. "I told you about that one, that Zoya," the husband-of-the-friend said. "You can't trust her." He turned back to me.

"If you wish to speak to her, she's here in the village."

"Zoya is here?"

He nodded. "She borrowed my donkey, but I told her if it wasn't back this morning, I'd come after her myself. She returned with two donkeys—the one I lent her and another she said she'd bought. . . ."

"After she sold my brother to the Magus."

His face remained still—all but his eyes, which widened a little, as if in surprise. "She told a different tale. We know she left with the boy last night and came back later without him.

We know she got herself another donkey. She told us the boy was in peril, needed sanctuary."

Grimly I lurched back the way I had come. The men and children followed in a ragged half circle behind and around me. I tripped once and fell to my knees; another time I stepped into a deep place and sank in water nearly to my chin. And all the while they followed—solemn, graceful, at ease in the marsh water, suiting their pace to mine.

Yet soon my head began to clear and my legs grew strong. A jolt of rage surged through me, merged with the beating of my heart: *Babak. Babak. Babak.*

And now the village rose above the reeds, and now I could see a gathering of women, watching us come near. "Fetch the old hoaxer!" the husband-of-the-friend called. "Fetch Zoya!"

But there was no need. A figure appeared in a doorway; she hobbled down among the assemblage of women. *Zoya.* And then I was running—or as close to running as I could manage—rushing at Zoya through the last remaining reeds and up onto the shore.

"You old hell hag! Fork-tongue! Lizard spawn!"

Zoya raised her walking stick to fend me off. Someone grasped one of my arms; I struggled against him; another man took hold of my other arm; they held me fast.

"You sold Babak, you demon's get! Scorpion! Bloodsucking daughter of a leech!"

"Eh, stop it, Ramin," Zoya said. "You're making a spectacle of yourself."

"Give him the donkey."

I whipped my head round; it was the husband-of-the-friend.

"I paid good coin for it," Zoya said. "It's mine."

"If what he says is true—and knowing you, I doubt it not—you got plenty for what wasn't yours to sell. Give him the donkey. The saddlebags, too. Maybe he can find his brother before it's too late—if only to say farewell. Come sunrise I want you away from here and back in the hole you crawled out of. I don't care how much peril you're in."

Zoya's glance flicked toward me and away. She shrugged. "Eh, it's a bony old nag. More trouble'n it's worth."

The man turned to the children. "Fetch the donkey. Fill a waterskin for the boy, and a sack of food. Get him a head-cloth, too—he'll have need of it." To the men holding me he said, "Let him go."

I shook out my arms, glaring at Zoya. "I trusted you," I said. "I knew your greedy old soul was pinched and dry, but I thought there was at least a drop of human kindness in you."

"I've done you a favor and you don't even know it, you little whelp. *Ramin,*" she added, a pointed reminder that she had kept that secret.

"You pretend to care for others," I flung back, "but truly you serve only yourself."

"And who do *you* serve, oh high-and-mighty one? We're more alike than you think." Zoya turned to leave, then hesitated.

"I would've given it to him myself, that donkey," she said to the husband. Then, to me, "You won't find them at the caravansary. They left this morn, heading for Sava."

She was the oldest, skinniest, feeblest donkey I had ever set eyes on. She let me mount, but she was balky and slow. I'd have set a brisker pace if I'd straddled a toad. Some of the marsh urchins guided me along the pathways through the marsh. When we came to a road, one of the older ones pointed west along it. "This road," he said, "leads you to another one, a bigger road. Sava's south and west."

I hesitated, for I had heard that the Magus would soon be journeying east, to Margiana. Might Zoya have lied again?

But it hadn't felt like a lie, what she had said. It had felt like a grudging gift.

A girl about Babak's age reached into her sash and held out the one-eyed kitten to me. "Here," she said. "For Babak."

I almost didn't take him. But the kitten let out a hoarse

meow and scrambled eagerly toward me, so I tucked him into my sash.

"Move along!" I admonished the donkey after the children had vanished into the reeds. I clouted her ribs with my heels; she put her head down, flicked a great, hairy ear, and refused to budge.

I dismounted and hauled on the donkey's lead; she pegged her heels to the ground and strained backward. I sighed, let the lead go slack. *Then* that ornery donkey began to walk.

I darted in front of her so at least I would seem to be leading. Looking back north to where the Elburz Mountains shimmered in the distance, I tried to find Rhagae, but it was too far away.

Rhagae. It was nearly two years since we had come there. We had been hungry, too hot and too cold, scorned by the lowest of the low, forced to beg and steal and to live in the City of the Dead. Even so, I felt a strange hollowness in my heart to leave the city behind.

We had been family there, my two brothers and I.

Now we were each of us alone.

PART II

THE JOURNEY

———

✳

CHAPTER 15

THE CARAVAN ROAD

It wasn't much of a road, just a narrow rut in the dirt. We followed it west, toward the blue, humped shapes of the Zagros Mountains. I walked and rode in equal measure; the donkey's spine was knobby and uncomfortable, but not long after I dismounted, the hot sand and lacerating stones on the road drove me to mount again. When the sun stood directly overhead, another road came into view—wider, longer, one of the ancient trade routes. In days of old this road had been paved. Now broken stones littered the edges of a wide dirt track. I could see that a large caravan had recently passed, because of a churning of sand and dust, and the fresh mounds of horse and camel dung. Here and there I could make out the clear print of a horse's hoof. It seemed the caravan was going southwest. I squinted in that direction, for I could see far along the desolate plain.

But there was no sign of them—neither the caravan itself nor its telltale plume of dust. They must have left early, perhaps not long after Zoya came to them with Babak.

If it was the Magus's caravan.

If Zoya had spoken true.

Something stood out from the dust a little way down the road. I urged the donkey forward; for once she obeyed. I dismounted and picked it up.

It was a potsherd, with a fine green glaze. Part of a very costly pot. I rubbed it on my tunic to clean off the dirt. There was the winged insignia of those who worship the Wise God.

It might have belonged to someone besides the Magus. But it could very well have been his. I stuffed it into one of the saddlebags—the kitten was napping in the other—and mounted again. "Hurry!" I said, switching the donkey's flank. She turned her head, eyed me reproachfully with her huge, sorrowful eyes, then eased into a disconsolate slog.

Still, a caravan does not move quickly—especially one so large. This one would surely crawl, with its heavy-laden camels, with its women and entertainers and cooks. And even if I traveled more slowly than they, they would stop to rest, in time.

I would not. I would ride until I found Babak.

The afternoon sun stabbed like a dagger in the eyes. I could not get relief even by looking away, for shiny bits of rock spit back the light in blinding flashes that pricked my eyes like so many needles. The heat weighed me down, sapped my strength. Little whirlwinds arose from time to time, flinging grit into my eyes and mouth. Even after wrapping my head-cloth about my face, I still breathed in the smell of scorched dust and salt.

The water went fast, rationed out in gulps to me, in dribbles to the kitten, and in half calabashes to the donkey. We came across a stream, where we all drank of cloudy, silted water. I refilled the waterskin; we went on.

We met with few travelers on the road. There was one caravan—a small one, with only a few horsemen and a dozen or so pack camels. Later, near a tiny village, I passed a man and a woman leading a small donkey carrying great bundles of thornbush. I feared meeting up with brigands, but one good thing about poverty is that no one deems you worthy of the trouble it would take to rob you. I would be clear to view if the Eyes and Ears came this way. But they were seeking a five-year-old boy.

And still no sign of the Magus's caravan! This donkey covered ground more slowly than any beast I had ever seen.

It was not that she couldn't go faster; she could. Every so often, for no reason I could surmise, she would break into a tooth-jarring jog. But in a moment she would halt—again for no reason—and switch her tail at flies or root in her fur for fleas or simply gaze, seerlike, into the distance. Neither kicking the sorry beast, nor scolding her, nor lashing her with a rope, nor dismounting her, nor mounting up again, made a jot of difference. "Gorizpa," I took to calling her, mockingly. *Fleet-of-foot.*

Still, our laggardly pace gave me time to ponder. What would I do when we reached the caravan? Would I throw myself on the Magus's mercy, ask him to take me with him? Or . . .

How difficult could it be to snatch a small, willing boy from a caravan while all about him slept?

I've done you a favor, Zoya had said, *and you don't even know it.*

What had she meant? Not the donkey, surely. Had she meant that she could have sold Babak to the king's Eyes and Ears instead of the Magus?

Pah! Just like her, to pretend it was for us she'd done it.

Nevertheless, it had been only yesterday, after the Eyes and Ears had shown themselves, that she'd turned up with the white sash. Maybe she did truly worry about what Phraates would do to Babak.

Or maybe she was using us to serve herself, as ever!

And who do you *serve, oh high-and-mighty one?* she had asked. *We're more alike than you think.*

I felt the barb of truth in that. But truly it was different in my case. Everything I asked Babak to do was for his own good!

On we trudged, until the sun set the western sky aflame. The mountains glowed like molten gold, then faded to the pink of my mother's dog roses, then darkened to the color of ripe plums, and then blackened against a deep blue sky. Stars flickered into view, shedding a pale luminosity that we could see by. The winds died down and the plateau seemed to sigh, possessed by a great peace. There was something comforting about the rhythmic clop of the donkey's feet, about the coolness that gathered about my shoulders. The kitten clawed his way out of the saddlebag and climbed up my trousers into my lap, hooking his tiny claws into the fabric. I set him within the folds of my sash, from whence he surveyed the scene about us with his good eye as if all were his to rule.

"Little lion," I said to him. "Ferocious beast."

I had meant to keep on until I overtook the caravan. But sometime after the moon had risen, I found that I could not. The pleasant coolness of early evening had sharpened into a biting chill. My feet and legs ached from walking; long ago Gorizpa had begun to stumble, either from weariness or because she could not see well where to put her feet in the odd shadows cast by moonlight. A few outcroppings of rock stood near the side of the road ahead, extending in broken rows back toward the foothills. I stopped behind one of the outcroppings, out of sight of the road. Brigands, at least, might pass us by.

A snake slithered away on the ground; I shivered.

Gorizpa, once unloaded, rolled over and flopped about in the dust, scratching her back. When she had done, she began to crop a clump of dry scrub, making loud, grunchy noises. I drew near to hobble her; she swiveled an ear round and gazed at me soberly with great, brown, liquid eyes. I must be getting soft, I thought, stroking her grizzled muzzle. I reached inside one hairy ear and rubbed a smooth place with my fingertips. The thin, disapproving line of her lips went slack; she moaned and began to drool.

"Silly old creature," I said.

Shirak stalked off into the darkness and, despite his one blind eye, soon returned with some kind of small rodent, probably a mouse. He tortured it mercilessly for a little while, then ate.

I made short work of a pomegranate, a handful of dried

melon seeds, and several dates, then wrapped my coat about me and curled up on the hard ground. My coat had conferred some small protection against the blistering sun, but the nighttime chill of the plateau cut through it as if it were made of shadows and stitched together with threads of air. In the distance I heard the howling of wolves. Once, I heard a lion roar. I tried not to think of snakes.

My own lion leaned against me and began to give himself a bath. He delicately licked his paws and rubbed them across his eyes—the bad one, then the good one—scrubbing the high planes of his cheeks. At last he nestled into the curve of my body and began to purr with a sleepy, trilling sound. He was warm and yielding, almost liquid.

Not that it made any difference to me. But Babak would be glad of his company.

The next day we plodded on through the dry pebble-and-scrub terrain. From time to time we came upon a pond or stream surrounded by lush vegetation; then I refilled my waterskin and let Gorizpa graze and drink. By now the tracks of the Magus's caravan had merged with those of thousands of caravans before. We saw places where they might have stopped—where the scrub was flattened and the ground trodden by many hooves and feet—but it was impossible to know for certain who had stopped there. Just go on, I told myself. Still, by late afternoon the heat had sucked the life out of me, and fatigue crept over me like sand before the desert wind. We stopped again to rest and set off at sunset.

I think it was because darkness obscured the dust plume, until I saw it drift across the lowest stars, that I was so late in noticing him. A single rider, on horseback, galloping down the old road toward me. One, not two; that was a good sign. He was far enough away that he might not have seen us; at any rate, he gave no sign.

A messenger?

Or something more ominous?

Best to be safe. I cast about quickly for somewhere to hide. Outcroppings of boulders dotted the landscape to the west, toward the foothills. *Hurry.* I picked the nearest cluster and urged Gorizpa toward it; for once she did not resist. When we reached the rocks, though, she balked. *Hurry.* I dismounted and, scrambling up the gap between two large boulders, pulled on Gorizpa's lead. She snorted, brayed, and struck sharp, echoing clops on the stony ground. "Shh!" I told her. I prayed that the rider couldn't hear, comforting myself that I couldn't yet hear him. Out of sight of the road, I stuffed Shirak into a saddlebag. I rubbed Gorizpa's soft muzzle, then scratched all along the dark stripe on her back, hoping to keep her quiet. She made a little humming sound in her throat, pressed the bony front of her massive head against my belly and chest. Shirak mewed softly. "Shh," I told them both. "Shh."

I tried to close my mind off from the rider, tried not to think about who he might be or what might happen if he were to find us. But I couldn't quite stave off thoughts of brigands. Or of the king's Eyes and Ears.

I could hear him now, could hear the crunch of his horse's hooves on the sand and loose rock of the road. I waited a long while, until the hoof sounds receded in the direction we had come. At last I peered out, saw nothing, let out a sigh.

He came out from behind a rock. I heard a swish of metal on metal, caught the quick gleam of a dagger.

"Ah," he said. "I was hoping it was you."

✳

CHAPTER 16

HE CRIES for YOU

Lean, leathery face, fiercely lined and hollowed, covered with the dust of travel. Watchful eyes, faded to the color of honey. Cropped, graying beard. High, jutting cheekbones. Hawk nose, slit in one nostril:

Slit-Nose.

He sheathed his blade, and the ghost of a smile flickered across his harsh features. "So I should thank you, then," he said. "You've done half my work for me. Come along."

I backed away. I had wanted to meet up with the caravan, but not like this.

"Your brother. He needs you."

Fear shut my throat. "Is he . . ." It came out as a whisper; I couldn't finish.

"Nay, he is well. At least, not badly ailing, other than missing you. He cries for you day and night, refuses to tell the Magus his dreams, refuses to eat—"

"You call that well?"

"His health is in no danger at present. But we fear it will be soon, unless . . . He needs you." The man put his fingers to his mouth; a whistle pierced the night. A horse appeared from behind a rocky crag some distance away and began to trot toward us.

The man turned back to me. "The Magus is generous. He invites you to stay with your brother. He promises you will be well treated."

I pulled myself up to my full height, as so often I had seen my father do. "Are we free, then? Free to come and go as we please? Free to dream—or not dream? Pah! The Magus did not invite my brother—he bought him."

The man's eyes grew hard. "Your brother cries for you. Will you refuse him?"

Babak. My heart clutched as I pictured him crying, with no one to give him comfort. And I knew it would make no difference whether or not I refused. This man wouldn't return to the caravan without me. We were stripped of our freedom already. The only question was whether I would come willingly or no.

The man—Giv, he was called—grumbled about taking Gorizpa, but I wouldn't leave her behind. She was the only thing I owned, besides her saddlebags, the clothes on my back, and the small cache of coins. I didn't count Shirak. No one can own a cat. Besides, Gorizpa, slow as she was, might come in useful later. Babak could ride her when he and I escaped. As we *would*.

Muttering, with that slight rustic lilt of his, Giv tethered her behind his horse.

I climbed up pillion behind him, holding him loosely, my right knee knocking against his bow case and quiver. I hoped he would not feel my body through my garments and perceive that I was a girl. Though there was precious little to feel, I knew. My cousin Atoosa, at my age, had blossomed like two ripe peaches. But I was still skin and bones.

I tried to shift Shirak round to the back of my sash, but he hissed fiercely and let out an indignant cry. Giv twisted round, scowling. I feared he would fling Shirak to the ground. Instead Giv plucked him up by the scruff of the neck and, cupping him in a massive, dark, and callused hand—adorned only by a horned thumb ring such as archers wear—set him gently into a saddlebag. Shirak gave a single protesting yowl, then yawned, curled up, and promptly went to sleep.

A gibbous moon had risen by the time we came to the

caravansary. A guard hailed us; Giv replied; the tall gate creaked open to admit us. The courtyard was dark but puddled with golden light from torches set in cressets in the walls and lanterns tucked into niches. From a dim corner wafted a soft, sad flute melody; across the courtyard three men sat on a spread-out carpet playing a hushed game of draughts. Someone was cooking in an iron pot on a stick fire set on the cobblestones. The rich, fat smell of simmering meat made my mouth water. Other men, nestled against bundles and carpet rolls, snored in droning counterpoint.

I slid down off the horse; Giv dismounted. A servant approached and led horse and donkey away.

"The donkey is mine," I called to him.

The draughts players broke off their game, turned to stare at me.

Giv's scowl deepened. "No one would steal that donkey," he said. "Now, come."

I stood with my feet rooted to the stones. "Are you taking me to Babak?"

"Not yet."

"I want to see Babak."

"And so you will. But first you must see my master, Melchior."

Melchior. The Magus.

I had seen Magi before, of course, in our home in the hills above Susa. They would come to visit my father, to stay with us when they were on journeys. Revered priests, they were, servants of the Wise God, Ahura Mazda. Although we had honored Ahura Mazda and his prophet, Zoroaster, we had been neither pure nor regular in our practice, especially our mother and her women. So there was always a frenzy of cleaning and purification on such occasions. My mother's household gods would vanish as if they had never existed, to reappear mysteriously soon after the Magi had departed.

My grandmother, though—my father's mother—had

spoken to me often of the Wise God and of the teachings of his prophet. "There are the Light and the Dark," she would say, "and all who live have the power to choose between them. Good thoughts, good words, and good deeds lead the way to paradise."

Then she would exhort us not to forget that we were heirs to an old line of kings who truly revered the Wise God—kings who paid him genuine homage, not just empty words. "Remember who you are," she would say.

Sometimes, I had peeked through gaps in the arras while one Magus or another met with my father. I stared at their tall, domed caps with long tails and ear flaps; at the bundles of barsom rods they held; at their wide neckbands of hammered gold, graven with the winged symbol of divine grace. Now and then I stole up by the fire altar at midnight and watched them pray: washing the dust from their faces, hands, and feet; tying and untying the kusti cords about their waists; intoning solemn words in the old language; casting incense into the sacred fire.

I had sinned grievously since those days, having given up any pretense at purification. I had lived among bones and touched blood. I seldom prayed, and when I did, it might be to any of a number of gods. True, I was not yet fifteen years old and therefore considered a child, so the sacred obligations did not yet lie upon me. Still . . . what would this one think of me? Do to me?

Even more worrisome: Had Babak let slip that I was not a boy?

✳

CHAPTER 17

MELCHIOR

Giv, carrying a lamp, led me past the stables and servants' quarters on the lower level and up a steep, turning torchlit staircase. We walked along the roof terrace, past a row of wooden doors until we came to a large, ornately carved one that fit snug within a high stone arch.

Giv thumped on the door. It opened a crack; Giv murmured to someone, then motioned me within.

It was a small, square anteroom, tended by an armed guard.

"Stay," Giv told me. "I'll come for you."

He and the guard disappeared behind a curtained arch.

Light flickered from the crack between the leather curtain and the wall. I could hear many voices. I pulled aside the drape a tiny bit, peered into the room.

There, reclining upon a divan, was the Magus, a roundish melon of a man, swaddled head to toe in woolen blankets and coverlets of bright-hued silk. Beside him sat a silver tripod, from which issued clouds of incense. Many servants attended him. One brought him a cup of steaming liquid, another added coal to a brazier at his feet, still others offered him bits of food. The Magus's cap sat askew on his head; his gray beard bristled like an untidy bird's nest and harbored a collection of fallen crumbs. At once he wrinkled his nose and waved the food away. He drew in a couple of quick, shaky breaths. Someone thrust a cloth into his hand, and then, "Achoo!" It was more piercing than a donkey's bray and twice as loud. He sniffed, dabbed at his bright red nose, then jabbed one finger in the direction of the cup. A servant hastily gave it to him. The Magus slurped, then made as if to set down the cup in thin air. There was a scramble of servants, and an inlaid table, no bigger than a round of flatbread, appeared beneath the cup, just in time.

"Ah, Giv! Come, come!" His voice croaked; he clutched at his throat; someone offered him the hot liquid again, but he waved it away.

Giv bowed, then rose and whispered something into the Magus's ear. The Magus sat up straight and made a grand, shooing motion. "Begone!" he bellowed—with surprising strength and resonance, considering his infirmity. "All of you. Begone!"

Quickly I drew back, but it soon became clear that they were not leaving through the doorway near which I stood. I heard footsteps moving away and recalled a glimpse of a wider arch leading out of the room on the other side. Then Giv was at the curtain. "Come," he said.

I might have been tempted to regard this Magus as a foolish man, if not for his eyes. They regarded me with a calculating shrewdness as we approached. Giv bowed again, and I did likewise. "Here is the boy we sought," Giv said. "Ramin, Babak's brother."

"So soon?" The Magus spoke to Giv, but his gaze remained fastened upon my face. "I know you are swift, but this time you must have ridden the wind."

"I'd no need to ride clear back to Rhagae. I found the boy not far from here. Following us, I believe."

"Huh." The Magus combed through his beard, plucked out a seed of some sort, and flicked it away. "So you have come to join us?"

"I have come to fetch my brother," I said.

"Ah." He glanced at Giv, then back at me. Suddenly, it seemed, he had no need to sneeze, no interest in food or drink. "You must appreciate," he said, "that Babak is now my ward."

"The one who gave him—*sold* him—had no right. She is not kin to him. We are of noble blood." I longed to tell him exactly who we were, what legacy belonged to Babak. But the Magus might be loyal to Phraates. He might . . . A jolt of fear struck me. Might he have spoken with the Eyes and Ears? Might he be an agent of the king?

But the Magus did not seem the least bit interested in our ancestry. "Babak needs you," he said. "If you care for him, you'll see that he eats. Comfort him so that he may sleep."

"If I care for him!" Giv shot me a glance and made a low warning noise in his throat. I breathed in deep, tried to push down the rage, keep it out of my voice. "I care for him more than you do. More than anyone."

Melchior nodded, regarded me speculatively. "For that reason," he said, "I am prepared to offer you my hospitality. So long as you are helpful to Babak."

"Hospitality! You mean make me your servant, your chattel? I'm nobody's menial, I—"

"No, no, no." Melchior waved a hand and smiled the smile of an indulgent grandfather. "Think of me as your guardian. I do have . . . conditions . . . but you'll find I am a reasonable man."

"So, I may leave?"

He shrugged. "Yes. Babak would not be happy, but . . . I make no claim on you."

"Anytime I like."

"Of course."

"Your conditions?"

"There are six." He leaned forward and the shrewdness came back into his eyes. He ticked off his conditions on plump, beringed fingers. "First: You must not attempt escape with Babak, nor in any way undermine his work with me. Second: You must not tell anyone—anyone at all—about the nature of that work. Dreamwork—as I'm certain you have surmised. Further, no word of Babak's gift for dreams is to be mentioned. Believe me, I will know it if you do. Third: You will not have Babak dream for you or any other person of your choice. I'll not have the dreams of others intermingling with mine. Fourth: You will be purified and will keep yourself pure and not violate the precepts of the prophet Zoroaster. Fifth: You and Babak will stay with Giv in his quarters. I have put it out that Babak is under my protection, the orphaned son of a pious tradesman. I will say the same of you, and you need fear no harm."

"But we are of noble birth, not—"

"Your noble birth—such as it is," he said, taking in my raggedness from head to toe, "will not serve you here. Don't draw notice to yourselves. Sixth: It's best that you find ways to be of use. You're of an age where idleness would breed the contempt of others—or make tongues wag. My wife can see to Babak while you work. She is a kindly woman; Babak knows her; you need not fear.

"You are welcome here so long as you keep my conditions, so long as your presence comforts Babak and makes it possible for him to dream. If you try to escape or set him against dreaming for me"—he snapped his fingers—"you will be put out at the nearest inn or settlement. And . . ." He leaned forward. "If you breathe a word about the dreaming, we will put you out exactly where we are when I learn of it—settlement or no settlement. Do you understand?"

I nodded grudgingly.

"Do you accept?"

"Yes, only . . ."

His eyes narrowed. "Only what?"

"This dreaming, it wearies him. He has never been robust. And he has been crying for so long. It would be better to wait until he is rested."

Melchior eyed me steadily, combing at his beard. "I will consider your request," he said at last. He took a cloth out of the folds of his clothing, put it to his nose, and let out with a great, damp, trumpeting noise. "How old are you?" he asked when he had done.

I took two years off, for most boys my age would be bigger, their voices on the edge of change. "Twelve," I said.

"Hmm," he muttered. "If you were fifteen, *I* would perform the purification rites. But since you're underage, Giv will perform ablutions. Heaven only knows when last you washed."

Giv turned to me. "My master is very generous, offering his hospitality. It is well that you should thank him."

That stuck in my craw. But I swallowed it, bowed again. "I thank you, Lord Melchior," I said.

Giv looked thoughtful as servants carried a large vat up the stairs to his lamplit room, as they filled the vat, pitcher by pitcher, with steaming water. Smaller vats were brought in as well, and stacks of drying cloths, and a copper thurible, which soon set to billowing fragrant white smoke.

I was thinking too. What would he do when he discovered I was a girl? Clearly Babak had kept my secret safe. Would they turn me out? The Magus had mentioned his wife, so he might put me in custody of her. Still, he would be angry. And my freedom would be sorely constrained. So much more difficult to escape!

When the servants had left, Giv asked me, "So, you have done this before, then—this purification in the way of the Wise God?"

"My grandmother cleansed us so." She had regularly washed us head to foot, and made much of polluting neither water nor earth nor fire.

"Then you know how it is done."

I nodded, though I did not. Not how to purify deep pollution such as I had known.

"Good." Giv started to leave, which surprised me, because I had clearly heard the Magus order him to perform the ablutions.

"But . . ."

He turned back. *There have been bones,* I almost said. *And blood. And once, a corpse.* But if I admitted this, he would do it himself and discover I was a girl.

"I . . . I will have need of . . . of clean clothing," I said.

He pointed to a stack of fabric set beside a pair of short leather boots. "There," he said and, eyeing the garments I was wearing, added, "We will dispense with those."

In a while, when I was clean and dressed in soft linen and wool—brown trousers, sash, and tunic with a wide band of yellow-embroidered felt at the neck, a loose coat of rusty red with embroidered sleeves—I heard two sets of footsteps coming down the corridor, one heavy, one light.

Babak.

The door swung open, and his small, bony body hit me hard, nearly knocking me to the floor. "Ramin!" he cried. "Ramin Ramin Ramin Ramin Ramin."

I scooped him into my arms, held him tight. He began to weep—great, heaving sobs that wracked his entire body. Out of the corner of my eye, I saw Giv slip out the door. "Hush," I said, patting Babak's back the way I always used to do. "Hush, hush, hush, little brother, no need to cry. All's well."

Though I was far from sure of that.

Later—when Babak and I had long since curled up together on a single sleeping mat, when his breathing had long since settled into the rhythms of sleep—I heard the door open. Footfalls in the shadows. Before I could make out a face in the gloom, a massive cupped hand reached down, spread wide, and out stepped something small and dark.

Shirak. He staggered a little, found his balance, then bounced across the floor and, leaning into the curve of Babak's body, commenced to lick himself clean.

*

CHAPTER 18

A PLACE of MANY SECRETS

It seemed we had just gone to sleep when Giv was shaking my shoulder, urging me to rise. "We leave today for Sava. There's work for you." Then he was gone. I quickly relieved myself in the chamber pot, then Giv returned with a ewer of water, some cucumbers, and a round of flatbread. I woke Babak; the three of us broke our fast quickly, by lamplight.

I was disturbed, this morning, to see how poorly Babak looked. He was as thin as he had been when we had to beg or steal all our food. He seemed tired, and the circles beneath his eyes had darkened.

Shirak lapped some water out of my hand but turned up his nose at the bread Babak offered. The kitten tiptoed to a corner of the room, tail held high, and commenced to feast upon a mouse he had killed the night before.

Babak, too, had been divested of his rags. It did my heart good to see him garbed in good wool and shod in sturdy leather. But he did not want to stay with Melchior's wife. He wanted to stay with me. Giv considered this, the lines at the sides of his mouth deepening, framing his habitual scowl. "Nay," he said curtly. "Later, perhaps."

Babak instantly broke into tears and clung to me. "I want to go with Ramin," he pleaded. "Ramin, don't go without me, please!"

"Hush, little one. It's only for a short while this time. I'll soon return—I promise."

But he would not be consoled. He was still clinging and

sobbing when the Magus's wife came, a rotund woman of middle years and a calm, smiling countenance. I pried Babak off as gently as I could.

"Would you like to come with us?" she mouthed so Babak couldn't see.

I shook my head and departed, feeling as though I'd torn off an arm. The Magus wanted me to "be of use." And a boy of twelve would not bide all day with the women.

Besides, if I didn't get out and about—learn the lay of things—how would I plot our escape?

No sooner had I set foot in the courtyard than a youth, a little older than I, accosted me. "Ramin?" he asked.

I nodded.

"Giv said I'm to show you what to do," he said, looking me over and stroking the faint beginnings of a beard. "This way." He set off at a brisk clip, throwing back over his shoulder, "My name is Pacorus."

The large, square courtyard, though still dark, had come to life. I followed Pacorus as he wove with a fluid, long-striding gait through the pools of lantern light—among camels standing and camels kneeling; among heaps of rolled carpets and hangings; among bowls, goblets, platters, chests, feed sacks, calabashes, jugs, casks, nets filled with melons, nets filled with cooking pots, and wicker cages full of clucking chickens. Bundle-laden men were shouting, striding back and forth from the courtyard to the rooms and stables built along two sides of it. Horses whinnied and donkeys brayed. I tripped over a man who, miraculously, yet slept, and nearly fell headlong into the middle of a squabble—two men, each claiming a single sack of barley as his own. A host of scents assailed me: smoke, cooking spices, incense, feathers, dust, animal sweat, and dung. We passed the tall, arched stable doors, where camels let out great protesting groans as they rocked to their feet and followed their masters into the open. I peered inside, looking for Gorizpa, for that was where the

man had led her when we'd arrived. But there was a darker
darkness in the stables, dappled with flares of lantern light,
yet untouched by the faint hint of the coming dawn. I could
not see her.

Pacorus halted when we came to the well. He handed me
a waterskin and instructed me to help fill the trough, for
many animals had gathered to drink now and the water was
running low.

I was strong for a girl but no match for Pacorus, who
would draw up a large, brimming waterskin as if it were filled
with feathers, then stride past me with sinewy grace and fling
it into the trough before my waterskin had cleared the lip of
the well. At first I thought he was annoyed with me, watching
me struggle with the skin. After a time he showed me to
another of the Magus's servants, one who was packing and
tying bundles. "He can help," Pacorus said to the servant. I
thrust out my chin, my face warm with shame, but there was
no contempt in Pacorus's voice, and he squeezed my shoulder in a reassuring way as he left.

Packing I could do: rolling up robes and blankets, laying
out pots and bowls and cups and swaddling them in layers of
cloth so that they would not break. Though I could not pull
the tying strings as taut as some of the other packers, I did
know a few special knots, which I had learned from Suren, for
cinching saddles and repairing tack. Someone handed me a
frayed girth strap, and with a little cutting and braiding and
tying I soon returned it to serviceable use. As I worked, a thin
man with the swaggering gait of a bantam rooster drew near.
He squatted beside us and watched with interest the twists and
turnings of the knots. When, for a moment, the men beside
me were distracted by a nearby commotion, the short man
drew yet nearer and said, "The likes of you shouldn't be doing
this. It shames your bloodline and all your kin."

My head snapped up; I stared at him. I knew him from
somewhere—the pointed beard, the pockmarked cheeks, the
reedy voice.

He laid a hand on my shoulder. "I can help you escape. You and your brother."

A throat cleared behind me; I whirled round to see Giv.

"Ramin," he growled. "Come with me."

When I glanced back at the man, he had vanished into the swarming hubbub of the courtyard.

My heart was pounding in my chest. *It shames your bloodline,* he had said. Might this man know who we were? And if he did know, how? Was it possible he'd met up with Suren somewhere? And . . . escape! *You and your brother.*

"What did the juggler want?" Giv demanded, leading me toward the stables.

Juggler! Was he the same juggler I'd seen in Rhagae, the one Babak had collided with? "He, ah . . . thinks he knows me, but he is mistaken." No use in telling Giv, rousing his suspicions. Besides, with the Eyes and Ears of the king looking for Babak, the fewer who knew who we were, the better.

Giv favored me with an appraising glance. "If he approaches you again, tell him only what the Magus instructed: that Babak is the son of a poor but pious tradesman, and you are his brother, and the Magus has taken you both under his protection."

I nodded, then, gathering courage, asked, "Which way is Sava from here?"

"It is south," he said, "and west."

"Will we stay in Sava, or go on from there?"

He eyed me oddly. "So many questions, then. Why do you ask?"

"I only wondered."

"You will see," he said shortly.

And so I will, I thought. So long as we traveled west, I was content to stay with the caravan. No need to risk escape. But the moment we halted for good, or bore east, or came within easy reach of Palmyra . . . nothing in this world would prevent it.

✳

CHAPTER 19

PROCESSION of THE DOOMED

The stables were warm and dark, the gloom only partly relieved by the myriad lanterns hanging from the rafters and the lamps flickering in niches in the walls. The smells of dung and hay lay thick in the air. I followed Giv among the horses, camels, donkeys, and men until I espied Gorizpa, tethered to an iron ring. Giv took a lamp from a niche, moved it along her flanks, legs, and hooves, then pried open her mouth and examined her teeth. He shook his head. "Best put it out of its misery. It won't fetch much, though, I warn you."

"You mean . . . slaughter her?"

Gorizpa's ears swiveled at the sound of my voice; she turned toward me.

"Aye."

And give me the proceeds. So the Magus hadn't claimed all I had as his.

I had no need for coin while in the caravan; it seemed that all of my needs would be attended to. Still, it would be good to add to my sackful of coins for when Babak and I escaped. And yet . . .

Gorizpa made a sound deep in her throat. She came and leaned her great, long forehead against my chest and belly. I let my arms slip about her; the tufts at the tips of her ears twitched against my cheeks. Truly, I had grown soft.

"No," I said. "I'll take her."

Giv regarded her with narrowed eyes. "So then," he said. "This is a slow caravan. Were it a fast one, I would not permit it. But if this beast"—he jerked his head at Gorizpa—"holds us back, I will slaughter it on the road, and purification be damned. That is a promise. Now, go tell Pacorus I want him to find you something to ride." With that, Giv departed.

"I hope you appreciate what I just did," I told Gorizpa, scratching at the base of her mane. She flicked an ear in my direction. "Did you hear Giv? Better not hold us back." I reached a hand into her great, hairy ear and began to scratch. Her eyes glazed over, her lower lip softened, and a bead of drool dropped upon the stable floor.

I found Pacorus in the middle of the courtyard, facing the woven and betassled saddlebags on a haughty-looking camel. He seemed to be looking at something he was holding. When I cleared my throat to make my presence known, he spun round, startled. The thing flew from his hands and landed with a *crack* upon the cobblestones.

It splayed open on the ground: a small, intricately carved wooden casket, inlaid with copper and gold. Pacorus scrambled for it and picked up something that lay within. A strange-looking object—a bronze disc with a flat bronze bar riveted to the center of it and a ring attached at the top. All round the edges of the disc were rows of tiny etched marks and figures.

"Ahh!" Pacorus threw back his head, eyes closed. "It didn't break," he said. "Thanks be to God."

"What is it?"

"It's a thing he uses at night. A *star-taker*, I have heard it called. I can't say that I understand it. But *he* sets great store by it."

Stars. Like the dream Babak had had when Zoya gave him the white cloth from the Magus. *Two stars. Near, apart. Near, apart.*

"Does he use it to study the stars?" I asked now.

Pacorus shrugged. "They say that is what it's for. I never saw him use it, though, until the night before we left Rhagae. For so long we'd been told we were heading for Margiana, and then one night he turns his gaze to the stars and"—Pacorus snapped his fingers—"suddenly it's Sava! Oh, no. Look!"

One of the casket's hinges had come apart. "I'll take this to the coppersmith. He can repair it before we leave." Pacorus leaped to his feet.

"Wait," I said. "Giv says you're to find me a mount."

"A mount! Did he say where I was to find one?" Pacorus demanded. "Every horse we have is spoken for, and nearly all the riding camels besides! There are a few pack camels left, but their gait's so rough they'd jog you right off—and most of them will bite you as soon as look at you. Am I a conjurer, that I can summon a suitable mount out of smoke?" But he was already looking about for one, I could see. He accosted one man and then another: "Do we have a riding camel to spare? How about that one Hormoz was riding yesterday? No? Well, how about the one the messenger rode in from the west? Is that ours?" Finally he turned to me. "I do know of one, if Giv will allow it." He looked me up and down in a way that nearly made me blush. "It's good you're a scraw—that you don't weigh overmuch," he amended. "Nor does your brother. Come. Let's leave this with the coppersmith, and then we'll see."

The camel stood hobbled at one corner of the courtyard, chewing her cud and staring into the distance with a sort of melancholy dignity. I saw at once why no one wished to ride her. Patches of bare, reddened skin splotched her muzzle and made inroads into the long hair on her flanks. Mange.

"Are you sure you can't find a horse?" I asked. Horses I knew how to ride. But not camels. Besides, this one seemed piteous.

"She's the best I can do," Pacorus said. "But she'll weaken fast on the road. You'll have to anoint her, morning and evening, with butter. She was culled for slaughter, but . . ." He shrugged. "She's good for a while yet, with a light load. Wait here; I'll find you a saddle."

Another animal marked for slaughter. I gently touched the festering skin; the camel flinched and looked down at me with reproachful eyes. Procession of the doomed, we were. Two refugees from the City of the Dead traveling with three ill-fated animals: the aged, the sick, and the half blind.

It was good that I did not place much faith in omens.

CHAPTER 20

A GREAT JOURNEY

There is a lightening of heart that attends the setting off upon a great journey, whatever your fears and misgivings may be. The camels' bells had a gaiety to them, as did the bright, swaying tassels of the horse and camel regalia, as did the flute-and-tambour chorus that arose from a corner of the court-yard, as did the sweet smells of wafting incense, the moving constellations of torchlight, and the thin rim of dawn that set the low clouds aflame. There was a roaring of many camels as they rocked to their feet in the dim courtyard, and a shouting of men, and a clopping of horses and donkeys. The whole of it—the whole pageant—stirred something inside me, some strange joy, frightening and wonderful.

Now, awaiting our place in line, I found my thoughts stray-ing more and more to Palmyra. To our kin, who would care for us, would restore us to the noble life we were meant to live—despite what sour Old Zoya had predicted. To Mother . . .

Soldiers . . .

Soldiers through the gates.

I shook off the memory. She *had* to have made her way to Palmyra. And perhaps Suren, too, when . . .

I pushed past something in my mind.

When he escaped and found us gone from Rhagae. And Father . . . Well, anything seemed possible. Who knew why Melchior had decided to journey west instead of east, but it was all to the good for us. At this moment the way ahead felt bright—or at least much brighter than the dismal lives we had been leading, with grimness stretching out before us without respite.

We would ride, Pacorus had told me, near the end of the first string of pack camels. First, on swift horses, came our guide and his men—with fierce eyes, sun-blackened skin, and daggers flashing at their belts. They had knowledge, Pacorus had said, of every water hole and stream between Rhagae and Ecbatana. Next, also on horseback, came the escort of the Magus, five or six men clanking with weapons—bows and arrows, knives and spears. Then some lesser priests and the bearer of the sacred coals. Behind them rode the Magus himself, regally mounted on a great white horse bedecked with so much finery that it seemed to shimmer and sway like a mirage: mirror-studded headdress, betasseled saddlebags, beaded necklaces and drapes. After him, more of his escort. Then, on camelback, the musicians and entertainers, and the howdahs of the Magus's wife and her women—bright-colored tents that shivered and shook with the movement of the camels' gait.

We came next. I squeezed Babak's hand as Giv tied our camel's nose line to the camel in front of us. This nose line, I saw, was attached to a wooden peg that poked out of one nostril. I clambered onto the saddle, nestled between the camel's two humps, and Giv lifted Babak to sit in front of me. Shirak, tucked inside my sash, peeked out and surveyed all with his one good eye.

"Huh!" Giv said, tapping our camel's flank with a stick. "Huh, huh!" With a beleaguered roar, she rose to a kneel, then abruptly straightened her back legs, pitching us sharply forward. "Lean back!" Giv shouted. Our camel's front legs straightened; Gorizpa, tethered behind, let out a frightened bray. A couple of members of the Magus's escort, laughing, joined the caravan behind Gorizpa—whether to protect us or to prevent our escape, I did not know.

It was high up here, and I could see more of the terrain—small hills and stony plateau to the sunrise side of us, and mountains to the other. In time I accustomed myself to our camel's gait, a swinging, loose-legged shuffle. It was comfortable enough, but utterly unlike the riding I had done in Susa, clinging tightly to my pony's body so that his rhythms became my rhythms; we were one and the same.

Morning spread like a spill of golden oil across the sky. The day grew warm. My high spirits soon evaporated beneath the white-hot glare of the sun and the drudgery of the long, hard trek. The silence of the high plateau soon deadened the hubbub of our setting out, until all I heard were the creaking of saddles, the jingle of camel bells, the crunch of animal feet and hooves on stone and grit. And the wind. Ever, ever the wind.

I tried to fix my mind upon the question of how to escape when the time came, but my thoughts kept drifting, and from time to time my head jerked suddenly upright, snapping me awake. In a while a different question began to occupy me: When would I be able to make water, and how would I do so without revealing my sex?

Babak looked about with interest at first, then started to squirm, then pestered me with questions. Where were we going? When would we stop? When would we eat? Could I make the camel run? Was Gorizpa growing weary? Finally his questions gave way to silence and he slumped back against me in sleep.

Pacorus came to ride beside us for a while, then joined a group of horseback youths—bareheaded and wearing loose, pleated overtrousers for riding. A couple of them greeted me before they took off, ranging up and down the lines of tethered pack camels when the road was wide. Every so often Giv would ride past, scowling as ever—checking nose line, girth, and crupper, casting a keen eye upon the animals' mouths, eyes, legs, and feet. He was neither guide nor caravan master, yet he seemed to have authority over all matters pertaining directly to the Magus, and the guide and caravan master often consulted with him. He frowned for a long while at

SUSAN FLETCHER

Gorizpa, but the old nag seemed perfectly content to slog along apace with the caravan. It seemed she balked only for me.

I was not the only one with a need to relieve herself, for we stopped from time to time for that purpose, the women pouring out of the howdahs and screening the entire group with large, flowing lengths of cloth. I found it was not difficult to be inconspicuous; there were many rocky outcrops to squat behind. Shirak, more modest even than we, would disappear entirely and reappear again. Giv, however, never seemed to be far from us—though not once did I see him glance in our direction.

When the sun stood high in the sky, we stopped beside a small stream. Those wearing the sacred kusti—women as well as men—made their devotions. I watered our animals, hobbled them, then put them out to graze in the sparse grass. Babak helped by standing on a rock and scratching in Gorizpa's ear. I looked about for the juggler—his name was Pirouz, I had discovered—and spotted him in a pavilion erected for some of the merchants. I wondered if he would approach me again or if Giv had frightened him off.

Well, if the right occasion arose, I would approach him.

Pacorus and the other youths set out what was needful for the Magus and his priests and escort. Babak and I helped them spread cloths upon the ground and laid great trays of food upon them. We supped with the young men, saying little but listening to the tales they told, laughing at their jibes and filling our bellies until they bulged. At first I was shy about getting into the scramble for food. But Pacorus, seeing Babak or me gazing at a heap of flatbread or a hunk of cheese or a mound of cut-up melon, would flash us a quick smile, then reach into the swarm of arms to fetch it for us. Soon Babak and I were boldly reaching in—even scavenging small scraps of lamb and goat for the kitten.

Watching Pacorus among the other youths, I noticed how

96

well favored he was—the grace of his movements, the roguish smile, those clear, penetrating eyes. Pacorus's speech was refined, as if he had spent time among the nobility, and there were black stains on his fingers, like the ink stains on the fingers of Suren's old tutor. Though Pacorus was tall, like Suren, the resemblance ended there. Suren had a weight about him, a meatiness-on-the-bones, a gravity of countenance—down to the squarish, solemn jawline he had inherited from our father. Suren always seemed content to be exactly who he was. Even if he was a beggar, I thought bitterly.

But Pacorus . . . There was a restless discontent about him that I recognized in myself.

A chorus of laughter arose from the circle of women, gathered about their meal. It transported me back for a moment to Susa, with my mother and aunts and cousins. Sitting idly in the shade of the garden, with women's talk and laughter flowing around me. Splashing my feet in the cool waters of the fountain. Stitching designs in soft linen with lengths of brightly colored thread. A deep-down knowing that I belonged.

And would again. If not in Susa, then in Palmyra. I would.

When we had finished with the meal, Pacorus gave me a small bowlful of melting butter, and I went for the first time to anoint our camel's ravaged hide. Babak reached for the bowl, wanting to help. "It's too perilous for you," I said. The camel looked down at us, disdainfully, it seemed. Warily, perhaps. As I nudged Babak back, my hand brushed hard against an open sore on the camel's side. She let out a sort of coughing, sneezing sound, bucked in her hobbles, and chomped out at me with great, yellow fangs.

I leaped back just in time. "You devil!"

The camel let out a groan, more pathetic seeming than malicious. She eyed me from behind her long lashes as if she knew she'd misbehaved.

Babak stood beside me and patted my back as I waited for

my heartbeat to slow and my courage to come out from where it was cowering. "I'm going to do this whether you like it or not," I told her. "Do you hear me?"

She shuffled her feet, looked abashedly at the ground. Her skin shivered where the sores were. That mange must hurt. She reached down to sniff at the bowl of butter, which I had dropped. Then she fixed me with a mournful gaze and groaned at me again—a pitiful, quavering plaint that slid all the long way from treble to bass.

I sighed. If only they'd given us a horse! I approached the camel slowly, speaking softly, as I used to do with my pony in Susa. "There now. You're a beauty," I said. This was an outright lie. But my pony—who truly was a beauty—always liked it when I told her so. "Ziba," I said. *Beauty.* Gently, I teased off some of the shedding hair that hung from her body in shaggy patches. Then I picked up the butter, dipped some out, and touched it to one of her sores. She moaned, low in her throat. Cautiously I rubbed it in. She moved her head until it was just above mine, until I could feel her breath stirring my hair.

I held my breath. *Don't bite,* I willed.

At last, she nuzzled at my hair with her soft lips. Just as, in Susa, my pony used to do.

CHAPTER 21

✳

SWEET DREAMS

Late that day, when the sun had slid down to the tips of the western mountains, we arrived at the caravansary outside the village of Sava. I was leading our animals to water across the bustling courtyard when Giv summoned Babak and me to follow him.

"But who will tend to Gorizpa and Ziba?" I protested.

Giv raised an eyebrow. "Gorizpa, is it? *Fleet-of-Foot?* And Ziba? *Beauty?*"

I held his gaze, daring him to challenge or laugh.

He did not. "Pacorus will tend to your animals," he said. "Just leave them and come."

"But the butter . . ."

Something shifted in Giv's eyes; I thought I saw his scowl lift at a corner of his mouth. When he spoke again, his voice seemed not quite so harsh. "I'll instruct Pacorus to anoint your . . . Ziba, never fear."

I reached up to Babak, high above Ziba. He leaned down and slipped, yawning, into my arms. We followed Giv up the stairs to the gallery; he pointed to the large rooms at the end. "Go, Ramin. Alone. The Magus wishes to see you before the sunset prayers."

I swallowed. "Alone?"

Babak said, "I want to go with you!"

Giv took Babak from me, set him down beside him. Babak started for me, but Giv firmly took his hand.

"We will wait," Giv said.

I followed the strains of music down the long, open gallery. *The Magus knows I'm a girl.* The thought flitted through my mind, but I swept it aside. How would he know?

Two guards stood in front of a curtain hung from a wide arch. They motioned me through.

Four musicians—plying a harp, a horn, cymbals, and a small drum—blared out a lively air in a corner of the room. The Magus, attended by servants, reclined upon a divan, eyes closed, seeming to relish some delicacy that a hovering servant had just popped into his mouth. Behind him, on a pedestal, the sacred fire burned, and the air smelled of sandalwood and incense. The servant whispered something into his ear. The Magus opened his eyes, saw me, and waved a commanding hand. Everyone left.

His nose was still red, I saw, but his eyes did not seem so watery as before, nor his voice, when he greeted me, so hoarse. The swaddlings of wool were gone; a fine white robe, embroidered in gold, now compassed his considerable girth. His gray beard had been cleaned and oiled and was not so bristly as before, though stray tufts still escaped and went curling off in odd directions. In a deep, rich voice the Magus asked after my health and comfort; he asked if I had passed the journey tolerably well; he asked if there was anything I desired.

"Melon, if you please, my lord," I said. Zoya would call me brazen, but he *had* asked. "And butter. Much butter, for my . . . well, butter. And a flat wooden box filled with sand for Babak's kitten."

Melchior clapped his hands; a servant entered. He repeated my requests with neither comment nor curiosity, and the servant left. Then, leaning forward with the first real interest he had shown, the Magus inquired about Babak.

"I have heard he slept all night without crying. Is this so?"

I inclined my head. "Yes, my lord."

"I have heard that our food now pleases him, and he eats until his belly is full."

"Yes, my lord."

"I have heard even that he smiles."

"On occasion, my lord."

"On occasion?" Melchior snorted. "What I have heard is this: All told, he fares passing well now you're here. He sleeps. He eats. He smiles."

I could see where this was leading, and I didn't like it. "Well enough, my lord," I said.

The Magus craved something more from me. He frowned, drawing together his brows until they loomed like snowy mountain crags above his eyes. He combed through his beard with his fingers, beringed with costly gold and gems. Soft, plump fingers on soft, plump hands—and yet they gave the impression of strength. Power seemed to crackle around him, to radiate from his body in waves.

I did not give him what he wanted. I would delay as long as I might. To touch the dreams of such a man . . . It could burn you.

"So," the Magus said at last. "Well enough, you say. Rested enough to dream for me?"

"I don't know for certain. It would be best to wait—"

"I don't . . . have . . . time." His eyes hardened, held me. At last he leaned back, smiled, and picked up a folded white square of cloth. Larger than a sash this time. An undertunic. He held it out. "Let us try it, shall we?"

So preoccupied was I when I left that I didn't see Pirouz in the shaded edge of the gallery until I had nearly walked straight into him. The tunic flew from my grasp and dropped on the tiled floor. I grabbed for it, but Pirouz was quicker. He ran the cloth through his hands, smudging it with gray.

"So," he said, "what's this?" Smiling, he handed it back.

I clasped it to myself.

"Don't be afeared, I won't tell. You've as much a right as he to the feel of finespun cloth against your skin. It's a shame you have to steal for it."

"I didn't—"

"Nay, of course you didn't." He smiled again. His teeth were white and small, like the teeth of a child or a fox—too small for his face. "Tell me," he said, "how is little Babak?" He shook his head sadly. "Babak—chattel to the Magus. No better than some foreign slave. What'd your father think? And you, a slave in all but name. Is this how the great bloodline's to end? And Suren . . ."

I drew in breath.

He laughed softly, expelling a gust of reeking air. "He *is* your brother, then."

"What of Suren? Do you know him? Do you know where he is?"

"Know him? I can take you to him!"

The creak of a door behind us, and footsteps. I whirled round.

Giv.

"Go," he said, glaring at Pirouz.

"We were only talking," Pirouz protested, turning his smile on Giv.

"*Go.*"

Pirouz shrugged. There was no way out for him, except by passing Giv. He sauntered past, plucking a leather ball from his sash and tossing it, catching it, tossing it—until Giv made a sudden move, and the next I knew, he had shoved Pirouz against the wall, dagger to his throat. The ball bounced once, twice, and dribbled away down the gallery.

"Leave them be," Giv said, "or I promise you'll live to regret it." He flicked the dagger in the air, then stepped back. Pirouz sidled a short distance along the wall before turning and scuttling away with a great deal less dignity than before.

"What did he want?" Giv asked.

I could not look at him. Was this a trick of Pirouz's, to trap me in some way? Or did he truly know of Suren? "The same as before," I said. "He thinks he knows me, but he does not."

Giv sheathed his dagger and scowled after Pirouz. "I'll watch him," he said.

I felt myself slowly unclench. It was good to have Giv on our side, but he was not a man you would ever want to cross.

Still . . .

Suren!

"Babak," I said.

He leaned against me, sleepy eyed. I stroked his hair; the downy strands on the back of his neck were moist. Shirak crawled into his lap and began to purr. Giv had left us alone in his quarters—a small room down the gallery from the Magus—but two men sat outside our door. I could hear their low murmurings and, from time to time, a rattle of dice on the tile floor. For a long while after speaking with Pirouz my heart had raced, but now it had settled again. Pirouz had said he could take us to Suren, but it might be a trick. I must be sensible. I mustn't do anything rash. But I had to speak with him again.

In the meantime, there was another matter to attend to.

"Babak," I said, "I want to talk to you."

He yawned. "I don't want to talk."

"The Magus wants you to dream for him again."

"Um."

"Last time . . . with the stars . . . it didn't trouble you?"

He moved his thin shoulders in a shrug. "I don't mind." He reached out for the cloth, and something about that gesture—the small, sun-browned hand, stretched wide—made tears prick the corners of my eyes. So accustomed he was to having his own dreams shunted aside, to being used for the purposes of others, that now he offered without question to have it done to him again.

I didn't give him the cloth. Not yet. "You're not afraid?" I asked.

Babak tipped his head back, gazed up at me. "Not if you are here."

Something twisted inside me; I looked away, struggled to keep my face from caving in. In a moment I had mastered myself again. I gave him the tunic, which smelled strongly of incense. I tucked it in next to his skin. He closed his eyes; soon his breath came even and slow. I drew my fingers along his eyebrows, felt the rough ridge of his scar.

"Sweet dreams, Babak," I whispered.

✳

CHAPTER 22

THE fORTRESS

This one began, like the other, with stars. Babak told it to me, then I to Giv, and then the Magus wanted to hear it for himself in his chambers. The same two stars as before, Babak said: near and apart, near and apart, near and apart. And then something different.

A king.

Babak did not want to tell of this king. I had not pressed when he and I were alone. But Melchior craved to know everything about him. Babak ducked under my arm and buried his face against my side. I looked down, fearful for him. He had never been like this before. Not just balky, but truly loath to tell.

Now he let it out in bits and pieces, whispered to me with a hand cupped to my ear.

"He says it was a strange king," I told Melchior. "His cloak was deep purple, and he wore it draped over one shoulder, leaving the other shoulder and arm completely bare. Long purple tassels hung down from the corners of this cloak. But he wore a narrow diadem, made of cloth, as our kings do. He lived in a great palace, and many attended upon him."

"Could be Roman," Melchior muttered. "But those tassels. Hebrew, perhaps. What else?"

Babak didn't want to tell. "You must," I said.

He whispered.

"He says the king was angry. His feet had open, oozing sores, and they stank. He says there were sores on his body as well, and a spell of palsy on him. He says . . ." Babak whispered again. "He says he was afraid."

"Who was afraid?" Melchior demanded. "The king?"

"Babak was afraid."

Melchior rose from his divan, shuffled toward us across the carpet, and stood glowering down. "Where was I in this dream?" he demanded. "How am I to know this dream was for me? He speaks of stars. He speaks of a king. How is this mine?"

To my surprise, Babak poked his head out from under my arm. "You saw it," he said. "I am telling what you saw."

Melchior retreated a bit, and when he spoke, his tone was softer. "How did he receive me, this king? How was his comportment toward me?"

Babak cupped his hand to my ear and whispered again. "He says he sought you out," I said. "He welcomed you. He treated you with honor."

"Hmm." Melchior settled back down upon his cushions. He combed through his beard again, thoughtful.

Even so, I wondered, why had Babak been afraid?

We stayed at Sava overnight and left after dawn prayers the following day, heading southwest, off the main trade route, past the lush greenery that rimmed a wide blue lake and then across a vast, desolate, windswept plain. Babak seemed spent, either from this last night's dreaming or from the mounting strain of travel. He had eaten little since the dream, not even the melon the Magus had sent. Now he leaned back, limp, against me.

I kept an eye out for Pirouz. He glanced at us from time to time. Once, he caught my eye and nodded. He was often in the company of one of the stable hands, a large, meaty man with sleepy eyes, who kept his head hunched between his shoulders. Again, I asked myself: What did Pirouz know of Suren? Could he take us to him? And if he could, was Suren just waiting for us someplace? That would be so like him, the way he was now! Not to come seeking, but to wait.

But then, maybe it was dangerous for him on the road. Maybe he had escaped capture. Maybe he was hiding and had sent Pirouz to find us. Maybe . . .

The possibilities buzzed round my head until I was dizzy with them. Take care, I told myself. You don't know Pirouz; you don't know who he is.

He couldn't be one of the Eyes and Ears of the king. They were all soldiers in disguise, and Pirouz hadn't the look of any soldier I'd ever seen—not at all.

But maybe the king's spies . . . had spies?

Still, it felt right that Suren should be alive and free. Hadn't I thought so before, when Zoya had been so sure of disaster? I must speak with Pirouz! But Giv was everywhere, it seemed. For now, I didn't dare.

The next time Pacorus rode up beside us, I asked if he knew where we were going. "There are rumors," he replied, "that we're making for the great fortress."

"What great fortress?"

"I've only heard tell of it. High in the mountains, they say. A fastness for the priests, a great fire temple of the Wise God."

"Is it . . . near Palmyra?"

"Palmyra? No, Palmyra is very far. Deep into Roman territory."

I recalled what Melchior had said under his breath when Babak described the king he'd dreamed of. *Could be Roman.*

"Is this fortress in Rome?" I asked.

"No! Rome is yet farther. Their territory begins at the western banks of the Euphrates River, but the city of Rome itself lies beyond the Syrian Desert, beyond Antioch, beyond Thrace, beyond even Macedonia."

"How many days' journey to Roman territory?"

"I don't know!" he said, waving my question aside. His camel snorted impatiently and drew ahead; he pulled her back. "Why do you ask of Rome?"

I couldn't tell him why.

He sighed, relenting. "I could draw you a map. A small one. I'm hoarding my parchment, but there's some to spare."

"Then, you *are* a scribe. So why do you also . . ." *Haul water,* I almost said. *Tend to animals like a common caravan hand.* But I didn't know him well enough to say these things without risking grave offense.

Sill, Pacorus seemed to sense my meaning. "It's a long story," he said. "You don't want to hear it."

"But I do." It would abate the loneliness I felt to find another in my position. Of noble blood, brought low by circumstance.

"Well." He looked at me quickly, then away. I settled Babak more comfortably against me. "My mother was of the Magian tribe. But she displeased her father, and he married her to mine, a merchant. Prosperous enough to set up six of his sons in the enterprise, but not eight. I am the eighth."

A Magian married to a merchant. Half noble. "But surely there was something better—"

"Than this?" He shrugged. "I was schooled in letters. I craved to be a priest. But no priest would take a merchant's son to apprentice. Save for Melchior, and he only if I would do his bidding—as a servant—for three years. He has little need of a scribe," Pacorus said, and I could hear a sour note in his voice. "He has two other apprentices, and they are of full Magian blood. But . . ." Pacorus straightened. "Only a year remains, and then I'm *certain* Melchior will do as he has promised."

The way he came down hard on *certain* let me know that he had doubts.

But now he was back to speaking of the fortress again, the fire temple for the priests. I only half listened. That way led his dreams, not mine. My eyes sought Pirouz and found him a little way ahead. "In Phraates' court," Pacorus was saying. I pricked up my ears. "He used to attend upon the king, but he caused offense and was expelled."

"Who?" I asked. "Who used to attend upon Phraates?"

"Why, Melchior!" Pacorus exclaimed. "Have you heard a word I've said? Melchior is banned now from Phraates' court—and bitter he is about it."

By the afternoon of the second day after Sava, I still had not managed to speak with Pirouz. Giv never seemed far from him, and at every stop he stationed one of his men to watch over us. Now we came to a small settlement, stopping for devotions, to procure food, and to water our animals. Then the track bent due west, straight toward the mountains, which stretched out before us in tiers, each tier taller and paler and more jagged than the ones in front of it.

Giv, when I asked him, had told me not to fret myself about the fortress. There would be priests, but he did not think that Melchior would tell them about Babak. Priests were not all of a single mind, he said. Often one priest would vie for supremacy with another. Melchior, Giv opined, would keep knowledge of Babak's gift to himself.

Still, the looming fortress plucked a new note in the discord of my mind. How long would we stay there? Would escape be possible in such a place?

Soon the wind picked up again, flung bits of grit and dirt into my face. Black clouds scudded in from the north and soon patched over the sky entire, turning day into near-night.

We halted briefly so that we could fetch cloaks and hats and blankets from our saddlebags. The Magus had provided Babak and me with thick woolen garments, but nothing was proof against this wind. It set our cloaks to flapping against our legs; it knifed clean through the wool to pierce our bones with ice. Clutching Babak tight against me, I could feel him shiver.

The road had begun to ascend; it grew steep and rough, and Ziba often stumbled. We seemed to be heading right into the mountains, through a deep cleft in the rock. All at once, as we approached the far opening of the cleft, I sensed a stirring in the caravan before us.

"Look!"

"See there!"

The cleft fell away on either side of us, and then I saw.

Dark in the distance loomed the high, jagged spine of the Zagros Mountains. Nearer, at the crest of a steep but smaller peak, it appeared as if a many-tiered fortress—tower, wall, and arch—had sprouted out of the solid rock.

We stopped beside a spring at the base of the peak. Men began to unpack and set up camp. As I hunched against the wind, toting an empty calabash to the spring, Giv approached me, with Pacorus in tow.

"You and Babak are to come to the fortress with the Magus," Giv said. "We've found a horse for you to ride, and I've charged Pacorus with your protection while we're there."

The smoldering uneasiness I had been feeling now flared to the surface. "Why can't we stay here with the others?"

Giv flicked a glance at Pacorus, then looked hard at me—warning me, I surmised, not to let drop word of Babak's dreams. But I remembered what had happened in Rhagae, that part of the caravan had not waited for the Magus, but had split off and made for Margiana.

"How long will we be at the fortress? What about the others? Will we join with them again, or will they travel to another place without us?" *Suren!* I wanted to shout. *How will I find out about Suren?*

Giv scowled. "Ours is not to ask," he said, "but to obey."

✳

CHAPTER 23

HE SLEEPS

It was another hour before we reached the fortress. An hour of winding up the steep, narrow track; an hour of horses groaning, their hooves slipping on a moving stream of scree; an hour of heart-stopping stumbles with nothing between us and the abyss. Soon the plain stretched out far below. The wind abated—blocked, no doubt, by the mountain's bulk— but the bone-piercing chill did not ease. From time to time I could peer down and see the lights of the campsite, which had shrunk to mere pinpricks. My hopes of hearing news of Suren seemed to shrink along with them.

We did not stop for evening prayers, but toiled onward. As we neared the summit, the clouds drew back from the face of the sky. The sun had set behind the mountains, but a luminous dusk limned the contours of the fortress. Thick, spiraling walls studded with watchtowers and arched gates. Stonework so cunning, I could scarcely see where mountain left off and edifice began.

At last we came to two gated watchtowers. The fortress guards hailed us; Melchior responded; the vast gates creaked open. We entered a flat courtyard enclosed on three sides by stables.

We dismounted—grooms led our horses away—and followed a servant up a torchlit spiral flight of stairs. Giv had gone on before, deep in consultation with Melchior. Babak was spent. Though I held his hand, he kept slipping, scraping his knees. I took him on my back. Pacorus appeared at my side as we entered through a pillared archway and veered into a smooth stone hall lined with closed doors to either side. The servant opened one of the doors and beckoned to us.

Inside more servants were at work—unrolling pallets, arranging skins and blankets upon them, setting out trays of food, filling lamps with oil. Carpets, soft and richly colored, lay spread across the floor, with gold-tasseled cushions upon them. A brazier filled the room with blessed warmth, and an incense-burning thurible, hanging from a chain affixed to a rafter, released clouds of fragrant smoke. Steam wafted up from water in a large copper bowl.

The servants left. We washed the dust off our hands and faces, then sat down to the feast. Two kinds of melon: green and orange. Three kinds of olives. Roasted lamb and partridge. A tall stack of freshly baked bread. A platter stacked with squares of goat cheese. Pastries dripping with honey. Shirak kept trying to nibble food from the serving platters, so I settled him in my lap, and Babak and I took turns feeding him bits of meat.

At last, licking our fingers, bellies filled to bursting, we lolled back upon the soft cushions. Pacorus set a low table over the brazier and covered it with a large blanket; Babak, Shirak, and I nestled together inside the tentful of heat. Warmth filled up the spaces beneath the blanket, seeped deep into my body, eased the aches and pains of travel.

The door swung open; the lamp flames leaped and stretched. It was Giv. He surveyed the room for a moment, then turned to Pacorus. "Go find one of the fortress servants," he said, "and tell him we have need of more blankets."

"Blankets?" Pacorus echoed. He looked pointedly at the large blanket that covered us, but Giv growled, "Go!"

The moment Pacorus had left, Giv handed me a length of white cloth.

"Tonight?" I asked, dismayed. "But he's worn out from the journey. He needs *peaceful* sleep."

Babak sat up beside me, took the cloth. A sash. He rubbed

it between his hands, held it to his face. He sniffed it. Seeming puzzled, he looked at Giv and then at me.

"You must do as you're told," Giv said irritably. He pointed a finger at me. "*Tonight.*"

"Ramin. Ramin, wake up!"

I opened my eyes. Lamplight flared before me, making it hard to see. A face—Pacorus's—behind it. "Where is Babak?" he asked. "Where did he go?"

I sat bolt upright, instantly awake. I yanked up the blanket spread across the brazier, picked up the blankets on the floor.

There lay Shirak, curled up in a tight ball, one paw covering his face.

But Babak was gone.

"Perhaps he just wandered off," Pacorus said. "We'll find him."

I was already out the door.

Which way? The hall was long and dim and full of moving shadows cast by fretted lamps in niches.

"Look." Pacorus pointed at a length of white cloth crumpled on the floor a little way down the hall. I picked it up and kept going, Pacorus right behind.

All quiet in the fortress. I breathed in a whiff of incense, felt the cold stone floor against my hurrying feet. Ahead, more niche lamps—and now two lights moving. A whisper of footsteps against the stone floor, a cluster of robed figures.

"Wait!" Pacorus whispered. He grabbed my tunic and pulled me back.

I stilled myself—though not my heart—until the moving figures had vanished. We crept forward along the hall. A little way on, it opened out into a wide, high-roofed, circular court. In the center stood a stone altar, where burned the holy fire. Beyond that rose a narrow flight of gleaming white stairs. The fire flickered, stirred by a draft.

"There!" Pacorus whispered.

Something moving near the top of the stairs.

Babak.

He slipped between two carven doors, which stood slightly ajar. And I was running—running across the circular court, running up the stairs.

Pacorus plucked at the back of my tunic before I slipped between the doors; he hardly slowed me down.

Starlight burnished the surfaces of things with a milky radiance: the great, wide tiled floor of this terrace; the sphere that sat atop a copper pedestal; the charts and maps that ruffled in the wind, anchored to a low table by a host of smooth, round stones. And Babak—there he was—making his way slowly toward a far curved edge of floor where stood a man I did not recognize, a man dressed in the tall cap and white robes of a Magus.

I ran to Babak and scooped him up, silent as an owl on the wing. He did not stiffen, nor cry out, nor even seem surprised, but only gazed at me, blank eyed, and rowed a little with his legs. And now Pacorus was there, leading us toward the back edge of floor to a low wall, behind which we might secrete ourselves.

I set Babak down and, kneeling, turned him to face me. "Babak," I breathed, "don't you *ever*—"

Pacorus set a finger to his lips. He put his two hands together and leaned his head against them, as if to say, *He sleeps.*

Sleepwalking.

Babak leaned against me; I wrapped my arms about him. I could feel him sag against me, and his breathing seemed to come slower, calmer. I looked down and saw that his eyes had drifted shut.

Pacorus tapped my shoulder. He nodded toward the outthrust apron of terrace, where the man stood, unsheltered by the fortress walls, his cloak snapping and billowing in the wind. This man was not tall, I saw, but his bearing put me in mind of my father—straight as a taut bowstring. His dark hair glistened with oil; his beard was neatly trimmed and squared off at the bottom. He seemed to be holding something—a chain or a string—from which suspended a flat metal disc like the one Melchior owned, the one I had seen with Pacorus. The man seemed to be sighting along some meridian toward the stars.

Stars. This journey of ours seemed full of them. Babak's dreams of stars for Melchior. And Melchior with his star-taker. What had Pacorus told me that first day? *I never saw him use it until the night before we left Rhagae,* he had said. And later: *For so long we'd been told we were heading for Margiana, and then one night he turns his gaze to the stars and suddenly it's Sava.*

Shivering in an icy wind gust, I looked up at the sky. The stars were bright and moist and clear.

What, I wondered, had Babak's dream told Melchior? What secret, embedded in the stars, would move him to turn from Margiana and journey to this forbidding place?

CHAPTER 2 4

✴

THE WANDERERS

The next morning, after the devout had said their prayers, Melchior summoned us to his chamber. It was only the three of us: Babak, Melchior, and I.

I had not asked Babak about his dream. He was weary upon awakening, wearier than I had ever seen him. The flesh about his eyes had gone purplish and bruised looking, and some lightness of his spirit seemed to have gone dim. Even so, he seemed less cowed by Melchior this time. He wished to tell his dream himself, and not through me. He stood as he spoke, and moved his hands to better show what he had seen.

It was another dream of stars. Stars, Babak told us in his way, moving east to west across the dome of the nighttime sky. But very, very rapidly—all ablur—circling and circling as in many nights, many months, many years, many thousands of years. And as they moved through the years, they shifted. If you watched the rising of a single constellation—the fish, for instance—it would come up first in the east, and drift over time along the horizon until it was rising in the south, and then west, and then north. And as it approached an eastern rising again—full circle—everything slowed and slowed and slowed, until each individual star, and not just the patterns of stars, became clear. Two stars, then—two of the wandering stars—drew very near to each other, then apart, then near again, then apart, and a third time near.

When he had finished, no one spoke. Not Melchior, who simply stared at Babak, nor I.

Babak leaned against me, spent.

At last Melchior stirred. He furrowed his great, shaggy brows and leveled his gaze at Babak. "Who has been talking to you about the stars?" he demanded.

"No one," he said.

"You?" Melchior asked me.

"No, my lord. I know nothing of stars, save for what everyone knows."

"Does everyone know about the precession of equinoxes? Does everyone know about Great Years?"

I opened my palms in an expression of bewilderment; he harrumphed and turned back to Babak. "What are the wanderers?"

Babak ducked his head, his former high spirits quenched. "He—," I began.

"I am asking you, Babak—not your brother. You said 'two of the wandering stars.' What are they?"

"How is he to know this?" I asked, impatience welling up within me. "He dreams for *you*, he—"

"I saw them," Babak piped up. "In the dream. There are stars that wander through the others. They are not"—he hooked two fingers together—"not fixed to the other stars, but wander."

Melchior combed through his beard, in which were lodged a collection of bread crumbs and a small scrap of cheese. "Have *you* heard of these?" he asked me, more mildly.

I shrugged. "Who has not, my lord? Except young children."

"Can you name them, the wanderers?"

It was so long since anyone had spoken to me of stars. Back in Susa, Suren used to point them out to me. He often showed me the wanderer Venus, star of Anahita, and the red star, the wanderer Mars. "Venus," I said. "And Mars." I couldn't recall the rest.

The Magus murmured something; I thought he said, "Not those." He sat brooding awhile, and no one dared to interrupt him.

But something was pricking my memory. Babak had behaved strangely when we gave him the new sash. He had seemed puzzled. And I knew from the gossip that Pacorus had told me late last night, that Gaspar—the Magus we had seen on the roof, Pacorus thought—that Gaspar was the one reputed to know everything about the stars, or everything that might be known.

Had Babak dreamed again for Melchior?

Or might Melchior have slipped us Gaspar's sash, and tricked Babak into dreaming for him?

Over the next several days I bided my time, impatient to depart the fortress and rejoin those we'd left below. I feared that they might leave and that Pirouz—and my chance of finding news of Suren—might vanish along with them.

Pacorus, freed from menial duties while here, was eager to explore. Babak and I tagged along behind him, through streams of servants bustling to and fro in the hallways; between the walls of high stone chambers that smelled of incense and echoed with the chants of unseen priests; to the guarded doors of the rooms of the various priests' wives. I cared little about the mystery and intrigue of the fortress. But my interest quickened when we came upon a heap of chests and baskets mounting up in the lower courtyard. Preparations for a journey?

"Whose are those?" I asked a group of white-clad priests who hurried past the piled goods.

None stopped, save for one, who favored us with a friendly smile. "For Gaspar and his party," he said. "He's joining your caravan."

"When?" I asked.

"I don't know," he said. "But soon."

"Going where?"

"Ecbatana," he tossed over his shoulder, hurrying to catch up to the others.

Ecbatana! The summer fastness of the king. Surely Phraates

would have left by now, with autumn newly upon us. But it was worrisome.

"Why Ecbatana?" I asked Pacorus. "Do you know?"

Pacorus shrugged. "It's the first I've heard of it, and I've kept my ear well to the ground. Perhaps Melchior's only just decided."

"Where is Ecbatana from here?"

"I'll show you."

We returned to the high, windy rooftop, the one where Babak had walked in his sleep. By daylight I could see far back along the caravan road we had taken—nearly all the way, it seemed, to Rhagae. At the base of the winding road that led up to the fortress I made out the tiny tents of the encampment we had left behind. "Ecbatana is there," Pacorus said. To my relief, he pointed due west. But when I gazed in that direction, I saw only mountains and mountains—the near ones sharp and dark, fading in more and more distant, craggy ridgelines to a pale and shimmery blue.

How far, I wondered, to Palmyra? Across all of those many ridges to Ecbatana. And then there would be more mountains, and the land of two rivers, and a vast desert after that.

Was Suren in Palmyra? Or somewhere nearer? And Mother. How had she managed to cross all of those ridges before us?

A heaviness settled over me, a weariness I could not dispel.

And still Pacorus wanted to explore! He wanted to see everything—every niche and passage, every fire chalice and barsom rod. He tapped his foot in the hubbub of the stables as Babak and I slathered butter on Ziba's sores. He paced the floor as Babak slept. More and more Babak craved sleep, and between sleeps he grew listless. At last I snapped at Pacorus, "If you can't bear to wait as he rests, just go!"

Pacorus sighed, grinned sheepishly. He was charged with our protection and likely not permitted to leave us. In a while he turned to rummage through a bundle of his things on the floor. He drew out an ink cake and began to grind it on a stone. The acrid, smoky tang of ink filled my nose. When he had done, Pacorus took out two sharpened reeds and a scrap of parchment and began to write.

I watched in the flickering lamplight as the characters flowed beneath his pen—mysterious points and arches, flourishes like flags. Though I could not properly read, I found I recognized what he was writing. The alphabet.

I leaped back in memory to the times when Suren had shown it to me, patiently tracing out, for my edification, the rudimentary signs by which meanings might be known. Suren, I used to think, knew everything. Each morning he used to meet with his tutor, because learning was important to my father. For sons, at any rate. I was content to be out on my pony, or wading in the cool stream that ran through our estate, or watching a nest of birds in a nearby tree, until Suren was released from study and could join me.

I studied Pacorus as he wrote. Half noble, he was, and perhaps one day a priest. In time I closed my eyes and drifted off to the sound of reed scratching on parchment, to the bitter smell of ink.

*

CHAPTER 25

HE WAITS for YOU

When the time came, we left the fortress, rode horseback down the steep, winding track, and came into the encampment below. Catching a glimpse of Pirouz, I sagged with relief. Still here. But we met with much dissatisfaction among those left behind, as it had been harshly cold at night even with braziers inside the tents, and many of the company were little used to hardship. Melchior disappeared into the women's quarters and emerged not long after, short tempered and disgruntled. He bellowed out a rebuke to a passing musician, who blatted a rude sound on his horn, then ran to hide himself somewhere among the clustered tents.

I could not help but remark the wry smile of the Magus Gaspar, who, though he added a small cadre of horse archers to our company, brought no women, no musicians, no birds in gilded cages, no amphorae filled with rose water, no stacks of silk-embroidered cushions, and far fewer attendants than his colleague.

And so we set off again.

The air warmed as we came down out of the mountains. We shed our caps and cloaks. Though the months of summer were past, the clime in the flat plateau had not yet robbed the sun of warmth. Babak seemed to draw strength from the heat, or perhaps it was from the few days of respite from dreaming. He spoke more often, and the dark flesh beneath his eyes paled a bit. Yet he did not come fully back to his old self. He had lost his joy in food; I had to coax him to eat, and still he grew thinner. There was less joy of any sort about him, even when he dandled Shirak in his lap. Shirak, I noticed, was no longer "brave" and no longer roared. More and more often Babak stared off into the distance, eyes vacant, and hummed.

Things that I had pushed aside in my mind now began to nag at me again. This latest dream of the stars seemed much grander than the ones before. Not just two stars together and apart, but the whole of the sky, over ages beyond imagining. *Might* it have been for Gaspar, with his great knowledge of the heavens? I had asked Babak whose dream it was, but he'd shrugged and turned from me, not wanting to be pressed. I worried, though. If Melchior were going to parcel out dreams as favors to powerful men—or use dreams to spy on them—what would become of Babak?

And then there was Ecbatana. Despite the season, might the king still be there? Might his Eyes and Ears?

Phraates, Pacorus told me when I asked, would be well away to his winter residence in Ctesiphon by now. Before too long the mountain roads to Ecbatana would be blocked by snow.

"Will we stay in Ecbatana until Phraates returns?"

Pacorus shrugged. "This, no one knows for certain. But they say Gaspar wishes to consult with another priest in Ecbatana, one more powerful still."

I felt these new priests crowding in on us. If they knew of Babak's dreams, surely they would seek to make use of them. All the more reason to flee with Pirouz. To Suren! More and more I felt certain we would see him again. I looked about for Pirouz and found him in a cluster of riders ahead. There had still been no chance to speak with him. Although Pacorus no longer stayed with us—Giv required him for other chores—another man sat just outside our quarters at night. But I must find a way to speak with Pirouz, and soon.

✳

We reached the main road to Ecbatana late on the second day after leaving the fortress. I had thought that we would travel through the night until we came to a caravansary, but at sunset we stopped near a stream for devotions. Afterward there was a convocation among Melchior, Gaspar, and Giv. The two Magi, I had noticed, did not seem to have much to do with each other, except for brief consultations like this one. Gaspar refused the rich food Melchior offered him, and shunned his entertainments, preferring to gaze at the stars, sighting along that disc of his, or to retreat to his quarters, alone.

Soon the call went out to set up our tents. The animals were weary, Pacorus told me; it was best to give them a rest and start fresh in the morning. He handed me an armful of camel gear—girths and cruppers, nose lines, a headdress, a torn leather pad. "Word of your nimble fingers has reached Giv. He would like you to repair the gear of other people's animals, as well as your own."

I groaned, but couldn't suppress a little glow. *Word of my nimble fingers.* Nimble not in stealing now, but in respected work.

I had fed and watered our animals and was dressing Ziba's hide with butter when I heard a footstep behind me. I turned to look.

Pirouz.

At last! "What do you know of Suren?" I asked.

"Shh." He peered furtively about. "He waits for you. Tonight, after midnight prayers, I'll come for you. Be ready."

"But—"

"Shh. I've a sleeping potion for your guard, and . . ." He nodded significantly toward the camp. Giv was striding our way, scowling more deeply than ever.

"Tonight!" Pirouz said. And he was gone.

"What did he want?" Giv demanded.

"Nothing. He still thinks he knows us. I tried to tell him no, but—"

"Stay away from him—I told you!" Giv growled. "Don't talk to him again. Do you hear me? *Do* you?"

Mutely I nodded, taken aback by his outburst. Men had turned round to gawk at us. Giv stared after Pirouz. "If the Magus weren't so fond of his useless juggling tricks, I'd get rid of him today," he muttered. Then, to me, he snapped, "Get back to your tent. Go!"

I turned away. Giv would be livid if we escaped. But Pirouz's words echoed in my ears:

He waits for you.

What should I do?

Darkness fell. I tucked Babak in for the night; Shirak tiptoed across the carpet and over Babak's shoulder, then curled up against his chest. I lay beside them, listened to the night sounds: the quiet rumblings of men's talk, the scattered snores, the shifting and groaning of camels, the whickering of a horse. From the distance came the eerie howling of jackals, or wolves. Nearby, someone began to strum a soft tune on a lute. Just outside our tent I heard liquid pouring into a cup and the rough, mumbled thanks of the man Giv had stationed there.

I've a sleeping potion for your guard.

He waits for you.

Tonight . . . Be ready.

I tried to think clearly, decide what to do. But my mind would not still; it hopped like a flea over the past weeks of my life, alighting on faces and incidents and fragments of things said.

Ecbatana, summer residence of the king.

Does everyone know about the precession of equinoxes?

Stars, all ablur, circling as in many nights, many months, many years, many thousands of years.

That sleepwalking dream, so much vaster in scope than the others, had seemed to sap the life from Babak.

How many such dreams could Babak endure?

To touch the dreams of such a man . . . It could burn you.

I leaped to my feet, prowled up and down the length of the tent space—quietly, so as not to wake the guard, whose rumbling snores now overwhelmed the other night sounds. Sleeping!

It's my guess . . . Suren's been captured.

Maybe this was a trap. Maybe Pirouz was one of the Eyes and Ears, despite all appearances. Maybe he would take us straight back to where Suren was held prisoner, if he took us to him at all. Maybe he would take us to the king.

But the Eyes and Ears, once they located their quarry, would have no more need of disguise—they would reveal themselves and seize whatever it was they wanted.

Or maybe he was a spy for them. But if so, he was not a good spy, for he had aroused Giv's suspicion right away. And if he were a spy, wouldn't he, having found us, ride back to tell the Eyes and Ears and let them seize us? On the other hand, if he was loyal to Suren—or at least expected a reward from one of our allies—he would likely have to fetch us himself.

I've done you a favor and you don't even know it.

Favor! Ha! I kicked a basket, tipping it over and sending a cache of dried chickpeas spilling out across the carpet. That old crone! We didn't need any favors from her. And we wouldn't remain chattel. Wouldn't. We were noble born—kin to kings! Should I spurn this chance—even if uncertain—to seize back the life we deserved?

Shirak, staggering out of Giv's massive, cupped hand.

Pacorus, hastening to search for Babak.

I shoved them out of my mind.

He waits for you.

Grandmother, beside me on her divan in our old home in Susa—drawing me close, setting her powder-soft cheek against my hair:

Granddaughter! Remember who you are!

*

CHAPTER 26

ACROSS THE PLATEAU

When Pirouz came, I was ready.

I roused Babak. He moaned softly and put his arms about my neck as I lifted him. Then I picked up the saddlebags I'd packed with blankets and a little food. Carefully I stepped over Shirak—curled up, sound asleep—and followed Pirouz out past the snoring guard. Though one of the larger tents glowed with lamplight and hummed with voices, nothing else stirred. We made our way down onto the dry bank of the stream and into the shadowy gloom of a dusty stand of trees, where we could not be seen.

The stable hand awaited us, along with two horses. Babak stirred, stiffened, let out a small sound of surprise.

"Hush," I said. "They're taking us to Suren."

"Suren!" Babak jerked fully awake, his eyes wild with hope.

"Shh. Come." Pirouz mounted one of the horses, held out his arms to take Babak.

He shrank from Pirouz, but I whispered assurances in Babak's ear and handed him up. I straddled the second horse, behind the stable hand. We set off.

We rode through all of that night. It was a rough, hard-pressed journey, traversing the high plateau at a tooth-jarring pace, shunning roads, clambering up and down the steep banks of wadis, stumbling on patches of loose rock and shifting sand. The wind stirred up. It swept away our tracks, for which I was glad. Giv, I knew, had some skill at tracking; now he could not follow. But this helpful wind also bit at my ears and spit sand into my eyes. The night grew piercingly cold.

And yet with every step we grew nearer to Suren.

At least, I hoped we did.

The knife-thin rim of moon was behind us as it set; after that, judging from what little I knew of stars and from the darker darkness of mountains against the sky, it seemed that we traveled mostly east. But sometimes there were mountains on two or three sides, and other times it seemed that we veered north or south.

If Suren had sent Pirouz to find us, why were we not headed south, to Susa? Or west, in the direction of Palmyra?

I pushed my qualms aside. Babak was no longer anyone's chattel. Soon, the gods willing, we would be reunited with our brother.

When the red morning sun shimmered up over the horizon, we were picking our way along the bottom of a barren wadi. We did not stop for devotions. When we came to a pool of brackish water, Pirouz pulled up beside us and told the stable hand to dismount and make camp.

"Where are we going?" I asked. "How long until we reach Suren?"

Pirouz didn't even glance at me, just turned his horse away.

"Where is Suren?" I asked louder.

"Put a muzzle on that one," he flung over his shoulder.

Before I could comprehend what was happening, the servant jammed a filthy rag into my mouth and tied it behind my head. When I lashed out at him, he clouted me hard across the face, sending me tumbling to the ground.

"Suren," Pirouz scoffed. He turned to the other man. "Suren," he repeated, as if they shared a secret joke. The man laughed, head hunched between his massive shoulders.

I closed my eyes and cradled my head in my hands, letting

the rage sweep through me, waiting for the bright, hot center of the pain to cool.

"When will we come to Suren?" Babak asked.

I looked at him. Didn't he understand?

Pirouz was lounging in the morning shade, idly tossing a ball and catching it, tossing it and catching it. The other man—Arman was his name—had hobbled and fed the horses, then unpacked from the saddlebags a waterskin and a small sack of dates. He had removed my gag but bound my ankles together and my wrists behind me, tight enough to chafe yet not so tight as to stop my blood. He'd bound Babak's wrists only, reasoning, no doubt, that my brother wouldn't try to run away without me, but that he might try to untie my bindings. Arman did think to settle us in the shade, which led me to believe we were worth something to them alive.

"When will we come to Suren?"

He must know that we would not. I opened my mouth to reassure him some way but found no words. A spreading darkness had come to pool about my heart.

"Where is Suren?" Babak said, his voice rising.

"Come here," I said. "Lean against me."

But he did not. "I want Suren."

"I want him too," I whispered.

Babak stared at me. Then, quietly, he began to weep.

This doesn't mean he's dead, I told myself. Just because Pirouz deceived us, it doesn't mean Suren was captured, or that he couldn't escape if he were. Pirouz might have met him on the road, and Suren might have told him too much. Suren was always too trusting.

That Suren! He had likely gone to ground somewhere and was crouching there, afraid to take a risk, afraid to go forward or backward without me to urge him on.

This doesn't mean I sent him to his death.

This means nothing. Nothing at all.

✶

In a while Arman untied Babak and made to free my hands so that we could eat.

"Let his brother feed him," Pirouz said.

Arman swept the barren landscape with his gaze, as if to say, *Where would they go?*

"Just do what I say."

Arman shrugged.

Babak roused himself to administer a few squirts from the waterskin and pop several dates into our mouths. His eyes were red from crying, and he wouldn't look at me. I motioned with my head for him to sit by my side. This time he relented. I felt him sigh, a sigh that seemed to release his anger at me into the desert air.

Or maybe it was hope he let go of.

The wind had died down, and a great stillness had come over the parched landscape, a stillness unbroken save for the buzzing of flies, the far-off cry of a hawk and, from time to time, a slide of pebbles down the side of the wadi as some small animal passed above. Inside an open lean-to Pirouz and Arman spoke softly, but I managed to catch most of what they said.

It was as bad as I had feared. We were headed for a caravansary Pirouz knew, where he could buy the innkeeper's silence. This caravansary lay on a different, more northerly road. We would join the next westbound caravan, skirt Ecbatana, and make for Ctesiphon, where Phraates and his men had gone for the winter.

Babak, listening, grew tense beside me. "Never fear," I whispered. "We'll find a way to escape. These men are low-born and stupid. We'll easily outsmart them." I tried to make myself believe the last part. If I didn't, Babak would feed on my fear. If I didn't, I would curl myself into a ball and wait for death to overtake me.

Soon I heard Arman ask for more dates, but Pirouz yanked away the sack, lounged back, and rested his head upon it.

"Watch 'em," he said.

"How could they get away? I can't go night and day on a couple of dates, I need—"

"If you want to give the orders, go find your own noble brood to ransom. Though you won't find any to fetch what these'll bring—of that you can be sure."

Arman, grumbling to himself, hunkered down to keep watch.

I lay with my chin against Babak's shoulder as the sun rose in the sky, shrinking our patch of shadow. I whispered words of comfort, words of escape. Gradually the tautness in his body eased. When at last his breath settled into the rhythms of sleep, the aches and pains in my own body rose up and cried for attention: sore legs and back, chafing wrists, shoulders cramped and twitchy. I strove to clear my mind and trace back through all I knew of Pirouz.

I could not recall seeing him in the original caravan when Melchior came into Rhagae. The first time I noticed him had been later. Babak had bumped into him once, when we were fleeing Giv.

Had I called Babak by name? It was true that Pirouz might have met with Suren on the road. Or—

The king's Eyes and Ears. What had Zoya said of them? They had come looking for a young boy named Babak and an older sister or brother. They had asked for Babak by name.

It was possible they'd just now—after all these years—come round to finding us. But more likely . . .

Suren.

More likely, they'd found Suren first.

Against my will the pieces of the mosaic seemed to click into place, forming a complete picture at last. Maybe Pirouz had spoken with the Eyes and Ears, in Rhagae or before. In the caravan he had recognized Babak from his name and description. When I showed up—*an older sister or brother*—I had confirmed his suspicions.

What a fool I had been! Babak had trusted me, and I had ruined us both.

And Suren. What had I done to him?

*

A PLAN

A while later a movement jerked me out of sleep. Babak was rising to walk! I hissed out his name, but he did not respond. His eyes seemed tranced, as they had that night in the fortress. I threw myself against his feet to stop him. He tripped and fell, then looked round, startled. At Arman, snoring, a little way off. At Pirouz, reclining in the lean-to.

Babak began to cry.

I itched to search beneath his tunic to find out if there was an alien piece of cloth there to cause this dream, but my hands and feet were bound.

"There, Babak." I tucked my chin atop his head and spoke into his hair. "Hush, little one." The sobs began to abate. Babak hiccoughed, rubbed his drippy face upon my tunic.

"What did you dream?" I asked. "Whose dream was it?"

"It was the shaggy beasties," he said. "The dream I had before."

How could that be? That dream had been for the Scythian's wife, and her dream cloth was long gone.

"What's amiss with him?" Pirouz approached with that swaybacked swagger of his; we must have awakened him. Suddenly a plan leaped into my mind.

"Don't say anything," I whispered to Babak. "No matter what I say, just nod. Do you hear me?"

Babak, sniffling, nodded.

I turned to Pirouz. "It's nothing," I said. "He's just had one of his dreams."

Pirouz grunted and turned back.

"I wouldn't trouble myself if I were you," I said, though clearly he was not troubled. "Babak's dreams don't *always* come true," I said.

Pirouz stopped. Slowly he turned round. Came back. Squatted before us. "What was the dream?"

I shook my head. "No need to bother yourself about it."

He seized a wad of my tunic and pulled me so close that the reek of his breath nearly brought tears to my eyes. "What was the dream?"

"Shh." I set my finger upon my lips, looked pointedly in Arman's direction.

Still snoring.

"Babak dreamed . . ." I hesitated. Was this wise? People had been known to kill the bearers of ill tidings.

Pirouz shook me. "What?"

"Someone stabbed you in the back with a dagger."

I felt Babak stiffen in surprise.

"Who?" Pirouz demanded.

I jerked my head toward Arman. *Quiet,* I willed to Babak.

Pirouz narrowed his eyes. "You said 'don't always come true.' So, sometimes they do."

"Sometimes."

"Often?"

I shrugged. "Often enough. He dreamed of a wedding for a Scythian and of winning a toss of dice. Those came true. And . . ." Here came another lie, but I needed to drive the point home. "And the death of an uncle by poison."

"Poison? Not just death, or death at another's hands?"

"It was poison." I turned to look pointedly at Babak. Obediently he nodded.

Pirouz let go of me. He gazed long and hard at his sleeping servant, then went off to brood alone.

Arman shook us awake as the sun slid behind the mountains and flooded the lowering clouds with crimson. He passed around the waterskin and doled out a few more dates, then untied us so we could ride.

Again we rode all night. Daylight found us moving across the plain toward a line of roundish mounds of dirt, like a string of giant anthills. Each mound, I knew, marked the well shaft to an underground irrigation canal, a qanat. Arman pointed to a spindly hoisting device, a well wheel, beside one of the openings. We rode toward it and stopped nearby.

Right away Pirouz and Arman set to quarreling. Pirouz favored moving down the canal to another well, as the well wheel indicated that people at a village nearby must have been cleaning the qanat recently, and they would doubtless soon return. But Arman said that the device was worth the risk, and that if we moved, Pirouz could haul his own water. Pirouz, muttering, dismounted and went to work erecting a shelter for himself, while Arman unpacked the horses. Neither had yet made a move to bind us. No doubt they would later, when they settled down to sleep. Arman had just set off to fetch water for the animals when Pirouz, sprawled out in his lean-to, clapped his hands imperiously and called to Arman to fill his waterskin first. Grumbling, Arman filled the skin, then ducked into the shelter. In a moment I heard Arman shout, "It's a lie!" Then all at once he jumped backward, knocking down a pole, collapsing the lean-to. Pirouz pursued him, dagger drawn; Arman unsheathed his knife. They began to circle, each one keeping eyes fixed upon the other.

I had hoped for this, for the poison to work in Pirouz's mind, but I hadn't expected it so soon.

"Follow me," I whispered to Babak. Slowly, we crept toward the horses. If we could take them both, the men would never catch us.

The first hobble was loose; I managed to untie it in no time. I helped Babak to mount and was fumbling with the knot of the second hobble, wedging my fingers into tight crevices of leather, when I heard Pirouz shout.

He had seen us. They were coming.

If I didn't loose both horses, we would never get away. "Wait for me," I told Babak, picking desperately at the knot with fingers now beginning to bleed.

Too late. Pirouz was almost upon us, and the knot had not begun to yield, but I couldn't let go of it, couldn't let go of hope.

Pirouz lunged for Babak, but Babak slipped off the far side of the horse. It whinnied and plunged. Pirouz fell backward, went sprawling. "It stepped on me!" he cried, holding his foot. I rose to go to Babak, but Arman flung himself upon me, pinning me to the ground—so heavy I thought my ribs would crack. I strained to lift my head. Babak was running. I squeaked out a call to him, for it was over now, he had no place to go. And when I realized where he was headed, I called again. Screamed.

"Babak! Don't!"

But he did. He scrambled up the side of the circle of heaped dirt and disappeared into the qanat.

✳

CHAPTER 28

QANAT

There was a moment of stillness, an indrawn breath of a moment in which I thought I heard a clattering of stones. Then I sank my teeth in Arman's hand, sank them deep. He roared, shook free of me, rolled off me to cradle his wound. I was running then, running past Pirouz—who lunged at me and missed—running across the hard, scrubby plain and up the loose dirt berm to the qanat. Deep. Deep and black. I could not see the bottom. I could not see Babak. But the rope from the hoisting device had come unwound from the wheel and hung down into the shaft. Had Babak climbed down the rope—not just flung himself into the well?

A shout. Arman was coming for me, Pirouz close behind. I crouched, grabbed on to the rope, and lowered myself down, setting off an avalanche of loose stones and dirt that rattled down the sides of the shaft and hit the water with a volley of *ploink*s. Down, down into the dark. My back scraped against the sides of the shaft. Feet slipping, knees slipping, rope burning through my hands, and now all of me sliding, all of me falling. A splash. A shock of cold. My boots knocked against the leather bucket, slapped down on solid, slippery rock.

"Sister!"

It was Babak. I couldn't see him; his voice came high and weak from the thick darkness beyond the dust-flecked light that streamed down through the shaft. I waded through frigid, thigh-high water toward the sound. Too slowly my eyes accustomed themselves to the dark. At last I found him, a small, hunched shadow against the rock.

"Are you hurt?" I asked. "Bleeding? Did you break anything? Tell me!"

He said no, but I felt him all over anyway. He did seem to have scraped himself—hands and forearms and maybe other places too. But he was whole. He was alive.

"You might have broken a leg," I said, "you might have . . ." My throat stopped up; I put my arms around him and clung to him, just clung.

Shouting up above. Pirouz. Shouting our names, shouting promises, shouting threats. His reedy voice echoed against the rock, sounded very far away. I unclasped myself from Babak and peered back up the shaft. I could see him now, looking down at us, though his face was all in shadow, backlit by the morning sun.

I had been able to see nothing when I looked down; likely he could not see me either. But he kept calling down the hole, urging me to save poor little Babak, urging me to set him in the bucket so Pirouz could haul him up.

"No," Babak said, very soft. "Please don't."

It was cool and still down here. Near the shaft, light rippled across the walls. I scooped up water in my cupped hands and drank greedily, then drank again. Pirouz must have heard something, because his importunings and threats grew louder, more insistent.

"I'll climb down there and fetch you out," he said, "I will!"

But he wouldn't, I didn't think—nor would Arman. Each would have to trust the other to draw him up again. Still, "We have to go up," I said.

Babak clung to my arm. "No."

"We'll escape another time," I said.

"No."

It would be foolish to stay in the qanat. We had no food, no place to rest. Likely there would be a village near the end of the qanat. But how far? This shaft was deep, and the string of mounds had stretched out long across the desert. I had seen no end to them.

I looked up at Pirouz, listened to him plead and rant. There was something snug about watching him from this cool, quiet place, out of his reach and seeing. To put ourselves back into his hands again . . .

No.

The water made echoey, rippling, purling sounds as we waded downstream. Pirouz's voice grew faint, and soon we could no longer hear it at all. I breathed in deep. The air was cool and smelled of fresh water: clean, metallic. The walls drew in close about us. Away from the shaft it grew dark. With one hand I felt my way along slippery stone; with the other I hooked fingers with Babak. I yearned for a lamp, but he was no longer afraid. Like a small, wild creature, he was comfortable in the dark.

But now there was light before us: a sheer column sifting down from above, a patch of shimmering gold in the water.

And a rope, with a loop at its bottom, hanging down into the shaft.

Pirouz. He must have gone ahead. He must have guessed that we would not push against the current, moving toward the deeper wells near the mountains, but would walk instead with the flow in the direction of shallower and shallower wells, hoping to reach the place where the water streamed out aboveground.

Babak stopped, tightened his grip on my hand.

"He can't reach us here," I said.

"He could come down the rope."

"He won't."

As we drew near, I saw that this shaft was wider than the last. Someone was lying on the ground above, head hung over the lip of the opening. The sun dazzled my eyes, so that I could not make out his features, but I knew from the narrow head and scrawny beard that it was Pirouz.

He must have heard us, or perhaps he could see, for he began to call to us—to wheedle, to plead, to promise—that he would treat us with the respect due to our bloodline, that he would take us straightaway to Suren, that he wanted only a small reward, a mere pittance to fine folks the likes of our kin. I pushed the rope contemptuously aside as we passed. He hissed out a curse.

We moved on, into the dark. Babak's grip on my hand eased.

"Are you certain he won't come down here?" Babak asked.

"Yes," I said, edging my voice with impatience to discourage him from asking again. True, it was likely that Pirouz would not trust Arman to haul him up. But he might ride along the row of qanat openings until he arrived at the place where the underground channel flowed out aboveground. He might enter the qanat and come to meet us, or wait until we emerged.

We were far from safe.

On we waded. The sky grew bright overhead in the shafts, merged in slow gradations from the cool blue of morning to midday's glaring white. Pirouz offered us no more ropes; he had either given up or gone on ahead. The coolness of the qanat had long since gone grim, driving through skin and flesh to lodge in bone. Often now we stood in the columns of sunlight beneath the shafts, trying to wick light and warmth inside us. My feet were numb stumps in my waterlogged leather boots, and I shivered without cease.

"I'm hungry," Babak said through chattering teeth. "I'm cold." I picked him up and held him in the thin slice of sunlight. He *was* cold. Too cold.

We ought to have taken that rope. I knew it now. With Pirouz we would at least have stood a chance.

Maybe he was still up there, still near. At the next shaft I set down Babak and called up into the light. "*Ahaii!* Help us! *Ahaii!*" My voice echoed off the walls and trailed away.

I half expected Babak to object, to plead with me not to let Pirouz know where we were. But he only stood and shivered. His lips had gone blue.

No one answered my call.

I took Babak's hand, trudged ahead. At every shaft I shouted, going through the motions, now without hope. Before long I had no strength left for shouting.

Soon Babak could walk no longer. I picked him up, slogged wearily on. I could feel death closing in about us, whispering in the water, echoing against the stone. I could feel it beating its soft wings against my cheeks.

I began to pray—first to the Wise God, then to the various gods my mother used to pray to, and then to all the gods at once.

I had doomed us. By refusing the rope, and before that . . .

Zoya had been right. She had done us a favor, selling Babak to the Magus. We would never have survived on our own, away from the City of the Dead, with the king's Eyes and Ears searching. If only I had not foolishly gone with Pirouz, we wouldn't be facing death in this qanat and might still have a chance at Palmyra.

And before that . . . Babak's dreams. I had known it was a sin to sell them.

And Suren.

Fearing that the king's men would *force him, by means of pain* . . .

I stumbled, caught myself.

By means of pain . . .

My feet slowed; they dragged against the bottom of the qanat. They stopped. I leaned my head against the cold, damp wall.

Who do you serve? . . . We're more alike than you think.

No.

Remember who you are.

Who was I, then?

A fool who dreamed old dreams of nobility and

consequence but in truth would never again have either.

By means of pain . . .

No, worse than a fool. Worse even than Zoya.

My knees buckled. I sank down into the water. It rose to my waist, numbing me with cold.

"Sister?"

Babak set his hands on my face; I could feel the warmth of his breath. Slowly I forced myself to rise, began to walk again. For now all that mattered was walking, placing one frozen foot before the other.

After a time that seemed at once like forever and like no time at all, Babak lifted his head from my shoulder, his body shot through with alertness. "Listen," he said.

I stopped. Set him down.

And there it was, so faint I could barely winnow out the sound of it from the soft, steady ripple of the channel. A water sound—not flowing, but a *swish* . . . *swish* . . . *swish*, echoing the *swish* we made as we waded. It did not cease when we stood still, as an echo would do. It kept on.

It seemed to be coming from the direction in which we traveled.

"What is it?" Babak asked.

"I don't know." It was constant, neither hastening nor slackening. Coming nearer, though. Coming this way. No clopping sounds, as a donkey or goat would make. Lions, I reassured myself, did not like water. Would never walk through a qanat. And there was a two-leggedness to this sound—one *swish*, another *swish*—that said *man*.

"Is it Pirouz?" Babak asked.

"I don't know." I groped for his hand, took it in mine. So cold. "But even if it is, we can't stay here any longer. We'll have to go with him."

"But—"

"We *must*."

We began to walk toward the sound again.

The light, when first I saw it, was an oval that flickered and bobbed.

Torchlight.

It divided now into two bright splotches—one in the air, one rippling below, mirrored in the water.

Babak tugged on my hand, signaling me to stop, and I did, for a moment. But the light pulled at me.

My first clear sight of him was sudden, as he rounded a slight bend in the qanat. I had an impression of solidness. Of relentlessness. He seemed taller than I, but not so tall as Pirouz or Pacorus or Giv. He was a youth, probably near my own age.

He stopped. "Who are you, then?" he asked. "Why are you here?"

Such easy questions—and yet, too difficult for me.

"I'm Koosha," he said. "Son of Ardalan, of the Village of the Red Mountain. We heard you call."

✳

CHAPTER 29

KOOSHA

He stooped down and held his torch before Babak's face. Babak blinked in the sudden brightness. Koosha stood, shrugged off his cloak, held it out. I picked up Babak and wrapped it around us both. The cloth was unusually thick and soft, and it had a comforting smell, of animal sweat and leather.

"Come along, then," Koosha said, and when I did not move, he repeated, "Come."

I followed. I knew nothing about him—whether or not he was allied with Pirouz or the king's Eyes and Ears, whether he would prove to be friend or foe. But we could stay no longer in the qanat. Besides, there was something about him, this Koosha. His eyes, when they caught mine in the torchlight, had seemed thoughtful and still. He seemed like someone I might trust.

Still, I had misjudged before.

He led us back the way he had come, his light dancing on the rough-hewn walls and gliding across the water, until we arrived at another shaft, where he pulled out a sheep's horn and blew a long, low note. The qanat rang with it, as if we stood within a giant bell. "Help's coming," he said, then asked again, "Who are you?"

The prospect of sorting out a safe reply weighed me down. My back ached from carrying Babak, who now hung lifeless as a sack of stones. I was weak from hunger and cold.

Though the upper part of the shaft shone bright as molten gold, neither heat nor light penetrated to where we stood. I shrugged.

The question remained in Koosha's eyes, but he did not ask again. He clasped his arms about himself—he, too, must be cold, without his cloak—and settled in to wait.

In some corner of my mind I knew that I ought to scent out whether he intended us good or ill. But it was too much to form the right questions in my mind, too much even to open my mouth to ask.

Before long I heard voices approaching, then a shadow blacked out part of the sunlight above. A man. Someone Koosha seemed to know.

"Did you find them, then?" the man asked.

"Aye, two bo—" Koosha turned to gaze at me, and I couldn't fathom his look. "Two of them. Savage cold, they are."

There was more calling back and forth, then a rope shivered down the shaft. Koosha began to tie a loop at the bottom. "'Tis my father and my uncle up yonder," he said. "Coming home, we heard you call. We were trading in the towns north of here, trading cloth. The cloth of our village is savage soft." He turned back to the knot, finished it, and tugged on the rope. It occurred to me that he was trying to make us easy with him. To help us trust him.

"So who'll go first, then?" Koosha asked.

"We will go together."

He shook his head. "Nay, it isn't safe. Nothing to anchor the rope. You must go one at a time."

"Babak." I jostled him in my arms to wake him. He looked up sleepily as I settled him within the loop. "They're going to take you out now. Hold on to the rope."

He clung to my neck. "No. I want to stay with you."

"I'm coming up next, never you fear. Let go of me now."

"Is Pirouz there?"

"No," I said, with a good deal more certainty than I felt.

"Now, let go." Forcibly I pried his hands from around my neck. He let out a piercing wail. "Cling tight to the rope!" I cried. "Hold on!"

He grasped it, his gaze fixed down upon my face as he rose up and up, as if, were he to glance away, some thread that bound us together would snap. So lonely, he looked, dangling from that rope in the blue black gloom of the qanat. It could pull out your heart by the roots.

Someone spoke to him from above. He straightened, looking up, and in the arch of his back I read hope. Voices. Hands reaching down from the light. And then Babak's voice, very calm.

He would not be calm, I thought, if Pirouz were there.

The rope slithered down again. I returned Koosha's cloak and slipped into the loop, holding on tight as daylight bloomed overhead, as a wave of warmth beat upon my body. Three shapes against the white-hot sky: A stocky, smiling man with a beard streaked with gray. A worried-looking man. And Babak.

The stocky man wrapped his cloak about me. I sat holding Babak while the two men pulled up Koosha. They spoke softly among themselves, murmuring, murmuring.

I remember someone helping me to my feet. I remember a tent, a sleeping pallet. I remember lying next to Babak, letting the heat of the high desert thaw my bones.

When I awoke, it was dark. I sat up in alarm, saw that I was in a tent. I scanned it for Babak—then heard his voice, along with others, outside. All the past day's events came back to me: Pirouz and Arman. The qanat. Koosha and his kinsmen. I lay tense and listening, fearful that Babak might have revealed something of who we were.

There was a rustic lilt to their voices, like Giv's only more pronounced. One of them—Koosha?—seemed to be speaking of their donkeys, of how this one was gentle and that one pricklish. Then Babak told how Gorizpa would purse her lips when you asked her to do something unwelcome, how she would swivel one ear round in the direction of his voice or mine.

The tightness inside me eased. Babak could sense things about people. If he was so easy with these men . . . Well, it proved nothing. But it was a good sign.

When I came out into the dusk, they all turned to look: Babak and Koosha, by the donkeys; the other two men, by the fire. I expected Babak to run to me, but after a glance he returned to what he had been doing, feeding one of the donkeys. "Babak?" I said. He indulged me with a cool smile. I stared at him, reminded of Suren, who, when younger, had been content to play with me only until the older boys let him join them.

But Koosha abandoned the donkeys, trotted over to me, and asked if I was feeling well. "Yes," I said. "Much better."

The stocky man now stood and introduced himself. There was an air of gravity about him, of steady strength, tempered by sadness. His voice was low and sure. He was Ardalan, of the Village of the Red Mountain. And this, the worried-seeming man with deep furrows graven in his brow beside the bridge of his nose, this was his brother, Kouros. "My son Koosha you have met," Ardalan said. I started to thank them—for the rescue, for the shelter—but Ardalan waved it aside. "Babak has been telling of your capture and your escape. He's saying you belong to a Magus."

Belong!

I almost told him my father's name, and of our whole noble lineage down to the early Parthian princes. But I clamped my lips shut and nodded.

"Will he be sending a man to search for you, then?" Ardalan asked. "This Magus?"

I considered. Yes, Melchior valued Babak—for his dreams, if nothing else. "I believe he will. One of them is said to have skill at tracking. But the wind swept away all trace of us."

"A good tracker," Ardalan said, "can follow a trail despite the wind—though it may take him longer."

"But the men who abducted us might search for us as well."

"And so we'll keep a lookout, then," Ardalan said.

"Father says we'll bide here a couple of days," Koosha said, "so the Magus'll have time to find you, and after that—"

Ardalan broke in. "After that, we shall see."

They fed us modestly but well: bread and cheese, date cakes and olives. The next morning, after the men had made their devotions to the Wise God, Koosha asked Babak if he would like to help gather thornbush for the fire. Babak jumped to his feet.

"Wait!" I said. "He is weak. He's . . . he's been ill." I stopped, hearing the pleading in my voice. What was wrong with me? I must remember to behave as a brother would, not as a sister.

"He likes to help," Koosha said simply, and continued on his way. Babak went tripping after. Koosha stopped and pointed out something in the distance; Babak looked up at him with adoring eyes. And Suren came back to me so strongly—Suren as he used to be, when he was willing to teach me, when I thought he knew everything.

They moved ahead together, Koosha's hand on Babak's shoulder. Darkness filled me, a kind of loneliness and shame. Not wanting to be left behind, I tagged along.

We did not stray far, lest Pirouz should appear. But there was plenty of thornbush; even Babak gathered a load nearly as large as he was and proudly dragged it back to the encampment.

Next we tended to the donkeys. Koosha drew up skins of water from the qanat as easily as Pacorus had done from the caravansary well, and poured them into calabashes. My gaze seemed to linger upon Koosha of its own accord. He was not tall and willow lean like Pacorus, but sturdy, compressed, like Ardalan and Kouros. I adjusted his age upward. Seventeen, perhaps, or eighteen.

We combed the donkeys' manes and tails with our fingers and beat great clouds of dust off their coats with palm fronds kept for that purpose. Babak joined in with gusto. Koosha, I saw, had a gentle way with animals. He lifted their feet and, with a stick, scraped dirt and sand from their hooves; they eyed him trustingly from beneath shaggy brows, and not once did they protest. He checked the smallest donkey's withers, gently rubbed her knees. "Are you hurting, then, old girl?" he murmured.

"Old?" I said. "She looks but half grown."

"She was sickly small aborning. Too weak to live without coddling. My father craved to put her down quick, but . . ." He shrugged.

"Why didn't he?"

Koosha grinned at me. "I made quite the plague of myself! Begged. Wheedled. Wept. All manner of rash promises passed my lips. Father let by, thinking to teach me a hard lesson, but he misjudged the flint in me."

"So, what did you do?"

"Fed her day and night, I did, with a teat fashioned from goatskin. Scarce slept a wink for weeks. But in the end she was thriving."

"My father would have called that a waste of effort—catering to the weak. She'll never be the same as the others."

Koosha bristled. "So, then! I have two working donkeys I wouldn't have else, and eleven goats besides. And—though your father'd call it a waste of time to hand-feed a brood of orphaned nestlings—we now have seven more larks in the trees, singing music that's savage sweet."

You and Babak, I thought. Two of a kind. But I held my tongue.

Koosha showed Babak how to saddle the donkey and stood patiently by as Babak began to fumble with the leather ties. But then the ties slipped from Babak's hands. His eyes went vacant and a look crossed his face, a look of listening to something no one else could hear. Koosha picked up the ties and was about to return them to him when Babak began to hum in that tuneless, absent way of his.

Koosha looked at me, questioning.

"I told you he was ill," I said, and abruptly turned away.

"Ill?" Koosha asked. "Perhaps I can help him, help you to heal him. I know how to—"

"He's not one of your strays," I snapped, "and neither am I."

Now Babak blinked, looked about him. Koosha shot me a level gaze, then handed Babak the ties and showed him again what to do.

I felt myself flush. Koosha had meant no harm.

Still, I didn't need some rustic telling me how to care for my own brother!

When Babak had finished saddling the donkey, Koosha laid a hand lightly on his shoulder. He smiled at a droll thing Babak said, and the smile lingered on his mouth while a faraway look gathered in his gray eyes. But he did not look straight at me again that day, even when he spoke to me. Which made it easier somehow—because the tenderness in him pulled at me hard, in a way that was new and strange and unsettling.

✳

CHAPTER 30

EYES TO SEE

Pirouz did not take long to find us. He turned up late that day—a cloud of white dust, then two horses, one of them riderless. No Arman. Ardalan motioned Babak and me into the tent. But Pirouz had seen us, Babak and me.

I felt a flicker of unease about the lie I'd told about Arman, about Babak's dream.

I did not hear all of what was said, for the convocation started out quietly. But soon Pirouz was ranting that he would come back with many men to fetch us, and that Ardalan and Kouros and Koosha would live to regret protecting us. Babak huddled against me, trembling.

I heard only Ardalan reply. He did not shout, but spoke firm and low. And I wondered how these villagers came by such nobility of manner—not deigning to honor Pirouz's threats with anger or fear—when they had not a drop of noble blood among them.

In a while I heard hoofbeats, then Ardalan and Koosha entered the tent.

"Is he gone?" I asked.

Ardalan nodded. "Aye. For now."

I breathed out slowly, released my hold on Babak.

"There's one thing puzzling me," Ardalan said. "This Pirouz. He claims he's returning you to your father, though he will not tell who your father is. A great nobleman, is all he says."

"He lies," I said. Which was true, at least partly. Pirouz was not returning us to our father.

"Then, if you'll pardon my asking, who is your father?"

I didn't like lying to him; he deserved better. But if Pirouz hadn't let drop who we were, best not divulge it myself. I held his gaze, said nothing. Ardalan waited. At last he sighed and said, "And so why did Pirouz steal you from your Magus, then, I'm wondering? Why does he come here to fetch you back?"

Still I held his gaze.

Ardalan frowned. He started to say something, then stopped and frowned again, this time to himself, as if deep in thought. He gazed out through the tent opening, across the plain. "So," he said. "We may yet have seen the last of Pirouz. But watch for him, that we will." He turned and left the tent.

Babak crawled into my lap and whimpered softly. I glanced at Koosha. "He's very young," I murmured. Though I knew it was more than that. Though I knew there was something soft about Babak, something that could not close itself off against the pain or rage of others and had nothing to do with his age.

"Don't apologize for him," Koosha said. "There isn't any need."

I felt my eyes drawn again to Koosha's, but I could read no disapproval there. Nor pity, either—that I could not abide. Only a kind of sadness—and a steady strength that warmed me like a drink of good wine.

On the third night it was Koosha's turn to stand the early watch. Ardalan offered the tent to Babak and me, but I declined. Babak craved to stay by the fire with Koosha, and it would be good for me to share the duty for once.

Babak lay with his head in Koosha's lap; I had to content myself with my brother's feet. The night was cool but, wrapped in warm wool, I didn't mind. Silence lay upon the land, broken only by the snap of the fire, a donkey's groan, the hoot of a nearby night bird. Babak wanted to know about the village where Koosha lived, and he asked a thousand questions—softly, so as not to disturb Ardalan and Kouros in the tent. "Is it a house that you live in or a tent? Do you have servants? Do you have a great stable with horses and ponies? Do you have a well in your courtyard? A fountain?"

Koosha answered patiently, laughing when Babak asked about servants and horses and fountains. "We're not of noble blood, Babak. We've only ourselves to do our work for us. We've sheds for the donkeys and sheepcotes carved out of the mountainsides, but neither horses nor great stables. They're for finer folk than us. As to wells," Koosha went on, "we've no need of them. There are three springs in the village, and a river flowing beside, with the sweetest water that ever cooled a man's throat."

"Does your father live there with you?" Babak asked. "Does . . . your mother?"

I felt the heat of Koosha's gaze upon me. Perhaps he wondered what had happened to our family, that Babak would ask such a question.

"Aye," Koosha said. "They do."

"I want to live there," Babak said. He turned to me. "Can we go to live with Koosha, in his village?"

"No," I said quickly. "No, Babak, we have our own ki—" I bethought myself. The less said about our kin, the better. "Think, Babak," I said, "of the delicious food the Magus gives us—five different kinds of melon. And of the fine leather boots he had made for us, and—"

"I don't want to go back to him. I want to go with Koosha!"

The dreams. He didn't want to dream for the Magus anymore. Didn't want to lose himself in that other place he went to—blank eyed, rocking and humming. And I don't want that for him, I told myself. That dreaming. I don't! Hadn't I taken him away from it? Hadn't I tried?

Still, giving up on Palmyra, giving up the chance of finding our true kinsmen and the life we were meant to live . . . That would be losing himself in another way. He couldn't see it now, but one day he would. Those dreams aren't truly hurting him, I told myself. Babak would survive.

But now it seemed I had offended Koosha as well, for he said to Babak, "Tell your brother that though we're not wealthy—not like your Magus, with his five kinds of melon—there's nothing in this world like melon grown in mountain air and fresh from the vine. Tell him that in our village there's fruit and grain and cheese sufficient and to spare for winter and into spring. Tell him that great trays of apricots and grapes are laid out on the roofs, so all through the snowy months we're tasting summer on our tongues."

"Snow . . ." Babak yawned.

"Tell your brother it's a savage lovely thing to live amid mountains garbed in snow, that they catch the light like jewels and dazzle the eye. Tell him that the breath of snow sets the lungs to tingling and the spirit astir. Tell him that our cottage nestles into the lee of the hills, sheltered from the wind, but the winter sun sits warm upon our shoulders as we overlook the valley from our terrace."

Babak's eyelids sagged; his breath came slow and even.

"Tell your brother," Koosha said, more softly now, "that the summer breeze goes whispering along the skin of the river. It wicks up the cool of it and sweeps it into every alley, every terrace. Tell him that the hillsides fill to bursting with tender grasses and blooms—savage good grazing for our sheep and goats. Tell him that the sighing of the willows and the rippling of the stream make music more tuneful than any lute you've ever heard. And tell your brother"—he turned from Babak, now asleep, and looked straight into my eyes—"that the women of our village crave neither fine leather boots nor robes thick with embroiderings. . . ."

I felt something leap between us, then all within me went still. At last I tore my gaze from his and looked down at the coat the Magus had provided, the embroidery on the sleeves now soiled and snagged.

"But they prize softness in cloth," Koosha went on, "and breathing air sweet with the scent of lemon blossoms, and freedom to stroll about the village as they please."

An odd, new, disturbing heat burned in my face. I became aware of his closeness, of the leather-and-animal smell of him. "I did not mean to offend you," I said in a low voice.

Koosha nodded, did not reply. The fire snapped. Babak's feet twitched, but his breathing did not alter.

I could see it now, this village. Though very different from Susa, it brought to mind the hill country there, where we used to live, before all had gone to ruin. Where you could gaze great distances across the land below. Where there were groves of fruit trees, and gardens lush with flowers, and good things to eat. Where brooks chuckled along beds of rounded stones. Where you had a place, among kin and friends. Where you were looked after. Cherished. And loved.

My chest opened up. I tipped back my head; the stars shimmered, blurred, swelled into bright, silvery globes that swam before my eyes. I breathed in the sky—all of it—swallowing stars. Something wet my cheeks; I dashed it away.

"You are no stray to be tamed or broken to a man's will," Koosha said, very softly now. "You are entirely yourself, no matter how you hide. I don't have to know who your father is to know this: The man who takes you to wife will have fire to contend with. He had best *like* fire."

I stared, could not think of a single word to say. At last I protested lamely, "But . . . but I'm a boy!"

"Oh, aye," he murmured. "So you say. But I have eyes to see."

✳

CHAPTER 31

HOW WOULD IT BE?

I couldn't sleep that night, haunted by Koosha's village—the red mudbrick houses nestled against the mountainside, the air perfumed with blossoms, the clear, rippling stream. And Koosha himself, the way he had looked at me. *Knew* me, it seemed.

I have eyes to see.

But no. I would not squeeze down my dreams until they fit inside his wretched village. I would not shape my tongue to the rhythms of his rustic speech.

I grew hot and threw off my cloak, then grew cold and drew it on, and then grew hot again.

Palmyra. Our kin, bloodline of kings. That was where we belonged.

And yet . . .

How would it be, I couldn't help wondering, to cease with struggling and let go of it all—of our hopes of finding Mother and Father and all our noble kin, of my life to come as a high-born lady among the Persians in Palmyra, of Babak's life to come as a scion of our great line? How would it be to let go of my longing to return one day to Susa, with its fine house and gardens and stables? How would it be to live out our lives and our children's lives and our children's children's lives as mere villagers in the mountains?

How would it be if Giv did not come?

✳

But come he did.

The following morning, under a low roof of clouds painted red with dawn, a dark speck appeared far off against the mountains to the north. It grew until it became a shimmering cloud of dust and sand, and then two moving things separated out: two horses. My heart seized. The Eyes and Ears? But in a moment I saw that only one horse was mounted, the other tethered behind. We five stood before the tent, the three villagers gripping the hilts of their daggers, and watched. The drumming of hoofbeats began to rumble beneath our feet. Pirouz again? Or . . .

"Giv," Babak said. He reached up his hand and slipped it into mine.

"Yes." I knew him now from the way he sat his horse—straight upright, but swaying easy in the saddle, like poplar boughs in a breeze.

A bit of the tautness drained out of the villagers, but they removed neither their eyes from Giv nor their hands from their daggers.

Something warmed inside me at the sight of him. After these long years of living among people who didn't care whether we lived or died, it seemed a miracle to have someone who would search so far to rescue us. Even though he had been sent by one who meant to use us. Even though we must betray him again, in time.

My eyes strayed toward Koosha and caught him gazing at me. Heat rose into my face; I studied the pebbly ground at my feet.

Giv, all-over gray with dust, greeted Ardalan first, introducing himself as a servant of Melchior. It was only after greeting Kouros and Koosha that Giv turned round to us.

He scowled, as ever, but his eyes seemed different, as if the hard, wary mask had slipped for a moment. Babak broke away from me and ran, flung himself at Giv, who picked him up and clasped him to his chest. I recalled some bit of gossip I had heard about Giv, that his mother and young brother had been taken by brigands many years before, that he had never seen them again.

Gently Giv set Babak down. He stepped forward, as if he might embrace me too, but then nodded gravely instead.

"Will you come in, then?" Ardalan asked him, motioning to the tent.

Giv ducked inside, followed by Kouros. Koosha began to do the same, but Ardalan stopped him. "Stay here with . . ." He nodded at Babak and me.

"Nay, but I must talk to you. To him," Koosha said, indicating Giv.

Ardalan's glance lit upon me so briefly that if I had blinked, I would have missed it. "Very well, then," he said grudgingly.

Giv peered out. "See to the horses," he told me. Trusting me not to ride off with them. For a fleeting moment I imagined leaping onto the back of Giv's horse, pulling up Babak behind me, and galloping, galloping toward the mountains, through the high passes, down into the great, crescent-shaped river valley Suren had told me of, and across the desert to Palmyra.

But I fetched water instead, fastening a waterskin to a rope and sending it down into the qanat. Babak followed, peppering me with questions and hope. "What will we do now? Can we go with Koosha to the Village of the Red Mountain? Giv could come too! Can we find Suren and take him there?"

Suren. A pang seized my heart to hear his name spoken aloud. Could Babak *still* have hopes of finding Suren?

"Babak," I said, "Suren . . ."

He turned from me and ran ahead to the horses.

Perhaps Babak truly didn't understand about Suren.

Perhaps he did, but didn't want to.

We gathered brush for fodder. The horses nosed through it and ate only the tenderest parts; donkeys would not have been so fussy. I turned again and again toward the tent, wishing I could hear what they were saying, wondering what was taking them so long.

And Koosha. What did he want with Giv?

The man who takes you to wife . . .

In time the tent flap rose and the men filed out. Each glanced at me in turn—Giv first, then Ardalan, Kouros, and Koosha—but I could not fathom the meaning of their looks. Giv took his leave, giving thanks to the villagers for their hospitality and many kindnesses. Then he turned to us and gruffly said, "Come." Babak let out a wail. Giv scooped him up and set him upon his horse.

So. It was back to the Magus.

Of course, this is the only way, I thought, as I mounted the second horse and turned it to follow Giv and Babak. Of course Melchior would not give up Babak, and Babak needed me, and anyhow, to sever him from me would be the same as lopping off one of my hands, one of my feet.

So.

When the caravan ceased going west, we would escape somehow and make our own way to Palmyra.

It was better this way. Koosha and his people were rustics. Lowborn. We would find our own kin, and the lives we were meant to live.

I did not look at Koosha as I passed him. I didn't intend to look back, either, and yet I did after we had gone a little way. Something pulled at me, forced me to turn.

Ardalan and Kouros, I saw, had returned to the tent.

But Koosha stood gazing after us, alone on the wide plateau.

✳

CHAPTER 32

IF YOU WERE A GIRL

We rode hard across the plateau all morning, heading west but shunning roads. I soon grew sore, though in my days in Susa I could have ridden thrice as long on my pony and never felt it. And yet to feel the horse beneath me and the wind against my face, to see the land go surging past . . . It brought back memories, and an ache for things lost. It reminded me of where I had come from. Daughter of Vardan, descendant of the great old Parthian kings.

When the sun had well passed its zenith, we came to a road and then a caravansary. As we entered the gates, some of the travelers halted in their work and turned their heads to stare at us. Giv looked about alertly, dismounted, then ordered me to water our animals and fill our waterskins. He strode toward one of the travelers and engaged him in conversation. The man twitched and shifted, and often cast a wary gaze at Babak and me.

Babak had given up crying for Koosha, but he did not seem happy, either. Now we both watched Giv, uneasy.

It was not long before Giv returned. "Mount," he said. "We'll not stay."

I tried to pry out of him what he had heard, but he would not say. Had Pirouz stopped by here, I wondered?

Later we halted to rest in the narrow strip of shade cast by an outcropping of rock. By now Babak seemed to have resigned himself to returning to the Magus. He curled up beside me without a word. "We will be fine, Babak," I said as Giv attended to the horses. "In Palmyra—"

Babak squirmed away from me. "I don't care about Palmyra!"

In a while, we fell asleep.

When I woke, the shade had stretched out from our outcropping to the next. Giv, currying his horse, motioned me to come near.

"How old are you, Ramin?" he asked. His brush moved across the horse's side in long, gentle strokes. He reached into a saddlebag on the ground and handed me another brush.

I drew it across the second horse's flanks, turning my head to avoid breathing the billowing dust. I remembered I had altered my age downward when Melchior asked, to make it seem more plausible that I was a boy. But had Koosha confided what he knew? "Twelve," I lied again.

"You ride very well, then—for a beggar and a thief."

I stilled my brush.

"And you speak well too. How did you come by that, I wonder?"

I didn't reply.

"I wish I had found Pirouz," Giv went on, tossing a blanket atop his horse. "I would have asked him this: 'Why did you abscond with those children? Was it because you had heard the Magus sets great store by the younger one? Did you know about the dreams? Did you plan to ransom Babak back to Melchior? Or was it for some other cause?'"

I swallowed. Did not look at him. Moved the brush slowly down the horse's neck.

"He told Ardalan some story about returning you to your father. So I asked myself then: Who *is* their father?"

"He—"

"Nay. Don't bother. You'd lie about that, as well."

A protest rose to my lips, but I squelched it. There had been many lies.

He hefted the saddle up onto his horse's back and began working with the cinch. "Two men—merchants, they said they were—came through that caravansary earlier this day. They asked if Melchior's caravan had stopped there. When told it had, they asked about a young boy named Babak and his older brother or sister."

Two merchants? *The king's Eyes and Ears?*

"Very well armed, they were, for merchants. They were told, I heard, that this Babak and his brother had been kidnapped and were no longer with the caravan. The men left the caravansary soon after—no one knows where they were headed."

"They mustn't find Babak," I whispered.

"No," Giv agreed. "They must not." He turned to face me, crossed his arms over his chest. "This'll amuse you, Ramin. The oddest thing! Koosha . . . he takes you for a girl. He pleaded to have me release you and Babak to his village— even offered to pay me for you, with animals and with cloth." Giv paused. "I believe he has some idea of marrying you one day."

I drew in a sharp breath, torn between the bewildering pull Koosha exerted on me and rage that he—a country youth, a rustic!—saw me as something he could buy and sell. "Was I to have a say in this? Or was I to be bartered, like one of his donkeys?"

"Oh, it would have been only with your consent. He was firm about that."

My hand halted with brushing, dropped to my side. I bowed my head, leaned in against the horse's flank.

"It is good that you are *not* a girl," Giv said. "You are of an age—which I suspect is older than you admit—you are of an age that you would not be permitted to lodge with me. You and Babak would have to stay with Melchior's wife, and I think she and her women will not journey with us if we go beyond Ecbatana. So then what would we do? Melchior will want Babak with him, and if you were a girl . . . it would be difficult, perhaps impossible, for you to come with us. Do you take my meaning?"

I straightened, nodded slowly, not looking at him. I thought I understood what he was saying.

"Aye, it's good you are not a girl. For if you were, you would be a woman before long, and if you were not isolated during your monthly courses, you would offend the Wise God and likely bring down his wrath upon our journey. Do you see that, Ramin?"

I nodded again.

"So if you were a girl, you would have to tell me if that happened. And I would make arrangements."

"Tell *you?*" I turned to glare at him.

"I wish you had your mother here to tell," Giv said, "whoever that *fine lady* might be. . . ."

Tears sprang into my eyes; I dashed them away.

"But for now it will have to be me. Would have to be. If," Giv added, "you were a girl."

We rode all the rest of the day and well into the night. Small white whirlwinds arose in the hot afternoon, far out on the rocky plain. The mountains loomed higher to the south and west, ridge behind serrated ridge, deep brown at the peaks, fading to soft blue and peach on the lower flanks. The following day we rode due west into the foothills, with mountains now cupping us on three sides. We stopped by a river in the heat of the day, fed and watered the horses, and had a repast of bread and dates. Giv and Babak curled up in the shade of some trees and straightaway went to sleep. Though I was weary, slumber did not come. I tried to cast out thoughts of Koosha but could not. And something else was troubling me, a *peck-peck-peck* of worry, fraying the edges of my mind. Softly I got up, took a large calabash, and made my way around a bend in the gurgling river, where hanging willow branches cast shade upon the surface of the water.

I took off my boots and waded over the shifting, rounded

pebbles into the shallows. I stripped off my clothes, folded them on a flat rock and, standing on the bank behind a screen of branches, poured cool water on my body, scrubbing off the grime with handfuls of sand. I washed my hair, teasing out the tangles with my fingers as well as I might.

Different. My body felt different from before. Not so many bones jutting out under the skin, but soft, curving places, hips and belly and . . . I looked down at myself. Small, rounded breasts. Riding the horse, I had felt a new, disturbing sensation, a looseness where it had used to be taut. And there, below my belly . . . wisps of coarse hair where there had not been hair before.

Quickly I pulled on my tunic and trousers, folded my arms across my chest. Was that what Koosha had seen? This new, womanly roundedness? But he couldn't have! The shape of my tunic revealed nothing. So what, then?

I walked along the pebbled edge of the river to where a small pool formed in the shallows. I squatted down and peered at the reflection of my face.

It was a small face, smudged with streaks of grime on cheeks and chin, and framed with a wet tangle of shoulder-length hair. A boy's face, you might think—if you didn't know.

I scooped up water in my hands, scrubbed and rinsed off the grime, then pulled back my hair from my face, as my mother used to do. I walked a bit upstream, where the water was smooth and clear.

Straight, determined mouth. Frowning eyes. The pointed chin I remembered from when I used to look in my mother's bronze mirror in Susa. Zoya was right; I was no beauty. Nor even pretty, like my cousin Atoosa. And yet . . .

The arch of my mother's brows was mirrored here. The high, wide prominence of her cheekbones.

Perhaps I could deceive people for a while longer by wearing the garb of a boy. But it would not last forever.

I have eyes to see.

Your monthly courses, Giv had said.

In Susa my mother and her women would cloister themselves in her chambers for some days every month. I was allowed to visit, if I liked—but never the men, not even my father. There would be storytelling, and laughing, and painting and daubing of kohl and henna and perfumes. They would brush one another's hair, I recalled, and plait it with ribbons. The women's gods came out, small figurines of Anahita, of Ashi, of Armaita.

Courses. I combed through my memory, trying to pick loose some clue. What exactly were courses? How did you know when you had them?

Blood. Hadn't I heard whispers of blood?

"Mother," I whispered to the reflection in the water, "why didn't you tell me? You should have told me."

All at once something swept over me—some longing or some grief—so fierce, it buckled me at the waist.

I knelt with my forehead pressed against the ground until it passed.

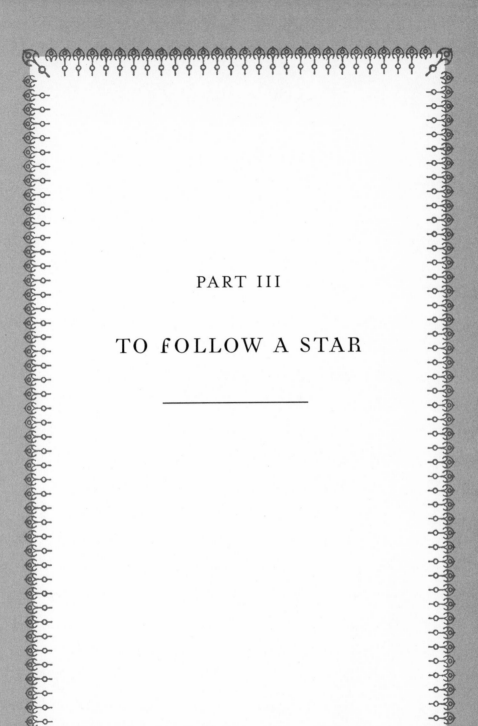

PART III

TO fOLLOW A STAR

✳

CHAPTER 33

ECBATANA

On the third day, not long after the sun had slid beneath the westernmost peaks, we spied Ecbatana in the distance, ringed with white-tipped pinnacles and flooded with ruddy light from a molten sky. The city's sevenfold walls rose in tiers that echoed the immense surrounding ranks of the mountains. It seemed that the city had simply grown there, a great, glowing rose having naught to do with masons and chisels and grout.

The heat had abated as we rode through the passes; now a mountain breeze played in my hair, bathing me in welcome coolness, perfuming the air with the fresh scent of trees and a distant, metallic whiff of snow.

Giv spoke for a time with the guard at the gate. "Our 'merchants,'" he told me when he returned, "may have stopped by here. But they soon left and have not been seen since."

I felt myself tense. "Did anyone follow them? What if they're lying in wait for us?"

"They have no way of knowing you'd be found. There are only two of them. They'll want to move on, to tell the king what they know."

Still, the peace I had felt at the beauty of this place was gone. And by the time we had passed through the outer gate, and thence through gate after gate until we reached the palace courtyard, all outward peace had shattered as well.

A roar of voices assailed my ears as the last gate creaked open. The courtyard was thronged. A groom came for our horses; I took Babak's hand and followed Giv through the lengthening shadows, among camels, donkeys, horses, heaps of rugs and bundles, cooking fires, tribes of roaming chickens, and men: men eating, men playing dice and draughts, men sleeping, men fetching water at a well. I breathed in the familiar caravan air, redolent of smoke, dust, dung, feathers, sweat, roasting meat and onions. Yet something seemed different. Men huddled in small groups, muttering and glancing furtively about. There was no music, I realized. No strains of flute or horn or lyre. And yet I did see a horn player—jabbing a finger at a patient-faced man I did not recognize, scolding him for some offense. And there, the drummer, wandering about, sullenly pounding his tambour. He caught me staring and made as if to pitch the drum hard at my face. I pulled Babak's hand and ducked into the crowd.

Something was amiss. It did not seem to have to do with Babak and me, which was a mercy. But Giv saw it too; he was taking it all in, somber and alert.

When we reached the palace door, he identified himself to a guard, who called another guard to take us to Melchior. Word of our arrival must have gone before us, for a third guard, the guard to Melchior's quarters, was waiting to let us in.

"You found him!" Melchior boomed. He heaved himself up from his divan and bore down upon us, scattering crumbs and morsels of food from his lap, trailing a wake of anxious servants.

He frowned at Giv, then turned to gaze with a kind of hunger at Babak. "Is the boy well?" Melchior demanded. "Whole and hale?"

Giv nodded. "Well enough."

"Who took him? Was it Pirouz?"

"Aye, and his servant, Arman."

"What of them? Where are they now?"

Giv hesitated. "They eluded me. I thought it best just to hunt down these two and fetch them safely back."

Melchior fluttered his hands at the others in the room. "Leave us! Away! Away!" When all but we three and the guard at the door had hurried out, Melchior turned and picked up a length of white cloth from the top of a trunk. "Here," he said, addressing Babak, thrusting out the cloth. "Dream tonight, boy. Dream as you have never dreamed before. I want to hear it all—first thing on the morrow. Don't forget a bit, do you hear me?"

Babak shrank from him. I started to tell Melchior that pressing Babak this way might well scare the dreams straight out of him, but Melchior was not interested in me; I was invisible. Giv spoke to Melchior in a soothing way. He took the cloth from him and then handed it to me, gesturing for me to tuck it into my sash. Then behind his back he made a shooing motion; Babak and I retreated slowly toward the door. Whose garment was it, I wondered? Melchior's? Or . . .

Giv made his prostrations and returned to us. "Send someone to find Pacorus," he told the guard. "Tell him—"

The guard started to open the door; there was a thump and a cry of pain. Pacorus appeared, rubbing a toe and looking sheepish.

"So, how many times have I told you not to eavesdrop, then?" Giv growled.

Pacorus grinned. "It is good to see you," he said. He turned to me and then to Babak. "All of you. What happened? How did you—"

"Never you mind," Giv said. "Have a room prepared for me and show them to it. Set a man to watch outside their door. See that they have plenty to eat and drink. Stay and attend to their needs. I'll come when I can."

Pacorus led us to a small room with high, narrow windows and a door that gave onto a gallery. He lighted the brazier. "Wait here," he said.

I had tried to push the news of the "merchants" far back into a corner of my mind, but now that we were alone, it began to rattle around inside of me. I paced up and down the carpet, trying to squeeze down my fear. They're gone now, I told myself. No one knew where to find us. We're well protected here.

But they had learned we were in the Magus's caravan. They had followed us so far!

Babak watched me, worried. "Sister, what's amiss?" he asked. I was trying to think how to comfort him when he jumped up and shrilled, "Shirak!"

Pacorus stood in the doorway holding a platter of meat and bread. He smiled, set down the platter, then plucked Shirak from his sash and set him on the floor. Shirak pranced across the carpet to Babak, who squatted, stroked the kitten's head.

"What about Gorizpa and Ziba?" I asked Pacorus. "Have you taken care of them? Have you anointed Ziba's sores?"

"Huh! *That* one. That Ziba, as you call her. She nearly bit off my head. But yes, I anointed her. And tended Gorizpa as well."

As we filled our bellies, leaning back against the soft cushions, Pacorus urged me to relate what had befallen us. Between bites I did so: told how Pirouz and Arman had come for us, how we had escaped into the qanat, how Koosha had found us, how Giv had tracked us down. I did not tell everything, though. Not why Pirouz had taken us, nor that I had gone willingly. Nor did I tell what Koosha had seen in me.

I tried to sense whether Pacorus saw it too, but I could read nothing beyond friendliness in his manner. He did not seem overly curious, either, being full of news himself. Melchior and Gaspar, it seemed, had indeed come to Ecbatana to consult with a third priest, one whom Gaspar revered. It had to do with the stars, Pacorus said. With something they had seen in the stars.

Babak looked up sharply at this. I itched to draw him to me and rub his back to comfort him, but instead I lay a brotherly hand upon his shoulder. He went back to feasting, but his ears were pricked, I could feel it.

"Do you recall that night in the castle south of Sava?"

Pacorus asked. "Do you recall the instruments Gaspar used—the globe and the chart and the disc? That star-taker disc, like the one Melchior has? Well, every night he consults these instruments, gazing up at the stars. And this third priest, this Balthazaar . . ."

Pacorus rose and pulled the door inward, leaving it just slightly ajar. Outside I heard the groan of a camel, the creak of the windlass by the well. "There are disputations among the Magi," he said. "I hear them at night, when they confer together: that bellow of Melchior's, and sometimes Gaspar's voice.

"And among the caravans themselves," Pacorus went on, "there is discord. Gaspar's archers take umbrage at the size of Melchior's party—the women and entertainers and their mountains of baggage. They chafe at the slow pace and sneer openly at the camels' gaudy tassels and chest bands and drapes. Melchior's party returns their contempt. The musicians refuse to play for Gaspar's men, and the women whisper, point, and laugh at them."

"What of Balthazaar's men?"

Pacorus shrugged. "They speak softly and seldom." He stared up through the high, fretted windows, where a few early stars pricked the darkening sky. Babak sighed and lay his head in my lap, with Shirak nestled against him.

"They say," Pacorus mused, "that something Melchior and Gaspar have seen in the stars compels them to take a journey to the west, deep into Roman territory."

My heart leaped. "To Palmyra?"

"I don't know. The territory of Rome is vast."

"But it's still west they will be traveling?"

"It seems so. They came here to consult with Balthazaar, but he had seen it too, the thing in the stars. They say that Gaspar presses him to come with us. But Melchior . . ."

Pacorus glanced toward the door and leaned in to me. "I have heard he sent someone to Balthazaar's quarters when Balthazaar was not there. To spy or to steal."

I looked quickly down at my sash. *To spy* . . .

"What is it they seek?" I wondered aloud. "What do they see in the stars?"

"Some say an auspicious event. A coronation or a birth."

I had heard rumors of this. Magi, it was said, had attended the birth of Darius the Great. And my father once told me that a band of traveling Magi came to my grandfather the night before the defeat of Rome at Carrhae.

"Others speak of the dawning of the age of Pisces or the coming of the Saoshyant. But," Pacorus continued darkly, "I have also heard tales of impending cataclysm. They say that Magi prophesied the birth of Alexander and the last Darius's defeat. There is talk of a great clash of armies, of the world's end."

The Saoshyant? The world's end?

Babak stirred, bringing me back to the present, back to what I must now do. I could feel his breathing against me, slow and deep. Shirak yawned, stretched, and made for the door. When Pacorus turned to watch him, I quickly tucked the cloth beneath Babak's tunic.

Sin. It still felt like sin.

I looked out toward the stars, now thick upon the heavens. It had begun so small, this dreaming of Babak's. Dreams of betrothals, of journeys, of the outcomes of small trades. But now it was a skyful of wheeling stars, and all they portended. The births and deaths of kings. The dawning of a new age. Cataclysm: the clash of armies, the end of the world.

How could these mighty dreams flow through such a fragile instrument, without cracking the instrument itself?

✴

CHAPTER 34

STAR-TAKER

Later, after Babak had fallen asleep, Pacorus and I stayed up talking. We leaned against the cushions, side by side. Up close, his eyes were uncommonly fine—deep and clear and flecked with gold, framed with long black lashes. Why had I not noticed that before? Something felt different, now we were alone. Some new kind of agitation. Each time his arm brushed against mine, the place where he had touched tingled strangely.

What was wrong with me? I wondered. I never used to feel this way.

Until Koosha.

With him I had felt . . . what? A stillness. A sense of recognition. But also this new, disturbing restlessness.

Now, intent upon his point, Pacorus took hold of my arm and leaned in to me. The musky scent of him filled my nose; I had to hold my breath to keep from trembling, or flinching or yanking my arm away.

Stop it, I admonished myself. What's amiss with you?

Forbidden. In Susa it would have been forbidden for a girl of my age to be alone with a young man not her kin. Perhaps *this* was why.

Meanwhile, Pacorus spoke of chaste and goodly things: of the Wise God, and of the Holy Immortals, and of purity of thought, word, and deed. Matters of which my grandmother had spoken to me all my life, though I had only half listened. But Pacorus seemed enthralled.

Once, Babak flailed his arms and moaned in his sleep. His face worked as if he were in pain.

"They say," Pacorus murmured, "that your brother . . . dreams."

"Of course he dreams. Everyone dreams." Except for me.

"Prophetic dreams, they say. Dreams that lead men to want to make use of him."

I kept my gaze fixed upon Babak. "Who is saying this, about the dreams?"

"Everyone," Pacorus replied.

I studied Babak's face in the lamplight—the troubled look of his brow, the dark circles beneath his eyes.

"It is also said—and this is only whispered—that Melchior hopes for the currency of dreams to buy his way back into his old position of power."

I looked up sharply.

"He seeks out the company of men of great renown, especially kings and princes."

"Phraates?"

"No. Too late for that, they say. But he had great power when he was Phraates' chief priest, and he wants it back—as priest and counselor to some other great ruler. And Babak's dreams . . ."

I sat silent, hoping he would not pry, hoping he would not himself use my friendship as currency, to buy *his* way into favor. An owl hooted somewhere nearby, and in the distance I heard the bark of a jackal.

Pacorus shifted, cleared his throat. "Well. They say that Melchior is a great man, that he is well known all throughout the provinces, that he hobnobs with nobility and high councilors. They say that Gaspar is a wise man, more learned in the secrets of the stars and the true nature of the heavens than any man now living. He has calculated the positions of the stars back nearly to the beginning of time, and out nearly to the end of all time to come. And Balthazaar . . ."

Pacorus broke off, gazed through the doorway into the night.

"Well? What do they say of Balthazaar?"

"They say he is a holy man."

And then it was the stars, and what might be foretold in them. It was the coming of a new astral age, and the Three Times of history laid out by the prophet Zoroaster.

The day had been long and hard. I began to let go of Pacorus's words, allowing them to flow over me without penetrating my understanding. My gaze strayed to the smooth planes of his cheeks in the golden lamplight, to the fine, straight line of his nose, to the ink-stained tips of his slender fingers. I felt warm, full bellied, and heavy. My eyelids were leaden; they wanted to close.

In time, sleep overtook me.

"Sister?"

I swam up out of a deep slumber to see Babak awake. Squatting. Peering down at me. I looked around for Pacorus, hoping he hadn't heard Babak call me *Sister*, but by the dim lamplight I saw we were alone.

"Sister, I can't sleep."

I sat up, took Babak in my arms. I rubbed his back, his bony back.

"Did you dream, little one?"

"No," he said, then, "Yes."

"Do you want to tell me?"

"No."

"Very well." Later we would have to tell Melchior. For now, I didn't give a straw for all his star signs and kings.

Babak scrubbed at his eyes and looked about him. "I don't want to sleep," he said.

Who could blame him? "What do you want to do?"

"Can we go see Gorizpa? And Ziba?"

I imagined the Eyes and Ears skulking round the palace

grounds, searching for us. But no. There are seven walls round the city, I told myself, and many guards at every gate. And it would be good to see Gorizpa and Ziba again.

"We will try," I said.

We did not leave through the main door of the palace, for I knew the palace guards would not let us pass. But at the far end of our gallery was a narrow stairway and, at the head of it, a slumped-over guard with eyes shut and mouth agape. I crept close enough to hear his snores, then motioned Babak to come. We tiptoed past him, down the dark steps to the courtyard. I surmised that it was well past midnight; he would likely not wake soon for prayers.

By the light of the stars we made our way among slumbering camels, the remains of smoldering fires, and shadowy humps on the ground that might be carpets or bundles of cargo or sleeping men wrapped up in their cloaks. A chicken clucked sleepily. Two men snored in a sonorous duet; one deep and booming, the other a high whistle.

The stables were dark and smelled of hay and dust and animal dung. I did not see how we were going to find Gorizpa and Ziba, but Babak would not give up, feeling his way among the animals—patches of deeper black against the gloom of the stables. I longed for light, and wished we had brought one of the lamps from our room. In time our animals found us— at least, Gorizpa did, giving out an indignant bray as we approached and pushing her great forehead against me. I scratched inside her ear; she let out a moan. I heard a wet, cud-chewing *crunch*, and then something nipped at my hair. "Ouch!" I said.

It was Ziba. I installed Babak upon an upside-down basket to continue with the ear scratching as I explored with my fingers along Ziba's neck and flanks, following the trail of hairless, puckered, crusty skin, trying to recollect how it had been before and to discover whether the mange had spread. Ziba grumbled deep in her throat, in a way that managed to convey both welcome and reproach. Though it was impossible to know for certain in the dark, it seemed that the mange was not much worse and possibly had healed a bit. My foot struck something hard; I reached down and picked up a wide, shallow pot containing a sticky liquid. I sniffed. Butter. So Pacorus was as good as his word. I scooped up a handful and rubbed it into Ziba's skin. Groaning, she brought her head down near mine and nuzzled my hair.

When the butter was gone, Babak and I made our way out of the stable and back across the courtyard. We had nearly reached the narrow stairway leading to our gallery when Babak pointed up. "Look," he said. "Pacorus!"

And indeed it was. I knew the lanky shape of him, and the way he walked, with a sinewy grace that somehow conveyed pent-up energy. He was moving along a roof terrace not far from our room.

"Shh," I said. "Don't call to him. You'll wake half the courtyard."

"Let's go with him. Can we, Sister?"

Somehow I doubted Pacorus would want our help.

"But you've hardly slept—"

"I don't *want* to sleep."

His eyes looked bleary, with that darkened flesh beneath them. To fear sleep itself . . . What had I done to him?

We crept up the stairs, past the still-slumbering guard, and up again, to a higher roof terrace. Babak nearly tripped, then caught himself. "Careful! Pay attention!" I whispered. We tiptoed past a room—Melchior's?—that rumbled with voices and glowed yellow with lamplight behind the fretted screens.

We'd seen Pacorus near another, higher terrace. A small ladder leaned against the wall, connecting this terrace to one above. Babak began to scale it; I took hold of the back of his tunic to stop him. I had begun to feel uneasy. What was Pacorus doing? *I have heard . . . To spy or to steal,* he had said.

"Pacorus might not welcome us here," I whispered to Babak.

"He *will*." Babak twisted away from me and scrambled up. Sighing, I followed.

We came out into a small private courtyard. Very bare, with only an unglazed water vessel standing in a corner. A thick oaken door stood ajar, and through the narrow slit I saw a flickering of light.

"Babak, stop!" I hissed.

Too late. He slipped through the doorway.

A clatter within. A whispered oath. I burst in to see Pacorus stooped over something flat and round on the floor. He swung round, frowned at me. "You shouldn't creep up that way!" he snapped. Babak pressed back against me. Pacorus picked up the thing on the floor, and I saw that it was a metal disc. A star-taker.

He'd dropped one of these before, on the day I first met him.

"What are you doing here?" I asked. "Do you have permission? Do you—"

"I had to see one up close," Pacorus said. "I want to know . . . I want to know *everything*. Look! Look at these markings—"

"What if you're caught? Whose room is this?"

It was a plain room, with a tattered straw mat rolled up beside a rude wooden chest, now open. A fire burned atop a small altar and, high up in the rafters, the shadows of cobwebs moved with the wavering of the flame. A faint whiff of incense hung in the air. On the floor I saw a spread-out scroll.

"It's Balthazaar's. But he is with the others in Melchior's rooms. Look," he said, holding out the instrument again. "I think these markings are for measuring angles, to see how the stars move and how they—"

"You are right," came a voice that was a bit raspy, yet somehow musical. I spun round and saw a tall, thin, white-bearded man in the open doorway, silhouetted against the stars. "That's exactly what they are for."

*

CHAPTER 35

BALTHAZAAR

He was a Magus. I knew it by the clothes he wore—the white wool tunic, mantle, and trousers, the hoodlike felt hat with long flaps that could be tied to cover mouth and chin. His beard, as white as his robes, was not bushy like Melchior's, but silky, long, and thin. Though I could not well see his face, I had an impression of ancientness, of solidity, like weathered stone.

Pacorus gazed at him fearfully. "I see you have my star-taker," the Magus said.

Pacorus held it out to him, but the Magus did not take it. "I . . . I wasn't stealing it," Pacorus said. "I know what I did was wrong, coming here to look. But I wanted to see it, see the markings on it, see if I could learn what it does, what secrets it reveals. There is so much that I . . ."

Stop, I thought. *Don't compound the crime of breaking into the Magus's quarters with the sin of prying into sacred secrets. Just stop.*

But he didn't. The words kept rolling out.

". . . that I want to know, so much I don't understand and crave to understand. I want to know about the twelve houses of the sun, and precession, and Great Years and what they have to do with the Three Times, and about paradise and the time to come, and . . ."

He glanced at Babak and me and was off suddenly on another course. "Don't blame them, Lord Balthazaar, they have nothing to do with this. They were sound asleep, and I thought I might, just for a moment—"

Balthazaar held up a long, thin hand to silence Pacorus, but even so, he did not seem angry. He turned, moving into the firelight, and looked at me and then at Babak. I could see the edges of his eyes crinkle, as if he were amused. But there was a look in them of something else, something sad and yet kind. "You needn't fear for them," he said, "nor for yourself. But I have a question. There is a thing missing from this room. Perhaps I have misplaced it, yet . . . Do you know aught of it?"

Missing. The sash? I tried to hold my face still so as not to betray my thoughts. Babak, seeming to sense my unease, reached up to put his hand in mine.

"No, my lord," Pacorus was saying. "I would never . . . I would never steal from you. I only—"

"Hush, boy. I believe you. Would you like me to show you how to use the instrument?"

Pacorus gaped, silenced at last, and then managed to croak out, "Yes," and as an afterthought, "If you please."

Now the Magus held out his hand for the star-taker. "Bring the lamp," Balthazaar said, and strode to a low wall at the far end of the terrace. Balthazaar held the metal disc carefully, reverently, laying it flat in the palm of one long-fingered hand. Everything about him was long: long, aquiline nose; long face; long arms; and a lean, tall, loose-limbed body that gave the impression, when walking, of an ancient crane or heron.

"We can derive the positions of all the stars in the sky and where they will be in times to come. And thereby . . . Well. See here." He held the ring attached to the disc so that it hung suspended below. Pacorus moved forward to attend him, but there were so many strange markings on the instrument, and I was too weary to attempt to follow. I put my arms round Babak's shoulders and looked up at the lovely, dark sky, bejeweled with countless familiar stars and constellations. Pacorus bent his head low over the instrument as Balthazaar murmured an incantation of unfamiliar words: *Projections. Latitudes. Azimuth. Zenith.*

"The stars have grammar and meaning," I heard him say. "They are an alphabet writ large upon the sky, in which we may read the smallest things—the pulses of the heart, the motions of the will."

All at once, Babak piped up. "I had a dream for you," he said.

The Magus stood perfectly still, and yet his face changed, seemed in some fashion to open up to an inner surprise. I looked down at Babak, tried to catch his eye, tried to signal *no* in a way that no one else would see. He was not supposed to tell about his dreaming. And heaven only knew what he had dreamed!

The Magus turned slowly. "A dream for me." His puzzled gaze came to settle on me.

I swallowed. Said nothing.

The Magus knelt beside Babak. "Was it a good dream?" he asked.

Babak seemed to consider. "It was a fearsome dream."

Balthazaar regarded Babak gravely. Then, before I knew what was happening, before I could stop it, Babak slipped out from between my arms. He reached up and laid his palms upon the Magus's face. Balthazaar carefully set down the star-taker and covered Babak's small hands with his long and thin ones. He released one hand and traced his fingers across Babak's eyebrows, forehead, temples, and cheeks. I started toward Babak, but Pacorus took my arm and stopped me.

"He is the soul of goodness," Pacorus whispered. "Can't you see that?"

"Just sleep tonight, little one," the Magus said.

"Do you want to know my dream?" Babak asked.

"No. Not tonight."

"Everyone wants to know my dreams."

"I want," Balthazaar said, "for you to sleep. Deep and peaceful sleep." He stood and turned to me. "See that he gets his rest. And you, son . . ." He held out his hand, seemed about to clasp my shoulder, but stopped abruptly.

He was still again, except for the *listening* in his face.

He lowered his hand. "Ah. Well. Take care of him," he said. "He grows weary."

Early the next morning I awoke to a commotion in the courtyard. Camels trumpeting, horses whinnying, donkeys braying. Clankings and bangings and shouts. Giv was gone, as ever; I was not certain he had ever been here. In fact, though we had occupied his rooms since joining the caravan, I had never seen him sleep. Had he known all along that I was a girl?

Babak lay peacefully; he had not wakened me with cries or thrashing all night. I opened the door to the gallery and looked out.

They were preparing to leave. Musicians and jugglers, courtiers and cooks. Melchior's people! A cluster of women stood on a far terrace—shouting, throwing bundles into the darkness of the courtyard, not yet warmed by the spreading light of dawn. Porters bustled past, toting caged birds, bolts of silks, rolls of carpets, chests and caskets, pots and pans and braziers, baskets of foodstuffs, jars of oil. They piled them in heaps on the cobblestones; other men loaded them onto horses and camels.

Leaving!

Why had no one come for us? Were they leaving us behind?

"Wake up, Babak!" I shook him; he yawned and snuggled back in to sleep. I hefted him onto my chest; he clung to my neck, his body limp and unwieldy and yet inexpressibly sweet. When we had nearly reached the stairs, I heard Giv call my name.

I waited as he strode along the gallery toward us. How long had I been plotting to escape? And yet now my cowardly knees buckled with relief to know we had not been abandoned. "Are we leaving?" I asked.

"Nay, not yet. Melchior's just paring down his caravan."

"Paring?"

"For the journey to the land of the two rivers. The other two Magi won't abide Melchior's overbloated entourage, thanks be to the Wise God," he muttered. "We're selling horses and buying camels. We'll all be camelback now."

I looked about and took note of the new camels. Their shapes, limned in the pale light, set them apart from the shaggy, two-humped Bactrians, like Ziba—and from the one-humped dromedaries I had seen from time to time in Rhagae. These seemed some combination of the two—short haired, with a single large hump with a dip in the middle. I had heard of these new camels, bred for strength and hardiness.

"What of Ziba? Will she—"

"The two-humped camels we'll keep as pack animals. And there won't be enough new ones for everyone; Gaspar's skimmed off the cream for his archers. You'll still be riding Ziba. Now—"

Belatedly it struck me. *The other two Magi,* he had said. "Will Balthazaar be coming all the way to the Roman territory?" I asked.

Giv looked at me oddly, and I realized that I ought not to have known Balthazaar, nor that we were going that far. "There is talk," I said. "I hear it."

He grunted. "Hurry. They wish to speak with you. What was hidden is now known—at least among the Magi."

What was hidden is now known. I followed him, wondering. So many things hidden! Our ancestry, that I was a girl, Babak's dreams. Some hidden thing was written in the stars. Which one—or perhaps more than one—was now known?

✳

LOSE THIS WORLD

When we entered the room, I saw that all the servants and guards had been sent away. Giv stood watch inside the door. The three Magi reposed in a semicircle upon carven benches: Balthazaar, pensive, in the middle; Gaspar to one side, arrow straight, his black hair and beard neatly trimmed and glistening with oil; Melchior to the other side, combing beringed fingers through his unruly bird's nest of a beard. I thought I detected a glint of something new—interest, perhaps, or only curiosity—in Melchior's eyes and in Gaspar's also. But it was difficult to tell. The blush of sunrise mingled with the glow of a small altar fire, making a moving pattern of light and shadow on the men's faces, like the ripples of a shallow stream over a bed of stones. The room smelled strongly of sandalwood and incense. I set Babak down, but he clung to me, sensing my unease, as we walked together to stand on the carpet before the Magi.

"Greetings to you, Ramin," Balthazaar said, "and to you, Babak."

We bowed and murmured our greetings. I glanced furtively at Melchior's face. He had striven so hard to keep Babak's dreams a secret, and now we had let it slip to Balthazaar. Did Melchior know he knew? If so, was he angry?

Balthazaar motioned us to sit on the carpet before them; we did. Melchior spoke. "You recollect what I said to you before, about the need to keep Babak's dreams a secret?"

I swallowed. "Yes, my lord." I flicked a glance at

Balthazaar. He nodded, almost imperceptibly; some of the worry I had held coiled within me began to ease.

"Well, now it is a secret to be shared. With these two lords only—and, of course, Giv."

"Yes, my lord."

"No others. Do you hear?"

"A bit late for that," Gaspar observed. Melchior glared at him. Gaspar's voice was flat, dry. "All the palace is abuzz with talk of Babak and his dreams," he said. "It's useless to shut the stable door once the horse has fled."

Melchior began to sputter; Balthazaar smoothly cut him off. "While it is true," he said, "that word of Babak and his dreams has spread beyond this room, it is likewise true that the less made of this the better—for Babak and for our quest. Are we all agreed to keep to ourselves what passes between these walls?" Seeing nods of agreement, Balthazaar motioned to Melchior, who cleared his throat and turned to Babak.

"So," he said. "I requested a dream from you last night and gave you, er, an item of clothing. What did you dream?"

Babak ducked under my arm and buried his face against my side. I looked down, afraid for him. That dream last night seemed to have troubled him. It was hard for him to relive such dreams. And now, with all three Magi sitting, waiting . . .

"Well?" Melchior demanded. "Tell us, boy."

Babak burrowed deeper. I squeezed his arm, trying to comfort him.

Balthazaar spoke. "Babak." My brother eased his grip on me, turned his head to look. "We will not harm you. Tell us only if you wish."

Melchior frowned. "He is my boy, not yours. You don't tell him what he may and may not do."

"But you agreed to this earlier," Balthazaar said mildly. "That the boy must not be forced. I repeat only what you've agreed."

"I agreed to too much," Melchior muttered.

Babak disentangled himself from my body, ventured forward into the rosy, rippling light, and knelt on the carpet before Balthazaar. Melchior began to protest again, but Gaspar shot him a harsh look and Melchior subsided.

Balthazaar smiled, wreathing his wise old eyes in wrinkles. He reached out his long-fingered hand and lightly touched Babak's shoulder. "Sit up, son. No need to kneel."

"It was stars at first," Babak told him. "The same as the stars when I dreamed for him." He flicked a glance at Gaspar, who gave a start, then looked daggers at Melchior, who frowned, peered down at the carpet, plucked at his beard.

Balthazaar, taking in all of this, raised an eyebrow. "So," he said, turning to Babak, "stars circling the sky for many thousands of years. So that each group of stars, each constellation, made a full circuit of the sky. Is that right?"

Babak nodded. "And then they stopped, and two of the wandering stars came near and apart three times."

"Yes," Balthazaar said. "And was that all?"

"No." He swallowed. "There was pain. A woman's pain. And blood. And then there was . . . a baby."

"Ah!" Balthazaar put a finger to his lips.

Gaspar spoke up. "Did you see more of this baby? Did you see his mother and father, or where he was, what sort of place? Was there aught remarkable about a blanket that may have been wrapped around him, or some cradle in which he lay?"

"No." Babak glanced quickly back at me, seeking reassurance. I did my best to smile, but I could see from the tight, hunched set of his shoulders that he was not cheered.

"Babak," Balthazaar said. "Will it trouble you if we ask some more questions?"

Babak shook his head. "Not if *you* ask them, my lord."

"Very well, then. These dreams you have, they are for others, not yourself?"

Babak nodded.

"And whose dream was this?"

"It was your dream," Babak said. "You were not in it, but I knew it was yours."

"Was it a sash you were given to sleep with? A white sash?"

"Yes, my lord."

"And I suppose you gave him something of mine to sleep with as well," Gaspar said, glaring at Melchior.

But Balthazaar made a calming motion. "And are your dreams . . . true, Babak?" he asked.

Babak looked back at me, confused. Melchior began to say something, but Balthazaar stopped him. "That is a difficult question?" he asked Babak.

Babak hung his head. I could tell that though he wanted to please Balthazaar, he was beginning to shrink from the questioning. "I dream," he mumbled, "of dreams."

Melchior crossed his arms, made an impatient sound in his throat. Balthazaar leaned back, as if to give Babak room to breathe, and turned to me. "Do you understand this, Ramin? What he is telling us?"

"I believe so, my lord," I said. Babak crept back and settled himself in my lap. My arms, hungry to comfort him, folded themselves around his body—light and brittle, a bundle of sticks. Balthazaar nodded for me to continue. "When we lived in Rhagae, Babak dreamed mostly of food. This was his chief desire, and mine also, because we were hungry much of the time. When he began to dream for others, he would dream, I think, of their desires. A healthy male baby. A wedding. A recovery from illness. A profitable trade. His dreams were true in this way: that they expressed the wishes of those he dreamed for. Their desires and most earnest hopes, or the secret wishes of their hearts."

"But did they come true? Did the dreamed-of events come to pass?" Balthazaar's tone was mild, yet he leaned forward and his eyes shone with a deep intensity.

"Many did," I said. "With others it is not yet known."

"I had no desire for whirling stars," Melchior protested, waving his hands in circles above his head.

I recalled the strange king of Melchior's second dream and marked what he did not say: that he had no desire to be welcomed by a king.

"And yet your tale of stars brought you my help," Gaspar said, "and you did desire that. If not for those dreams, I'd have—"

"Ah, well," Balthazaar said in a mollifying way. "Sometimes our dreams are wiser than ourselves." He turned to me. "How long had he been dreaming in this way before Melchior came to be his guardian?"

"I don't know for certain. A month, perhaps."

"And did he dream in this way every night? Dream for others, not for himself?"

"Nearly every night. I told her to let him rest, but—"

"Her?"

"The one who sold Babak to Melchior. She was our go-between. I tried to tell her—"

"Hush, child," Balthazaar said. "You couldn't know the harm it would do. Has he ever dreamed in this way without the token? Perhaps continued a dream from a previous night without the token near his skin?"

Fear lay a cold hand on my heart. I remembered the time with Pirouz, when Babak had started to walk in his sleep and I had tripped him. He'd said he had dreamed of shaggy beasties—that dream he had had long ago. Now the altar fire popped and leaped, sending light flaring across Balthazaar's face, then casting it into sudden shadow. Babak clung to me, his face pressed into my chest. "There was once," I said. "And he sometimes seems . . . absent, my lord. Not entirely here. He hums. . . ."

Balthazaar frowned and murmured something beneath his breath; I thought I heard "too late . . ." But he looked up again and spoke softly to me. "Dreams of this sort visit only a certain kind of soul, those who haven't built up stout walls between themselves and the sufferings of others. We don't know where these dreams come from—whether from the

Wise God or some other, earthly source. But touching the flame of the divine can burn us as well. When these dreamers dream for others, their own rightful dreams are stolen from them. They can lose their boundaries if they have crossed too often into other people's dreams. Then they swim in and out between this world and the dream world. And if they are too far gone, they lose this world altogether. Do you understand?"

Lose this world. I touched Babak's face, traced my fingers along his scarred eyebrow. His skin was too delicate, too thin, no protection against what might seep in. "So it would be as if he were . . . sleepwalking . . . all the time? In and out of other people's dreams?"

"Yes. And you could not rouse him."

"How do we know? How do we know if it has gone too far already?"

"We wait. But we must not use him thus again." He looked about at the group, fixing Melchior with a long stare.

Melchior, defiant, stared back. "I didn't agree to *never*. You said—"

"Only in the direst extremity," Balthazaar said. "I can take the two children off your hands, since Babak will now be of little use to you."

"No!" Melchior's face burned red; he seemed to struggle to restrain himself. At last he turned a milder countenance upon Balthazaar and said, "He's my responsibility, and I'll not shirk it. I'll care for him. For *them*," he said, glancing at me.

"But no dreams," Balthazaar said.

"Except in extremity," Melchior grumbled.

But I didn't trust him. He had kept us only for Babak's dreams. If he truly didn't intend to use Babak again, why wouldn't he let us go?

"Babak." Balthazaar's voice was gentle. Babak looked up at him. "You must rest. Dream only for yourself. Do you understand?"

"I would dream for you," Babak said. "If you wanted me to."

"*No.*" For the first time, Balthazaar's voice sounded harsh. He breathed out a long breath, his lips moving slightly, as if they formed the words of a prayer or incantation, then he smiled at Babak. But his eyes, when they rested for a moment upon mine, were full of pity.

✳

CHAPTER 37

TWO FAREWELLS

When the Magi had dismissed us, I stumbled through the bustling courtyard after Giv, gripping Babak's hand. The caravan sounds made an odd, distant rushing in my ears; men and animals and cargo blurred before me in the gathering light. My bones felt watery, as if the hardness in them had leached away. *Too late.* Time and again I stopped to peer into Babak's eyes to reassure myself that he was still with us, still of this world.

All at once Gorizpa stood before me, and Giv was saying something about a buyer. "What? A buyer?" I asked.

"Yes!" Giv sounded impatient.

I glanced at the man standing beside him. The buyer. I'd been worried about Ziba; I hadn't given a thought to Gorizpa. "She's not for sale."

Giv's scowl deepened. "Have you heard a single word I've said? She'll slow us down; she must go. No—don't dispute with me. She must. So then: This man has made a fair offer. His wife is with child; he needs a donkey she can ride when she travels to her mother's home."

Babak burst into tears and ran to Gorizpa, buried his face in her coat. I turned to look at the man, the buyer. A heavy man, with a great, bushy head and tiny, close-set eyes. If his wife was likewise heavy, she would break the poor donkey's back.

"What will you do with her after the baby comes?" I demanded.

"I will sell her then, of course," the man said. "But in the meantime I will treat her well."

I turned to Giv. "I will not sell my donkey to this man."

"Nay, but he'll find a good owner! Tell him that," he said to the man.

"Why should I? He's but a boy, and you know my price is fair!" Then, faced with Giv's implacable glare, the man turned to me. "Of course," he said, speaking slowly, as to a young child. "I will find another owner just as kindly as myself."

"No," I said.

"Ramin—" Giv growled.

"No! I won't! He can't have her. I don't care what you do to me, you can slice me up in pieces, you can hang me up by my heels, but I won't let you sell her to him so he can ruin her! I won't!"

Babak turned to stare at me, tears streaming down his face. The buyer held up his hands, backed away. "It's just a donkey," he said. "I'll find another."

I glanced at Giv, expecting him to be furious. But something had shifted in his face, had softened. I blinked back tears, tried to master myself, tried to stop shaking. What was amiss with me? She *was* only a donkey, old and broken down.

I saw Giv motion to Pacorus, saw him take him aside and speak to him. I saw Pacorus leave, and made to follow. "Stay here!" Giv barked, gruff again. "I don't want to have to send for you, then. You've squandered enough of my time." He strode off across the courtyard.

Babak reached up, patted my back, as I had done a thousand times to him. Gorizpa gazed at me with great, wide, melting eyes, then leaned her bony head against my chest. When I scratched inside her ear, she moaned and closed her eyes, lower lip loose and drooling. Stupid old thing!

In a while I spied Pacorus with a balding, stoop-shouldered, shuffling man. The two of them threaded through the hubbub to Giv and spoke to him briefly. Giv led them to us. "If you reject this one," he said low in my ear, "it's straight to the butcher with her." Someone called him away; he nodded at the stoop-shouldered man, favored me with a glowering eye, and left.

"Tirdad," Pacorus said, "is a weaver of cloth. He needs a donkey to help transport his work to the bazaar."

"Cloth only?" I asked. "Not stones or jars of oil?"

"Cloth only," Tirdad said.

"No pregnant wife?"

Tirdad laughed and pointed to his grizzled beard. "My wife and I are well past that, I fear."

"You will not overload the donkey?'

"Nay, I'll not."

"How long will you keep her?" I asked. "Only until you can afford a younger one?"

"I'll keep her so long as she can carry cloth to market."

"That's not—"

"Your Magus," he interrupted, pinning me in his gaze, "can afford to keep pets—monkeys and birds and such."

And children, I thought. Was that why Melchior wouldn't let Babak go? To retain possession of his most unusual pet?

"But I'm a poor weaver," the man went on, "and haven't the means for pets. When this donkey's too feeble to carry my cloth, I'll put her down mercifully. This I promise, but only this."

I could see in his eyes that he told the truth.

Well. There was nothing perfect in this wretched life. No matter how you tried, you couldn't keep from betraying those you cared for. But small betrayals were preferable to great ones.

"It is enough," I said.

But the last farewell was yet to come. When we returned to our room, Shirak was gone. We had not seen him since that first night, when he had greeted Babak and later slipped away. Now we searched for him everywhere; Babak began to cry again. Then, just as the sun burst over the courtyard walls, I was standing alone on the gallery and chanced to look down near the stables. There, tail held high, was Shirak, prancing across the cobbles with a small gray cat behind.

So. He didn't need us anymore, though Babak still needed him. Well, caravan life was fine for a kitten, but it wouldn't suit a cat.

"Farewell, Shirak," I whispered.

✳

CHAPTER 38

THE WAY to BABYLON

We left the next morning, followed the old trade route west through the mountains, stopping after a time at a temple of Anahita of the Waters, and then, over the next days and nights, up into the high passes, where the mountains loomed jagged and steep to either side. Wild goats stared down at us from the fells; from time to time there was goat meat in the pot at night. We passed some bas-relief carvings—cut, it seemed, by giants, high up into a sheer cliff face—a centuries-old tableau showing Darius, victorious over a group of rebel princes and protected by the winged symbol of divine grace. And, a sight that made me stiffen my spine with pride, a depiction of King Mithradates—our honored ancestor, my namesake—standing before four supplicants. Down near the road, so close I could nearly touch it, reclined a lifelike stone statue of the yazata Herakles.

We were a sober company, unleavened by music or jugglers' antics or the laughter of women. From time to time the Magi would peel off from the moving caravan to pore over charts—sky charts, Pacorus said. By night they would climb some nearby promontory and train their star-takers upon the mysteries of the heavens.

Though our numbers had been greatly reduced, the contingent of guides had increased, from seven or so to twelve. Nor were they the ones who had been with Melchior before; these were different guides altogether, men from nearby tribes who knew how to find water and knew which wells belonged to which peoples.

I looked about constantly for the distant puffs of dust that signaled riders. Now that I knew the king's Eyes and Ears had followed us beyond Rhagae, I was ever catching sight of their shadows out of the corners of my eyes, ever feeling their breath prickling at the back of my neck. Giv, too, seemed to be mindful of the "merchants," though he never spoke of such to me. But whenever we passed another caravan, he found some reason to surround Babak and me with high-packed camels, shielding us from view of the strangers.

Pacorus grew more and more consumed with the study of the stars. He insinuated himself into the presence of the Magi—Gaspar especially—fetching and carrying for them, finding pretexts for other work nearby, even slipping away from the caravan to eavesdrop on them as they gazed. Giv grew annoyed with him because he could never find him when he wanted him. "Pacorus!" he would cry, and then, when Pacorus did not reply, would fall to muttering about boys with heads stuffed with stars. Me, he loaded down with work—mountains of girths, cruppers, leather pads, hobble leathers, saddle frames, drapes, and chest bands to repair when we halted in the evenings. "Melchior desires you to earn your keep," he growled.

But sometimes, Pacorus pointed out to me what he had learned. The Magi bent their attentions upon one particular star in the sky—the brightest one. It was not a single star, Pacorus explained to me, but two of the wanderers drawn close together, so you could not see the space between them. A *conjunction*, he said. I remembered Babak's dream: *Two stars. Near, apart.* Pacorus explained that one of the stars signified the protector of the Jews. And the other, he said, was a sign of the birth of a king or some other great personage.

So: Two stars, coming near. A birth. A king.

The selfsame events that had appeared in Babak's dreams . . . were written in the stars.

★

The nights grew chill. The camels breathed great plumes of white mist, and each morning we wiped frost off our saddle-bags. Soon the mountains would be impassable, covered with snow.

Babak slept soundly, without calling out or thrashing or rising to walk in sleep. When awake, he could recall no dreams. The circles beneath his eyes began to fade. Although he did from time to time go blank and humming, it seemed to me that this happened less often now and for shorter intervals. Perhaps we were not too late!

Although Babak put on little flesh, it was not so with me. My new curves and rounded places seemed to grow curvier and rounder. I felt an unaccustomed heaviness in my breasts as I walked. Once, when I was stooping to hobble Ziba, I caught one of the guards staring at my chest. Hastily I turned away, feeling my face grow hot. After that I bound my chest with wide strips of linen.

Even so, I found my gaze drifting more and more to Pacorus, to the gold flecks in his eyes; to the high, chiseled planes of his cheeks. Sometimes, to my shame, I craved for him to look at me as Koosha had. To see me as a woman.

But no. He mustn't! No one must know.

Pacorus's eyes, when they chanced to catch mine, held only friendship, as before.

At last we came out of the mountains and down onto the great Mesopotamian plain. I grew more and more worried about Ctesiphon, where Phraates held his winter court. But I soon discovered, by listening to the talk that swirled about us, that we would not stop there. It wasn't just Melchior who wished to avoid Phraates, but the other Magi also. We would bypass Ctesiphon, and Seleucia as well, but stop in Babylon so that the Magi might consult about the stars with some Chaldeans.

"What did Melchior do to be expelled?" I asked Pacorus.

He shrugged. "Perhaps Phraates didn't like the way he dressed or spoke or held himself. It's not necessary to *do* anything to be expelled by Phraates," he said.

And to those who sought to overthrow him . . .

Blood spilling on the cobblestones, a din of metal-clash and bellow. Mother calling . . .

And Suren. *By means of pain* . . .

I tried to push the thoughts from me. But they never strayed far.

The days grew hot again. Unseasonably hot, even for the lowland territory. Giv provided Babak and me with headcloths to protect against the blazing desert sun, and many of the men donned them as well. Now I yearned for the crispness of mountain air, for the bracing bite of morning frost. More and more we traveled at night, both to escape the heat and swarms of stinging flies and to avoid notice by any brigands, who famously infested this road. The Magi, even Melchior, put aside their priestly dress and garbed themselves as ordinary merchants. The coals of the holy fire they kept in a nondescript iron brazier, kindling them only during the times of prayer.

At times I longed to pray along with them, but something held me back. The Wise God abhorred a lie, and I lied every day. About my sex. About my parentage. My whole life was a lie!

But Palmyra . . .

I could feel it drawing near!

I craved to know just where in Roman territory it was. I asked Pacorus to draw me a map, as he had offered to do, hoping that he would include Palmyra and I wouldn't have to ask. He did not want to waste precious ink, so he took a sharpened stick and drew in a patch of sand.

"Here," he said, "is the river Tigris. The king's residence in Ctesiphon is on the east side of the river, the side we are on now. Seleucia lies just across, on the west side. We will pass as far as we might from Ctesiphon. But it will not be as far as the Magi would like, because we must cross the bridge only a little way south of the city. Babylon is here"—he put a mark farther south—"near the banks of the Euphrates. We'll cross into Roman territory and follow the Euphrates, then cut off on the desert road to Palmyra. From there . . ."

But I heard no more, only gazed at the mark he had made to signify Palmyra. We would pass right through Palmyra! So Babak and I would not have to journey there on our own. All we would have to do was *escape.*

But first, we must safely pass Ctesiphon—and Phraates and his spies.

✴

CHAPTER 39

THE GARRISON

When the time came, I could make out the ancient walls of Seleucia, dark in the distance across the Tigris. Nearer, on our side of the river, watch fires illumined the newer walls of Ctesiphon. I wanted to tell Babak to turn his face away, as if Phraates—or his Eyes and Ears—might see him from there. Fear pressed down on me, as if they might sniff out our presence in the air or feel it in the trembling of the earth as we passed.

But then, a new thought: Might they have taken Suren to Ctesiphon? I turned to stare at the city walls. Would I feel his presence if he was here?

But all I felt was dread.

Soon I could make out the bridge, a string of wooden rafts lashed together, stretched out across the swift current in a thin, wavery line. As our party approached, Giv went to confer with the three Magi. Then he rode toward us, detached Ziba from the string, and led us toward the pack camels at the rear of the caravan. "There's a garrison by the bridge, and guards stationed at either end," he said, speaking so none but us could hear. "We don't know what's become of our friend Pirouz. But he may have guessed our caravan was coming this way. It's possible they'll be watching for us. Best for you and Babak not to be seen."

He loosened the tarp on one of the pack camels and began to pull out provisions—cushions and blankets and bedrolls.

"But how would Pirouz know we were back with Melchior again?" I asked.

"He'd know *I'd* fetch you back," Giv said grimly. "Duck your heads now; I'm going to cover you." He flung a blanket over us, then another. Now something different—sacks of grain, or wool? The weight of them bent me forward against Babak; I pushed back against Ziba's hindmost hump so as not to squash him. "Can you breathe?" I asked. I could, but it wasn't pleasant; dust clogged my nostrils, and one of the blankets reeked overpoweringly of sweat. I couldn't make out Babak's muffled answer, but I felt him nod.

The squeak of a rope; Giv must be securing the bundles. We moved slowly forward, then stopped. I heard a hum of men's voices, the deep croak of a bullfrog, a camel's groan. Behind that, the steady rush and gurgle of the river.

Now the voices seemed to grow louder. And now, the sound of a hoof striking stone. A horse.

Someone was talking to Giv. I could not hear much, just snatches. A stranger's words, rising at the end as in a question, and then Giv's voice: ". . . rebalance the load . . . overladen . . . while we wait." Then the stranger again, and then an odd *pok!* noise I could not place, accompanied by a little jerking motion. It was a piercing sound, short and somehow brutal, as if . . . as if someone was sticking a dagger through a membrane of cloth and into whatever the cloth contained.

I held my breath. *Pok! Pok!* To my left. *Pok! Pok!* Somewhere in front me—too high, I hoped, to hit Babak. *Pok!* Something scraped against my right shoulder. If there was blood on his knife, he would *know*.

I held myself still, willed myself not to cry out, not to flinch, not to draw up my legs and contract myself into a tight little ball. The heavy sacks weighed down on me, made me itch to fling them off.

Pok! Pok!

Such a vicious little sound. Had men like these captured Suren? If so, what had they done to him?

No. I didn't want to know.

Voices again, Giv and the other man. The clop of a hoof; the whickering of a horse, now behind us.

I let out my breath in a tremulous sigh.

"Babak," I said softly.

"Yes."

"Did the knife . . . Are you hurt?"

"No."

I reached for Babak's hand and squeezed it; he squeezed back.

"Ramin." It was Giv's voice, very soft. "How do you fare? How is Babak?"

"Well enough," I said. There was no purpose in telling about my shoulder. Not yet. "Was Pirouz there?"

"Not that I could see."

Soon we began to move again. Up ahead I could hear men shouting and camels groaning. The river sounds grew louder—a steady roar, sloshing, the creakings of many ropes. I felt Ziba's body tense. She began to pace uneasily, and then the ground dipped and slued sickeningly beneath us. Ziba trumpeted and balked. I murmured comforts to her; she groaned out a shuddering complaint but stepped haltingly forward. New smells penetrated the stench of the blanket: the bite of pitch; a green, reedy fragrance; and the silvery tang of fresh, running water. At long last, with a little stumble, Ziba stepped out upon dry, firm ground.

In a little while Giv led us aside from the caravan and removed the cargo that weighed on us. Babak did seem unharmed, though frightened.

I stretched to relieve my aching back, then checked my shoulder. Only a shallow scratch. No blood came off on my hand. "You've got heart, I'll give you that," Giv said, scowling. "Especially for a g—" He cleared his throat, flung a heavy sack atop a pack camel. "Well. You come from spirited stock."

I looked up sharply.

"So, what do you think the guards were looking for, then?" he asked. "You couldn't tell from a knife blade what lay within the bundles—unless it cried out and bled. I wonder," he went on as he tightened another knot, "would Phraates' men search so thoroughly on the word of a lowly juggler? Unlikely, seems to me. But the Eyes and Ears of the king, I've heard, have been seeking the children of the rebel Vardan. If they gave word to search the caravan, that would explain much."

I groped for Babak's hand, squeezed it, swallowed.

Giv threw a tarp over the pack camel's load, then turned to face me. "I've spoken only to the Magi about what I've long suspected. Your secret is safe with us."

"Which secret?" I choked out.

"Both of them, my lady."

✳

CHAPTER 40

THE KING'S MEN

We rode across the lowland fields between the rivers, fording a maze of small streams and canals as we wended our way south and west. At last, in a morning drenched with copper light, there rose before us on the flat horizon the great black walls of Babylon. The walls grew higher as we passed through yellowing fields of wheat, until they loomed above us—still mostly intact but decaying, the tops of them in places jagged as mountain crags.

It was half in ruins, was Babylon. The great road that led between the fabled Ishtar Gate lay pitted and buckled, with hollowed-out shells of palaces and temples to either side. I had heard that our Parthian kings had looted the stones and bricks of Babylon to build their winter capital in Ctesiphon, and I could well believe it. Sheep and goats grazed amid a stony rubble of tumbled-down pillars and walls, and a stork clattered its beak atop a half-fallen colonnade.

We made camp alongside the collapsed remnants of an old ziggurat. While Babak rested and I cared for Ziba, the Magi set off, word had it, in search of an old Babylonian astronomer who dwelt in the section of the city that had been restored.

I had not spoken to the Magi since Giv told me they knew who I was. Melchior and Gaspar gave no sign of this knowledge, other than, perhaps, to avoid me. But Gaspar had never paid me any mind, and Melchior seemed to notice me only when he needed me. Balthazaar, though, rode up beside us once or twice, and asked how Babak fared, and spoke of matters of no consequence. His manner was kind, and gave me to know that neither my sex, nor our father's treachery, nor my concealment of both, would cause him to hold himself aloof.

Now Giv dispatched some camel riders to patrol the road we had come from, and others to procure raftsmen to ferry us across the Euphrates. He stationed two men outside Babak's and my tent.

"Where is Pacorus?" I asked. I had not seen him for a long while—not, so far as I could recall, since crossing the Tigris.

"You leave Pacorus to me," Giv grunted, then left us.

One might think that he, knowing of my royal heritage, would treat me with greater respect!

After repairing a bent saddle frame and a few frayed cruppers, I settled in to sleep beside Babak, in the shade of the ziggurat.

I woke without knowing why and felt him sitting erect beside me. "Babak, what is it?" I asked. He did not answer. In the light that filtered dimly through the small openings in the tent cloth, I studied his face. He was staring fixedly into a corner where nothing could be seen but shadows. I passed my hand before his face; he neither flinched, nor blinked, nor turned.

Asleep.

Gently I patted down his tunic, looking for some piece of cloth or token that might have been thrust beneath it.

"Shaggy beasts," he said.

I froze.

"Salt," he said. "Stars, circling and circling. Many nights, many weeks, many years, many thousands of years." He began to rock and hum.

I rummaged through his blankets, searching. Melchior must have done this to him. Maybe he had given something to the guards outside our tent. . . .

But there was nothing. Only the blankets. Only his tunic and trousers and cloak.

Something was crumbling inside of me, collapsing to shards and dust.

Babak hummed and rocked, hummed and rocked.

"Hush," I said. I put my arms around him; he slumped against me. I leaned my head against his, breathing in the smell of him, dust and sweat and something purely *Babak*, something baby sweet.

"Babak, hush."

I awoke to a thundering in the earth, and shouts, many voices back and forth. I thrust my head out the tent flap and saw Giv and a cadre of camel riders amid a gathering crowd. By the light of dusk I made out Pacorus—talking, twisting round to point behind him and then turning back, with many animated gestures, to Giv. "Pirouz," I heard, and "the king's men—coming this way."

Pirouz? But we had passed unnoticed through the garrison at the Tigris. Hadn't we?

Then someone said "children of Vardan," and that one word—*Vardan*—stirred up spreading rings of echoes that rippled through the crowd, making the hair stand up on the back of my neck: *Vardan, the leader of the rebellion? Vardan's children here?*

A sudden hush, as if all the air had been sucked out of the world. Men turned to stare at Babak and me. And then an explosion: angry shouts and accusations, men scattering in all directions, camels groaning, and above it all Giv calling—calling for the men to wait, to mind their duties, calling out that they were cowards, deserters, traitors, vermin, dogs.

"You're the vermin!" one man bellowed. "Get us killed, you would!"

I stood rooted, unable to move as pandemonium surged around us: men swarming like beetles; tents shivering to the ground; camels roaring, rocking to their feet, speeding away. I saw Balthazaar appear at Giv's side. Giv listened to what he said, then pointed at the remaining men. "Pack up!" he shouted. "Now! We depart!"

Numbly I began to stuff our things into bundles. I handed them through the tent flap to the men outside, who took them quickly without meeting my eyes. Next I woke Babak— as well as I might. He blinked at me groggily; I picked him up and ducked outside.

We were but a fraction of our former numbers. No more than twoscore camels remained, and half as many men. Giv came striding toward us.

"Mount your camel, then," he said, "and be quick about it."

"Why? What's happened?"

"Just do as I say."

He vanished into the throng as suddenly as he had appeared.

I fetched Ziba, asked her to kneel. "Whoosh!" I said. She refused, looked anxiously about. "Whoosh!" I insisted, tugging on the nose line. Reluctantly, she knelt. Soon after, Pacorus appeared at my side, helped me to load and saddle her.

"What's happened?" I asked.

"It was Pirouz," he said, not meeting my eyes. "He came riding up to the garrison with two other men sometime after we had passed. They were heavily armed, and the guards obeyed them without question. The two men asked questions about our caravan and became enraged when they heard the guards had let us pass without calling them."

"So Pirouz is coming?"

"The king's soldiers are coming! Those two men— Phraates' spies—railed at the captain of the guard, and now they're all coming. They said . . ." Pacorus looked at me now, and there was something angry there, something of a dare. "They said you and Babak are the children of Vardan."

I stared right through Pacorus, seeing the crush of

horsemen careening through my father's gates, hearing the din of metal-clash and Mother calling.

"Mount!" he said. He pushed me toward the camels.

Babak and I mounted.

"Huh!" Pacorus tapped Ziba up and slapped her on the flanks. "Get along with you!" he snapped. "*Go!*"

*

CHAPTER 41

MADMEN and STARGAZERS

Ziba bolted. I hung on as well as I might, clasping Babak to me, straining to cleave myself to the saddle. Ziba's humps jiggled comically, but dread lay leaden in my belly.

Others streaked past us, bells jingling, tassels swaying, men and camels grunting. Melchior. Gaspar. Pacorus. Balthazaar hovered near us for a time, until Giv, who seemed everywhere at once, motioned him to move ahead and stationed men behind us. Soon we found ourselves near the rear of the pack. Dust clogged my nostrils, stung my eyes, coated my throat. Ziba's breath came labored and uneven—she was slower than all but the heavy-laden pack camels—but some sense of fear or urgency infected her now, for she put down her head, stretched out her neck, and strode out as never before. I clung tight to the strap on her forward hump, struggling to reseat myself and Babak after a hard jolt knocked us off balance. Babak had come full awake; he held himself taut.

I craned back to catch sight of the king's men, or the Eyes and Ears, or at least a dust plume that heralded their coming. But night had thickened around us, and the air was so clotted with our own party's dust that I could not have seen theirs.

We pounded across a wide bridge that spanned a black ribbon of river, lined with a garden of date palms. A shadowy field of ancient ruins went joggling past; then, to either side of us, the gateposts of the slumping city wall. We rumbled over the collapsed remains of what must once have been a moat, and then headed west across the marshy waste.

Soon, as the full moon rose, half obscured by a veil of dust, the main channel of the river Euphrates appeared before us, broad and slow and dark.

And soon again we had reached the river, and Giv was shouting at us—at all of us—to dismount. The emissaries he had sent ahead must have achieved their purpose, for a knot of men stood on the riverbank, holding tall rods, their heavy log rafts clustered on the water behind them.

Pacorus came to help us—a little grudgingly, I thought. He lifted Babak off the saddle and waited for me to dismount. We led our camels onto one of the smaller rafts. Although Ziba did not balk this time, she lifted her head high, minced cautiously with her feet, and grumbled loud and long. We pushed off.

I turned back, seeking some sign of the soldiers, but saw only dust and darkness. Pacorus, noticing my look, sighed and seemed to soften. "Across is Rome," he said, pointing to the far bank.

"That won't stop them."

"We'll take all the rafts. At least that'll slow them down. You're safe, for now."

For now. My heart beat fast from our headlong flight. A blister throbbed on my heel. The river was filling with rafts, like a flock of waterbirds paddling serenely toward the far shore. The Euphrates gurgled and splashed as our riverman plied his pole. A heron called mournfully; I could hear men murmuring nearby on the dark water, and the fitful groans of camels. This river smelled different from the Tigris—heavier, slower, muddier, older.

The sudden peace was unsettling. I sat on the edge of the raft, took off my boots, dragged my sore feet in the cool river. Babak came to lean against me. He seemed awake, but very weary. In a moment, Pacorus sat down to my other side. "You might have told me," he said.

I turned to him, looked him full in the face, trying to read the unspoken words that filled the silence. I might have told him . . . what? Who my father is? That I'm a girl?

"Why?" I asked. "What would have changed?"

"You are my friend. I could have helped."

Neither his eyes nor his words told me what I yearned to know. Koosha had *seen* me, with no one to tell him I was a girl. Did Pacorus?

And why should I want him to?

We drifted across the reflected face of the moon—captured like a great white fish in the river Euphrates. The Persian shore receded into blackness, along with the king's men and his dreaded spies. I breathed in the smell of Pacorus—a tang of ink, the musk of his sweat.

He is but half noble, I reminded myself. Beneath me. Not at all part of my plans.

Still, I could have stayed in this moment forever, in the space between two kingdoms, with Babak safe beside me, and Pacorus near.

All too soon we reached the far shore. Giv called out to all of the rivermen—something about buying their rafts, something about paying them well. Pacorus urged us to mount and be on our way; I tugged on my boots again and strained to see across the river. The Eyes and Ears. Were they there, waiting to follow us?

As we left the Euphrates behind, I heard the sound of splintering wood.

Later, when Giv rejoined us, I asked him if all the rafts had been destroyed. "Many, but not all," he replied.

"But surely, over time, the king will find or build more."

"Yes," Giv said.

"But would they dare leave Persia and follow us into Rome?"

Giv snorted. "Leaving Persia has naught to do with it. The Eyes and Ears would not hesitate to cross into Rome. But the great western desert . . ." His scowl deepened. "Only madmen and stargazers would dare it."

*

CHAPTER 42

ACROSS THE DESERT

We struck out across the trackless waste. At times Ziba's foot-falls echoed hollowly on slabs of rock; at times they swished through mounds of loose dirt or sand; at times I heard the crackle and snap of thornbush. Giv made no move to tether us to the pack camels. Ziba stayed near the other animals; when I desired her to move one way or another I guided her with the nose line. Once the moon had set, it was ever more difficult to see. Though starlight washed the landscape with a silvery glow, it lent no shadows to limn small hillocks or hollows. Ziba plunged and strained on the uneven ground.

Often and again I turned back to see if the king's men were following. But saw nothing, until a single man galloped camelback into our midst—a messenger Giv had stationed at the riverbank—reporting that the soldiers had detained the pack camels we'd left on the Persian side, but that there were no remaining rafts on which to pursue.

At this, Giv gave the order to slacken our pace—but only a bit.

The remaining men of the caravan looked curiously at Babak and me from time to time. *Children of Vardan.* Now they knew. But not, Giv had told me, that I was a girl. That must remain a secret. This new knowledge did not seem to change how the men treated us, other than perhaps to make them stare at us more often, yet hold themselves more aloof. But then, we had always been somewhat apart. Much as I had tried to make myself useful, Babak and I were not working men, but children. Melchior's pets.

The sun rose, laid a burning path across my shoulders. We stopped briefly for devotions and moved on. There was no sign of the Euphrates, only dry, gritty soil and stones as far as the eye could see. A sense of unease began to niggle at me. On the map Pacorus had drawn we were to follow the Euphrates for a long while and then strike out across the desert for Palmyra. I recalled what Giv had said: *Only madmen and stargazers would dare it.* But surely not everyone who journeyed to Palmyra was mad or a stargazer! Didn't all western-moving caravans go through there?

I urged Ziba forward and found Giv conferring with the guide and his men. "Where are we going?" I asked. "When will we meet up again with the Euphrates?"

Giv deftly tapped Ziba aside from the caravan. "We will not," he said.

"But I thought—"

"I know what you thought."

"But Palmyra—" The word flew out of my mouth; I couldn't stop it.

"Oh, aye. You thought to escape in Palmyra. But we will not be passing through there now. If you're looking for something to lose sleep over, it is there." He gestured wide, taking in the whole sweep of the desert. I could only gape at him, until he said more gently, "You can close your mouth now. You're not as clever as you think." Abruptly he turned his camel and left.

So he had known all along what I had planned, and never said a word. Once in Palmyra, he would have been watching for us to escape.

I felt all within me sag.

Palmyra, and my kinsmen, and my mother and my father, seemed to shrink from me, to grow more and more distant. I closed my eyes and tried again to see my mother's face, but it had dissolved altogether. Her soft hands, with many rings, moving in the air as she talked or brushing a tear from Babak's cheek—those I could see. But not her face.

Remember who you are!

The echo of my grandmother's voice pulled me up short.

I would bide my time, and soon, when Giv was least expecting it, I would act. I still had a small sack of coins secreted in the folds of my sash. And we were closer than ever, tantalizingly close! If we rode straight north, we were bound to reach the Euphrates, and then . . . We *would* get to Palmyra. It might take longer than I'd hoped, but we *would*.

Now Pacorus and Gaspar rode past, deep in conversation. I caught a faint whiff of Pacorus's scent, and the Euphrates crossing rushed into memory—the bright moon reflected in the water, and Pacorus by my side.

How would it be, I wondered, if he became my kin?

The sun climbed higher, turning the sky white and leaching the color from the land. In time, I became aware that Babak was dreaming. He hummed and rocked against me, murmuring words I could but partly make out, floating in and out of this life and into some other—some world of shaggy beasts and stars and weddings and ailing, angry kings. I tried to shake him awake. I tried to shout him awake. He hummed and rocked, eyes wide and blank. Sometimes, after a long spell, he seemed to come back, turning round to blink at me, asking for a sip of water. But soon he was gone again, gone to another place, a place where I could not follow. And all I could do was hold him—and pray to the Wise God to bring him back.

We made camp before the hottest time of day, setting up tents in a stand of dusty acacia trees and gray green scrub amid a desolation of sandy dirt and rock. But birds perched in the trees, and a hare peered out at us from the brush. Our new guide had found a well as promised, though I heard mutterings that he was not of the tribe who held the well, and that tribe, should they happen upon us here, would be mightily displeased.

I looked about at our company, now that we were gathered. No more than thirty men remained. It seemed that most of Gaspar's archers were still among us, and Balthazaar's small band had stayed. But of Melchior's original caravan, few were left.

They wanted nothing to do with the children of Vardan.

Later—after Babak had sipped a bit of water, eaten a few gritty dates, then lapsed back into his dream world—Balthazaar came to see us.

"How does he fare?" he asked.

I lay down the girth I'd been repairing. The tent cloth dimmed the glare of the sun, but light pressed, as through a sieve, between the threads of the fabric and stabbed in blazing shafts through the torn places. Babak did seem deep and soundly asleep. Still, the bruised hollows looked darker beneath his eyes, and the gauntness had deepened in his cheeks. His skin stretched dry and tight across his bones, and there was something old about his face that had not been there, even in the City of the Dead, when we were hungry most of the time.

"The old dreams have returned," I said. "In Babylon, and then again last night. Bits and pieces of the dreams he's had for others before, but with no cloth or other token to summon them."

Balthazaar bowed his head, pinching the bridge of his nose as if to ease pain.

"He hasn't walked in his sleep, though," I said. "Not since we were with Pirouz."

The Magus looked up sharply. "He has walked in his sleep? How often?"

"Three times now."

Balthazaar's eyes grew grave. "Well. If he has walked thrice in his sleep, he will likely do it again. I have an herb that may still the walking, if nothing else." He rummaged in a leather satchel he had brought with him, and handed me a small cloth bag. "Steep a pinch in hot water every day and feed him half a cupful. Otherwise he may put himself in danger."

I sniffed it. Bitter. "I could tie him to me when I sleep."

"And he could untie. If you were weary enough, you would not wake."

Babak shifted and groaned.

"Could you . . ." I began.

Balthazaar nodded for me to go on.

"Do you remember," I asked, "the first time we met you, how you moved your fingers across Babak's face?"

"Yes, child."

"That night he slept sound and sweet, as he had not since . . ." *Since I began selling his dreams.* "Since he began dreaming for others. So perhaps if you did that now . . . Would you? Would you touch him again?"

"Child, what I did was merely comfort, no remedy for what's plaguing him now."

"Could you try?"

Balthazaar hesitated, then stroked his long fingers across Babak's face. I could feel the tension in Babak ease, and he let out a little sigh. All at once the tent grew brighter. I looked up to see Melchior at the opening, glaring in at us.

"What are you doing?" he demanded.

Slowly Balthazaar withdrew his fingers. "Trying to comfort the child. He is not faring well."

"Comfort? What do you mean by 'comfort'? I no longer ask him to dream for me, and now *you* steal a dream from him? Remember whose boy he is. Remember that he is mine."

"The child is gravely ill. If you doubt me, come and see."

Melchior hesitated, then reluctantly came to crouch beside us. Balthazaar pointed silently at the hollows beneath Babak's eyes. Something came over Melchior's face then, a kind of surprise. The corners of his mouth dragged down. When he spoke, his voice was unusually soft.

"You may resume," he said.

✳

CHAPTER 43

BLOOD

We pressed on, traveling mostly by night to avoid the worst of the heat, stopping when the sun was high in the sky and sleeping until late in the day. Then, just as the last red rim of sun disappeared below the horizon, the world would go still, and the cool, dark, star-flecked curtain of night rolled down across the sky. It seemed, at times, as if our next step might take us right into it, out of this earthly realm and into the heavens.

The desert swept past us in moonlit undulations, dreamlike, seeming no more solid than the currents of a river: steep-sided wadis; stands of thorn trees and scrub; vast stretches of pebbly, sandy dirt and weedy grasses. The driftsand waxed and waned, sometimes just puddling round the roots of plants, sometimes mounting into great, wind-hewn dunes. And always restless—skirring in feathery eddies at the camels' feet; or lifting off the knife-edge of a dune; or whipping past our faces like billows of stinging smoke. From time to time herds of wild animals drifted across the landscape—gazelles, ostriches, antelope. Often we heard the distant howls of wolves. Once, we passed an ancient city gone to ruin—carved marble pillars thrusting up from mounds of shifting sand.

On the valley floors the taste of dust mingled with the sharp tang of the wormwood that spread up the sides of wadis, and in the damp hollows the fragrance of lusher growth perfumed the air like drifts of summer flowers. Often, silence lay so deep about us that the creak of a saddle seemed whip-crack loud, and a sudden rustling of brush beneath a camel's feet could make me jump.

At night, cold pierced through our cloaks, so I rummaged through the saddlebags for spare blankets and wrapped them about Babak and me as we rode.

But come morning, the desert sun rose with a fiery blast, drenching us in rivulets of sweat, its long, slanting rays striking sparks of light off the pebbles and sand before us. Our eyes perpetually ached.

I had begun to hoard food, thinking to take it with us when we escaped. But now was not the time for escape. Each passing day, I knew, took us farther from the Euphrates and a reliable source of water.

Balthazaar's potion must have tasted as bad as it smelled; I had to struggle to get Babak to drink it, sometimes pinning him to the ground and forcing open his lips. Afterward he would not talk to me. On occasion Pacorus held him for me, but Pacorus was often with Gaspar. He had taken to helping Gaspar pack and unpack, and they spent hours in conversation. Balthazaar came each day to trace his fingers across Babak's face—more to ease my mind, I think, than from any hope he held. Though this did at first seem to give Babak some respite, his phases of alertness grew shorter and shorter, and increasingly he was plagued by waking dreams. He hummed and rocked and murmured. If I held a waterskin to his lips, he would drink. If I led him, he would walk. But in his eyes you could see that he was not here, but in some other place.

When the sun rose, the dreams often released him, and sometimes, if he had relented in his bitterness toward me, he would tell me about them—the same old tales of babies born, and shaggy beasts, and weddings, and salt trades, and stars, and a king with weeping sores. Then, Babak would slumber as if he had not done so for days, as if the dreaming did not replenish sleep, but sucked the vitality out of him.

"Look at him," I said when Balthazaar came one day to

visit, after Babak had collapsed in sleep before I could persuade him to eat. "I try to force food upon him, but the labor of chewing tires him out. I can feel his ribs beneath his tunic. The potion keeps him from wandering in his sleep, but not from this."

Balthazaar swept Babak's hair from his brow. Gently he traced his fingertips along Babak's eyebrows, then bowed his own head, pinching the bridge of his nose, as I'd seen him do before. This time I noticed how knobbly and stiff his fingers were. How white his hair and beard. How thin and stooped his shoulders. At last, he looked up at me. "I know of nothing more. It's possible it will run its course."

"Then he'll get well?"

"I do not know," Balthazaar replied.

Then one morning, after Babak had gone to sleep and I had slipped out to relieve myself behind a tamarisk tree, I saw a spreading dark stain in my trousers.

Blood?

I stared at it dumbly. I had received no injury. So why . . .

All at once, I remembered my cousin Atoosa running to my aunt and my grandmother, crying. Had she said something about blood? The women's laughter, and whispers. My aunt spiriting Atoosa away.

The monthly courses. Blood.

I recalled that Atoosa, who sometimes ran and climbed and rode with Suren and me, never did after that day. She stayed close to the house and courtyard, always with the women.

No longer a child.

Did this mean that I was no longer a child? That I was a woman?

With Atoosa it had been some great, joyous secret that the women would not share with me. When she had emerged with her mother, she had been flushed and proud. I had pestered my mother to tell me what had happened to Atoosa, but she said no, not yet; she said I'd know in time. I begged Atoosa to tell, but she wouldn't either—just lorded it over me with a smug smile. If I had been older, I might have been able to pry the secret from her. I had been jealous of Atoosa, with all the women fussing over her.

But later, after my uncle sold her horse, I'd felt differently. If this secret meant an end to riding, perhaps I didn't want to know about it after all.

Now I peered around the tree at the men. Striding about, tending to their affairs, without fear that their very bodies would betray them and bring them shame.

Unclean.

I was unclean in a way they never would be, unclean in a way they could not possibly understand. Unclean, and alone.

Something caved in at the center of me and my body folded in half, knees against chest, head held in hands. To have a woman near, just one . . . Even Zoya would have been a comfort!

A camel groaned; I snapped upright, wiped myself quickly with tamarisk leaves, scoured my hands with sand. I yanked up my trousers, checked the back of my tunic. No blood had leaked there. I peered around the tree again, looking for the Magi or for Giv. Since they knew I was a girl, they might easily become suspicious. But the Magi had disappeared within their tents, and Giv was deep in convocation with the guides. I strode back to Ziba, trying to appear as if I hadn't a care in the world. Then I took calabash and blanket from the saddlebags, catching the eye of a man Giv had set to watch over Babak and me. He nodded. I had often gone off to wash alone. It was good that we were all Persians, save for the Bedouin guides, who never paid me any mind. Greeks—now *they* had no modesty, or so I had heard. They thought nothing of bathing and even urinating together. But we Persians were discreet.

I walked downstream from the oasis. When I was out of sight, I drew off water from the brook. I cleaned the stain from my trousers and laid them on a rock to dry. Ripping strips of blanket and tying them together, I devised a sort of swaddling for myself, something to catch the blood. I poured cool water over my hands and scrubbed them raw.

I sat back on my heels, swatted at the cloud of flies that buzzed round me. What now?

Giv had said I must tell him if this happened. But what would become of me if I did? I could see the horror on their faces—Giv, Melchior, Balthazaar. And Pacorus! With his love of the Wise God and his teachings, Pacorus would recoil from me.

Unclean.

Would they leave me here in the desert alone?

No. Balthazaar would not permit that. And Giv—no, he would not.

But perhaps they would leave me here with only a servant to shove food and water through a tent flap until the bleeding stopped.

Or perhaps they would let me ride far behind them and eat and sleep apart. Like a leper. Lower than a foreign slave.

I dressed again, tugging at my tunic to cover the wet place in my trousers, then walked back to our tent, unremarked by Giv.

I crouched beside Babak, watched his chest rise and fall in sleep, watched the flickerings beneath his eyelids.

I would not be separated from him now. I would not.

They called it sin for me to walk among men during the monthly bleeding. An offense against the Wise God. And it must be so, for everyone said it. Even in Susa women were confined. But now, looking down at Babak, at his old-man face, at the bruised flesh beneath his eyes, it seemed that it could not be so great a sin as this: that I—his very sister—had agreed to sell his dreams, despite the peril to him. I should not have listened to Zoya. I should have stopped the dream selling when I could. I should have run away in Ecbatana. I should have . . . I should have . . .

So many shoulds!

It was for his own good, I had told myself over and again. But was it, truly?

Or was it only to fulfill *my* dreams?

CHAPTER 44

*

MIRAGE

On the fourth night after my blood began to flow, when it had dwindled to a rusty trickle, our waterskin grew slack. We had not come across an oasis, nor even a well, since the first day of the bleeding. I heard mutterings against the guides, questionings as to whether we had passed this bluff or wadi days ago, wonderings whether they truly knew where water lay. Time and again, Gaspar peeled off from the caravan to gaze up at the heavens. Often Pacorus followed and wrote down on parchment figures that Gaspar seemed to be reading from his star-taker. It seemed that some new arrangement must have been made, for Pacorus now rode mostly with Gaspar, and Melchior didn't protest. But Melchior and the chief guide often exchanged harsh words. And whenever the guide rode past, the men nearby stilled their tongues in an uneasy silence.

Had the Wise God turned against us because I was unclean? Giv's words rang in my memory: *You would offend the Wise God and likely bring down his wrath upon our journey.*

Still, when I saw how the men eyed the guide, I was glad no one knew about me.

At last, as the sun rose one day, a shout went up from the front of the caravan: "Water!"

Water. Water. Water. The word hummed through the ranks.

I took a swig from our nearly flat waterskin as Ziba picked up her pace and jogged eagerly forward. The world set to jiggling—the sand-and-scrub hill before us and the humps of camels all around. Bells jingled. Saddles creaked. Metal pots and implements clanked. Babak shook his head and blinked, and I was about to tell him about the water when I heard angry shouts ahead. As we crested the rise, we saw men and camels trailing long, early-morning shadows and milling about in disarray. The men were grayish white all over, crusted with the accumulated grime and dust of travel. Several of the guide's party stood near a well, pulling on ropes. Something heavy was rising up out of it.

A mule. A dead, decomposing mule.

I slumped in the saddle, ran my tongue across my dry, cracked lips. Someone had poisoned the well.

The Magi, Giv, and the guides gathered in a circle about the mule. Melchior, I saw as we grew near, was frowning, stabbing a plump finger at the chief guide. He bellowed something back, and then they were all shouting, it seemed—all but Balthazaar, who made calming gestures as the voices subsided to a low growl.

I drew up beside Pacorus. "What's happened?" I asked.

"One feuding tribe has poisoned the well of another. Melchior demands to know why our guide didn't know this or anticipate it."

"How far to the next water?"

Pacorus shrugged. "The guide and his party wish to ride two days north, but the Magi say that their way is west, and they may be late already. They ask what if the northern well is likewise poisoned. The guide says it will not be poisoned. Melchior says he doesn't think the guide knows, that he did not know about this one and so he cannot be certain, and that it's common knowledge that there is water to the west. The guide says the western water is too far, and we're not carrying enough water to get us there alive."

The sun was a molten ball in the east. Already it had banished the nighttime chill so completely that I could no longer remember how it felt to be cold. A bead of sweat trickled down my brow; I captured it with a dusty finger and brought it to my tongue. Babak looked up at me, anxiety etched on his face. Fear was crowding in on me; I tried to push it away so that it would not infect him.

Voices swelled, the guide intoning that it was his responsibility alone to decide where to go for water, and Melchior flinging back that it was folly to entrust this mission to the judgment of a stubborn donkey. The guide went quiet, gathering his dignity about him. "I cannot lead if you will not follow," he said. Then he spun round on his camel, summoned his companions with a wave, and headed north across the desert.

We watched in silence as they shrank in the wavering distance. One man spoke agitatedly to Giv and pointed at the departing guides, clearly asking if he might fetch them and bring them back. But Giv lifted his chin, signaling *no*.

The desert stretched out parched and bleak on all sides, with no pockets of green grasses or trees to suggest where it kept its water hidden. Far away, the guides dwindled to flickering puffs of dust.

There was a convocation then among the leaders—the Magi, Giv, and a few others. Babak and I dismounted and let Ziba loose for a while to crop the brittle scrub.

Had I truly cursed this journey? Should I tell someone about the bleeding?

But what would befall me if I did? What would befall Babak? In any case, there was no water to spare for purification. And the bleeding had all but ceased. What was done was done.

Soon Giv came round inspecting waterskins and confiscating some. Water would be distributed so that no man received more than any other, he said. Then he surreptitiously tucked a full skin into one of our saddlebags. "Make sure he drinks," he said, jerking his head toward Babak.

We mounted our camels and set off again, west.

All the long day the sun beat down like a hammer on

copper, denting me, making me tender and soft. Heat rose in shimmering waves from the ground, wicking all the moisture from my mouth, from my throat, from the whole of the insides of me, leaving me dry as a shriveled husk.

We did not erect tents when we stopped, as we would not rest long enough to justify the effort. I found a hollow in the ground of the right size for Babak and me, and set up a makeshift shelter from a doubled length of blanket hung over a thornbush bough. When I fed him the potion, Babak was too weary to object. I held him in my lap, poured it slowly into a corner of his mouth, watched his throat contract with swallowing. When I was done, he turned away from me and slept. We were forced to shift after the moving shade the whole while we rested, scraping our bodies across the humpy, pebbled ground—damp with sweat, and beset by fleas and biting flies.

All too soon the call came to rise and set off again, straight into the glare of the setting sun.

Afterward there was an easier time, when the heat of the day eased and the night had not yet turned frigid. We stopped for a while as the Magi gazed up into the sky, and Pacorus took down figures for Gaspar. Later, Pacorus came by with water and inquired after Babak. "They're navigating," he told me. "Gaspar can find from the stars where we are; he can tell which way to go."

"But do the stars tell where water lies?" I asked.

Pacorus did not reply.

The following nights and days passed in a haze of milky blue starlit landscapes, then stretches of glittering sand that blazed like lakes of fire, shooting pain up through my eyes and crashing in dark waves against the back of my head. Sometimes I saw shimmering mirages, in which I could pick out the shapes of palm trees and cool, running streams. Am I dreaming? I wondered. At last?

As time went on, Pacorus came by less and less often to

give us drink. My tongue swelled up, dry and foreign in my mouth; my shrunken lips cracked open and bled. Sometimes Giv slipped us a half-empty skin, but the water did not suffice for long. There was not enough for Babak's potion, but I knew he would not sleepwalk, because he no longer had the strength to walk. He moved in and out of his dreamings, at times calling out one thing or another, which I had not the wit nor will to decipher. Once, Giv led us to a trickle of muddy water in a hollow; we knelt down and greedily sucked moisture from it through the cloth of our sleeves. In a while, we had eaten up all the stores I had saved for escape.

Escape! I couldn't even contemplate it now. It was all I could do to endure.

One day, the wind picked up. I heard it first, a rattling in the stiff thornbush, a low, dry rustling of sand on limestone, sand on sand. It beat a faint tintinnabulation against the camel bells and hissed against our robes, which bellied out behind us like sails. The horizon disappeared, engulfed by a rising tide of darkness. The air filled with sand and dust, dulling the sun to a dark gold disc. It smelled of hot metal. I drew my headcloth tightly across my nose and pulled the brow folds forward, leaving only a slit to see by, then helped Babak do the same. Nonetheless, sand began to burrow beneath my eyelids, to scratch my shriveled eyes. It crept into my nose, my ears; it crunched between my teeth. The edges of the caravan blurred until I could scarcely make out the shape of the camel in front of ours.

Ziba lurched, stumbled, recovered, slowed to a faltering walk. At last, with a plaintive bellow, she dragged wearily to a halt. Where were the other camels? I looked all about for them, but the land and sky had dissolved, and now there was only sand.

We were alone. We had escaped at last—just when I least desired it. The caravan had vanished; the sun had vanished; there was nothing to see or hear or feel but sand. I slumped in the saddle, turning my face out of the wind. I closed my eyes and slipped softly back in memory to another time of sand, when Suren and I had gone riding in Susa. A gale had come up suddenly, and the world had shrunk down to a tight cone of swirling dust and grit. I had been terrified—but not Suren. He had taken me up behind him, tethered my pony to his. He had enveloped me in his cloak and let his pony find the way home.

Now I squinted open my eyes, forced my hands to move. I swept my cloak over Babak's head and shoulders. I urged Ziba forward, and when at last she began to walk, I let her choose the way. After a space of time that could have been a moment, could have been an hour, could have been a day, I saw a figure in the blowing sand beside us. *Suren!* I thought. But no. It was Giv, tethering Ziba to his camel. I pulled my headcloth down over my eyes and let him lead us to the others.

And then, on a different day, the phantasm of trees and water that shimmered in the air before the caravan did not erode back into dust. Our camels hastened to an eager, jiggling trot as bit by bit the oasis took on substance: an oleander thicket; a convincing deep green thatch of palms; a clear, still pool in the midst of a running stream. When we were nearly there, Babak and I slid down from Ziba. Staggering, I carried him to the stream, found a spot among the men clustered round there. We scooped up water, gulped it down, let it drip in wasteful runnels down our chins.

"Look!" Pacorus pointed west, to where a ridge thrust up against the horizon. "The hills just this side of Judea. And not far beyond them . . . Jerusalem!"

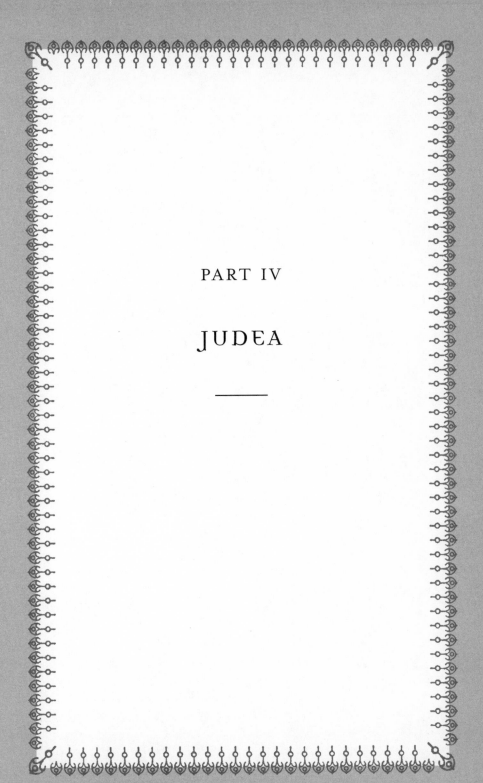

PART IV

JUDEA

———

✳

CHAPTER 45

KINGS

The next day we reached Jerusalem, high atop two hills, its great, crenellated walls gleaming gold in the late-afternoon sun. We put in at a caravansary outside the gates; the Magi retreated to their quarters, and soon I heard the chanted drone of prayers. As I led Ziba to water, I silently lofted two prayers to the Wise God. One, a prayer of gratitude, for delivering us from the desert. The other, a plea for Babak.

I set him beside me as I fed Ziba and dressed her sores with butter. Her mange was worse, great patches of angry, red, puckered skin, spreading across her flanks and sides. She had grown slower by the day.

I felt all my hopes unraveling. Babak drifted in and out, at times seeming present, at times taken over by waking dreams. He was so ill, I feared he wouldn't survive a journey to Palmyra, even if we managed to escape.

Still, we had survived Pirouz and the king's Eyes and Ears, the poisoned well and the sandstorm, the desertion of our guides. We had crossed the great western desert and, compared with where we had been, Palmyra was tantalizingly close.

And yet . . .

Sometimes in these recent days, Palmyra had begun to feel like nothing but a comforting dream, a dream I had conjured to keep my will alive.

I scanned the courtyard until I found Pacorus, pulling up waterskins from the well. He moved as gracefully as a dancer, despite the fatigue he must feel.

Koosha had not been as pleasing to look at as Pacorus. But I could not quite banish from my mind the steadiness of his gaze, nor the stillness I had felt between us. He had *seen* me. Had known me, it seemed.

Still, Koosha was a rustic, a villager. And he was far, far away. I would never meet with him again.

Something my mother had said long ago echoed in my mind. "One does not marry for love," she had said. "Yet it is good to marry someone you might come to love."

Did Pacorus know I was a woman? I wondered for the thousandth time.

And what would he do if I told him?

A while after we had retired to our quarters, as two servants poured water into a copper basin for our bath, a stirring in the courtyard brought me out to the gallery. Below, the Magi emerged into the open, arrayed in full ceremonial garb. Balthazaar came first, dressed in plain white, from his tall cap down to the thin satin bands of embroidery at the sleeves of his robes. Next came Gaspar, costumed likewise in white, except for a deep blue robe that called to mind the midnight sky. And finally Melchior, decked out in princely splendor— bejeweled cap and robes of rich purple and red, all thickly embroidered with threads of gold and studded with count- less pearls. All three wore the heavy, gold-wrought collars that marked them as Parthian nobles. My father had had one just as grand, which he had worn on great occasions.

Were they seeking the Roman king of Melchior's dream? The baby of the dream that was likely Balthazaar's? Or the king or great personage whose birth was written in the stars?

Perhaps all of them, I thought.

Now I saw Balthazaar motion for a few men—Giv among them—to accompany them to the city. When Gaspar crooked a finger at Pacorus, he leaped up with joy and began to bustle about so self-importantly that I turned away, refusing to catch his eye. But I watched him as he left, sitting straight backed upon his camel, his hair now clean and oiled, gleaming like polished mahogany.

I returned to our quarters, noting the guards at either end of the gallery. Giv and the Magi—gone! If it were night, and Babak well, and the guards asleep, and I myself not weary to the bone, I might have contemplated escape. I sighed, then set myself to bathing. My bleeding had ceased, and now was my first chance to purify myself.

When I had done, I crouched beside Babak, laid my hand on his brow, trying to feel if he was fevered. But he did not seem so.

A fly buzzed lazily round the room. A dove cooed from the rafters. The caravan noises had mostly stilled, as the travelers would be resting. I wiped the dust and grime off Babak with a clean, damp cloth as he slept—now a deep sleep, a sleep so deep, I turned him this way and that and he never stirred or spoke or even fluttered his eyelids.

Babak slept. And, after repairing a girth or two, so did I.

I woke to a sense of presence in the room. Was it something I had heard? I sat up, rubbing my eyes. The ruddy glow of sunset filtered in through the latticework of a small window. Caravan sounds had picked up in the courtyard. Had the Magi and their entourage returned? A sound at the door; as I turned to look at it, it eased quietly shut. Soft footsteps along the gallery.

Someone had been inside.

"Babak?" I laid my hand on his chest. Breathing. Peaceful breathing. I crept to the door and opened it, peered along the gallery. No one, only the guards. One of them turned toward me, caught my eye, twisted quickly away.

Had he been in the room? Or had it been someone else, someone he knew?

The courtyard was bustling, full of camels and men in the coppery light. Balthazaar and Gaspar I saw, consulting by the well. Giv was calling out orders to prepare the camels for a new journey, and Pacorus loped to and fro, fetching bundles of provisions. As I watched, Melchior strode out the doorway to the gallery stairs and joined the other Magi.

Had they found the baby they sought? If so, why the hurry to leave?

Later, as we moved with the caravan into the gathering dusk, with Babak still asleep and leaning back against me, Pacorus related what had befallen in Jerusalem. I had worried when I saw we were headed south, for I knew that Palmyra lay north and east, but Pacorus said we would not be going far.

"Where, then?" I asked.

"Just wait and let me tell you in my way! It was a wonderment, what befell us." He leaned eagerly toward me. "When we came through the great, arched gates of the city, the beggars halted their entreaties to gape at us. The tradesmen in their booths ceased with hawking their wares. A hush fell over the street. Women gripped their children's hands, pointed, and whispered, 'Kings.'

"The crowds parted before us," Pacorus continued, "and flocks of stray dogs and idle boys followed after. Hebrew priests on the wide steps of their temple paused in their preaching and turned to stare. A dove seller forgot himself and left the cage door open; a stream of birds came pouring out, raining down feathers upon all!

"And everywhere, the Magi asked about this baby who is to become the king of the Jews. People looked amazed when they heard what we sought. They had heard prophesies of the coming of a new and mighty king, but no one had news of the birth."

At last, Pacorus told me, a man had come quietly to speak with Melchior—he deemed Melchior the foremost of the Magi because of his lordly demeanor and the splendor of his garb. This man led the company up a hill to a grand, colonnaded palace encircled with ramparts and towers: the abode of Herod, the king of that place. "Then," Pacorus went on, "the Magi took from their saddlebags gifts for King Herod. There were other gifts as well, gifts they had brought for the baby. Gold, I heard, from Melchior, for he deems the child is destined to be a great earthly king. Holy frankincense from Gaspar, for he seeks, through knowledge of the stars, to unravel the mysteries of God's heaven and earth. And they say that Balthazaar, hoping to welcome a great healer to this world, brought myrrh." The Magi followed the man through a high door, Pacorus said, while the others waited in a court-yard among beautiful gardens with fountains and pools.

"An hour or more we waited," Pacorus continued, "all of us chafing to know what transpired within."

But when the Magi had returned, they said that King Herod did not know of the birth of the new king. Still, he had been most helpful; he had summoned his own priests, and they related what the ancient prophesies had foretold about the star-omened king of the Jews. He would be born, they said, in the town of Bethlehem, less than an hour's ride to the south.

"Did you see this king, this Herod?" I asked. I wanted to know if he was the king of Babak's dream.

"No. But I heard he was fearsome to behold, with a palsy on him."

"A palsy," I repeated. He *must* be the king of the dream.

"Yes. They said he was unsteady on his feet and had ter-rible, seeping sores. I heard he even stumbled, and his mantle tore."

"But why wouldn't this king know of the new king's birth?"

Pacorus shrugged. "Perhaps the stars know what he does not. The future king is not always the eldest son of the last. Perhaps this one does not have sons, or perhaps they will die, or—"

"But hadn't the priests of this place noticed the omens the Magi have seen in the stars?"

"I think their priests do not set so much store in stars as do ours."

"Still, you said 'star-omened.' How can this be if they do not set store in the stars?"

"I do not know!" Pacorus said impatiently. "You will see—we shall all see—soon enough!"

Perhaps. But it was strange.

We passed vineyards, with grapes ripening on the vines, and small watchtowers of sun-dried brick and stone. A cooling breeze sprang up, carrying the scents of dust and leaves, bringing relief from the day's heat. But soon Babak began to twitch and then to moan.

"Shh," I said, holding him tight. "Babak, hush." I peered down at his face. In the fading light I saw that it was twisted in pain, his eyes screwed shut. Some dark dream had come upon him. Pacorus glanced at me, his brow furrowed.

All at once Babak cried out, hoarse and shrill. Hair rose on the back of my neck; Ziba flinched and stumbled; the men ahead of us turned back to look. In a moment, Giv was there, having raced all down the line of the caravan. He pushed past Pacorus, and then the three Magi appeared beside us as well. Babak stiffened, arched his back, screamed again.

"Can't you do something?" I pleaded. "Some new decoction, or some words of power, or—"

Balthazaar shook his head. "Nothing I know can—No." He drew his fingertips lightly across Babak's eyebrows, eyes, and cheeks. "Peace, little one," he said.

Babak drew a shaky breath and opened his eyes.

Melchior crowded near. "What did you dream?" he demanded.

Babak burst into tears. I held him to me as he cried, great, heaving sobs. Balthazaar turned to Melchior. "Leave us," he said in a quiet voice that brooked no dissent. Melchior glowered but grudgingly acceded, motioning Giv to accompany him to the fore. Gaspar left too, shaking his head, and Pacorus with him.

Suddenly I recalled the presence I had felt in my room earlier in the evening, and how Melchior had come out the door into the courtyard moments after. I pulled back Babak's cloak and slipped my hand beneath the neck of his tunic.

There. Something affixed to the inside of it, by means of a plain bronze pin. I pulled out the pin and held the thing up to catch the light of the stars. It was a tassel, of deep purple thread.

Hadn't that king Babak dreamed of, that king with the weeping sores and the palsy . . . hadn't he worn a mantle of purple, with purple tassels?

I thrust out the tassel for Balthazaar to see. He took it between his fingers, puzzled, then his eyes went hard. He clenched it in his fist and urged his camel to the head of the caravan.

✳

CHAPTER 46

BETHLEHEM

We passed by gnarled old olive trees with dusty, blue green leaves, and stands of canopied fig trees. Far away, above dry, scrubby hills sliced by deep ravines, the stars came glimmering out. By their pale glow I could make out more vineyards climbing up the nearby terraced hillsides, and flocks of shaggy sheep. Once, a shepherd left off playing his pipe to stare at us, leaving the echo of his yearning melody lingering on the air.

Babak sobbed for a while, and then at last seemed to have cried himself out. He leaned against me, his breath ragged, shuddering harshly from time to time.

Now, low in the sky, I could see one star that outshone all others. For a moment I set my troubles aside and pondered over this journey we had taken. A journey omened in the stars. Perhaps to greet a great future king. Perhaps one as great as Mithradates, or even Cyrus.

I imagined him now, a great prince—father of the king-to-be—lifting Babak up, proclaiming to all present who he was, and then honoring me as well. Sending us both, in a royal entourage, to Palmyra . . .

I sighed. Truly, my mind must be addled with worry and fatigue! A high prince of Rome would find nothing to love in a lost prince of Persia. And who would even believe it, to see Babak now?

✳

At last Babak turned back to look at me, eyes clearer, I thought, than I had seen them in quite some while.

I wiped the tears from his cheeks, not wanting to ask him what the dream was, for fear it would disturb him again. And, truth be told, I wasn't sure I wanted to know.

"Are you thirsty?" I asked.

He nodded. I gave him a sip from our waterskin. "He is a bad man," Babak said, wiping drips of water from his chin.

"Who?" I asked.

"That king of my dream. His soldiers are bad. They bring death with them."

Death.

I sucked in a breath.

Soldiers through the gates, and women crying . . .

"Which king?" I asked softly. "Which king's soldiers bring death?"

"Melchior's king. With the palsy and the sores."

I waited for the pounding of my heart to settle. *Not Phraates.*

But that tassel . . .

Now I knew it for certain: Babak had been dreaming for Herod—the present king of the Jews.

Well before we reached Bethlehem, we glimpsed it in the distance, by the milky-bright light of the stars: a scattering of flat-roofed dwellings perched atop a limestone spur. I scanned the hilltop for some large edifice that might be a palace—but could see nothing remotely like. Just small, stone-built houses, some of which seemed to nestle into rocky outcrops or cliffs behind them.

How could a king arise from such a lowly place?

The air grew cooler as we wound up through the terraced hills. A breeze rattled in the olive trees, and a night bird called mournfully. Soon the waking dream came once more upon Babak. His face contorted as if in pain, and from time to time he startled in convulsive alarm.

I held him tight as we stopped just outside Bethlehem's gates while the Magi spoke with someone there. Then the great wooden door creaked open and we went shuffling through.

The town slept. All was still, save for the sounds of our camels: the crunch of padded feet on packed earth, the tinklings of bells, small groans and sighs. But presently I began to see pinpricks of light flare up in windows and courtyards as we passed. By ones and twos and threes, clusters of dancing lamplight collected about us, with the shapes of men dark beside them. Dogs gathered too, nipped at the heels of our camels. Too weary to strike back, the camels simply plodded along, as if the dogs were no more bothersome than gnats.

Balthazaar asked the men a question in the tongue of that place; they glanced round at one another in an odd way, as if they were mystified, as if they were afraid—but not, it seemed, as if altogether surprised. Hands pointed up a slope to where a cluster of houses nestled into the side of a hill.

Not one of them fit for a king. Compared with our home in Susa, these were just heaps of dried mud and stone.

Up the slope we went. A spray of bobbing lights marked the front of the procession, as a few of the villagers moved ahead to show the way. More and more people came to follow; we trailed constellations of lamplight behind us. I could hear the villagers' voices, kept soft: a rumbling of fathers, a crooning of mothers and, from time to time, the shrill, high piping of a child.

At last, near a well, the Magi stopped. Ahead I saw one of the villagers pointing: *There.*

It was a tiny limestone dwelling, set back against the side of a cliff.

Anger surged up inside me. They had traveled all the way from Persia for this? They had forced Babak, a scion of Persian kings, to spill out his life force for this? Some Hebrew pauper?

I glared up at the bright star. Either the Magi had erred in their calculations—or the heavens had played us for fools!

Balthazaar dismounted, his movements stiff and slow, and rummaged in his saddlebags. *He* had offered us nothing but kindness. *A holy man,* Pacorus had said.

Perhaps . . .

Perhaps this child-king had been separated from his kin, forced by chance or tragedy or betrayal to live among the lowly. Yes, surely that was it! And the Magi would lift him up again, return him to his rightful place, to the palace in Jerusalem.

And yet there was that troubling dream. *They bring death with them.*

Now Gaspar dismounted as well, but Melchior did not. Frowning, he barked out something to Gaspar, stabbing an angry finger first at the sky, then at the house, and then at Gaspar.

Gaspar answered crossly and began to open his saddlebags.

Melchior suddenly wheeled his camel round and came back to us. He stared into Babak's blank eyes, then turned to me. "Did he tell you of his dream?" he asked in a low voice. "Did he see aught of this hovel?"

I refused to meet his gaze, but pushed the words out between tensed jaws. "I know not what he dreamed, but I found the tassel you put there, from that king you saw, that Herod."

Melchior had the grace to flush.

"Babak says that king is a bad man," I said grudgingly, "and that his soldiers are likewise bad. He said, 'They bring death with them.'"

Melchior's brow furrowed. He looked with distaste at the dwelling, then turned to regard Balthazaar and Gaspar, who stood waiting, bearing fine wooden caskets that gleamed with inlaid gold.

Grumbling, Melchior returned to the head of the caravan. He dismounted, reached into his saddlebags and, with brusque, jerky movements, yanked out a gilded casket of his own.

They walked toward the dwelling with stately, measured steps, even Melchior now adopting the bearing of ceremony. The stars glittered above—one brighter than the rest—and a mirror of flickering lamplight circled about us. The flames stretched out long in a sudden breeze, pricking out, as the Magi passed, the gold of collar, hilt, and casket, of embroidered thread on flowing robes. Beside the humble dwelling the Magi seemed wildly out of place and oddly useless, like bejeweled rings on the fingers of a tiller of the soil.

A man appeared at the gate of the abode. He spoke briefly with Balthazaar and motioned them in. Several of the townspeople made as if to follow, but Balthazaar said a few quiet words in their language, and they held back.

One by one, the Magi disappeared within the gate.

✳

MERCY

We waited.

No one spoke.

Only the creak of saddles and the shifting and groaning of camels broke the silence. The breeze had stilled, and even the insects hushed. The night smelled of dust, and burning lamp oil, and the sweat of men and animals. And something else, too, something faint: the sweet tang of wood shavings.

Soon it became clear that the Magi would not simply bestow their gifts and depart. A few at a time, we urged our camels to kneel and dismounted under the curious stares of the townspeople.

A small boy, not yet past the age of suckling, broke free from the villagers, toddled up to Babak and me, and snatched at the fringe of one of Ziba's saddlebags. With a sharp cry his mother fetched him quickly back. But when another boy moved to finger the bow of one of Gaspar's mounted archers, the man knelt down, holding it out to him, and several young boys clustered round. One of the boys mimed a question, and the archer motioned up to where the bright star hung in the sky, the boys following with their gazes where he pointed.

I leaned against Ziba and settled Babak beside me. What would the Magi do next? I wondered wearily. Was the journey ended? Once he found what he sought, would Melchior let us go?

Babak began to whimper. I gathered him into my lap, but he flailed and cried out.

The boys scurried back to their mothers and fathers. The townspeople backed away from us; their lamp flames leaped, as if alarmed.

"No, Babak," I pleaded softly. "Not now. Please stop."

He screamed again, then kicked, wrenching loose from my grasp. He lurched, wobbling, to his feet and launched himself headfirst to the ground.

I lunged for him, turned him onto his back. He was limp now, eyes empty and staring. Blood gushed from a cut on his chin. Giv came running with a rag to staunch it, but the blood kept coming, soon soaked clear through the rag. Pacorus gave me a second rag, but before long that one was full of blood too.

A disturbance among the townspeople. I looked up to see a young woman, with a baby on one hip, pushing through the crowd. Another woman shouted angrily at her, plucked at her mantle, but the first woman shook her off. She knelt beside Babak, set a small clay bowl on the ground, motioned me to move the rag aside.

Whatever was in the bowl smelled foul. "No!" I said. "Giv, make her go—"

"Hush!" he said to me. He looked the woman full in the face; she clutched her baby tight against her chest but did not flinch. Giv picked up the bowl and sniffed at what lay within. "It's healing herbs," he said.

"What's Babak to her that she would help him? I don't trust her; she—"

"Don't you know mercy when you see it?" Giv snapped. "Do you think everyone sees those around them as mere steps to tread upon for their own gain?"

Chastened, I let him pluck the rag from my hand. He nodded to the woman.

She scooped up the thick, acrid-smelling paste in her free hand and slathered it on Babak's chin. Gradually the flow of blood ceased.

Babak blinked and looked dazedly about. His eyes found mine; he sighed and seemed to drift off to sleep.

I sagged with relief.

A movement in the crowd. While some of the townspeople held well back, others, I saw now, had drawn near. Another woman with a babe in arms. A spindly old man and his bent-over wife. One of the boys who had touched the bow. They gazed at Babak worriedly. The old man gave me a solemn smile.

Giv cleared his throat and nodded again to the woman with the herbs. *Thank you,* his nod said. She nodded in turn; he rose to his feet, motioned Pacorus to follow, and began to circulate among the men of the caravan.

The woman held out her hand toward Babak, but hesitated. Looking at me. Questioning.

I shrugged. Nodded.

Tenderly she stroked her fingers through Babak's hair, across his brow, and down one cheek. Then she shifted her infant back onto her hip, straightened her headcloth, and seemed about to rise, when her gaze caught mine. She studied my face so closely, it should have caused offense. But I felt no ill intention, only her surprise.

She knew.

It was the same look I had seen in Balthazaar's eyes when he realized I was a girl.

The surprise dissolved into something else, a kind of warmth, a smile behind the eyes. It came to me that she was not much older than I—maybe a year or two. It came to me what a comfort it would be to share friendship with such a woman.

A commotion from somewhere in the crowd. A man called sharply; the woman turned to look. She nodded to me, picked up her bowl, then rose and followed him through the clusters of flickering lights and into a nearby house.

Something was trembling inside me, something was welling up. Memories of past mercies swam into my mind: Of the man in the marsh, pressing Zoya to give us Gorizpa. Of Koosha and his family, bringing us out of the qanat, protecting us from

Pirouz. Of Giv watching over us, never sleeping in his tent. Of Pacorus. Of Balthazaar. Of Suren, patiently teaching me so many things, leading us safely away from Susa.

I tried to hold the trembling in, to press it all back into the tight space where it had been pent before, but it was leaking out, it was surging up, it was flooding into my throat, my nose, my eyes.

The scrape of a gate opening. And here they came again, shimmering beyond the glaze of my tears: Balthazaar, looking grave and pensive; Gaspar, dropping his head back to gaze up at the sky; and Melchior . . . he walked stooped and unsteady, like an old, old man. He blinked, his visage vague and bewildered, as if a bright torch had passed too near his eyes.

✳

CHAPTER 48

THEY BRING DEATH

Retracing our steps through Bethlehem, we were oddly subdued. The townsfolk had vanished back into the dark streets from whence they had come, and the sounds of our passing—the creaks of straps and harnesses, the jingling of bells, the muffled *thud*s of camels' feet on packed earth—rang loud against the hush of the night. No one of our company spoke of what had come to pass in the dwelling where the Magi had gone. No one even asked.

I studied the backs of the Magi up ahead, hoping to read in their bearing some sign of what they had found. But each looked straight forward and spoke to no one.

Melchior especially I watched. Would he have need of Babak after this? And if not, what would he do?

I peered down at Babak. He slept fitfully, his chin swollen and encrusted by herbs.

Was that all? I wondered. All this long journey, from Rhagae, from the great castle in the foothills, from Ecbatana . . . The whole of the heavens turning and turning over numberless years . . . All for an hour spent inside a hovel in some poor Judean village?

And what would become of us now?

Think, I urged myself. How to persuade Melchior to pass through Palmyra on our return? Or failing that, how to escape and make our own way there?

But a great weariness had come over me; I had no heart for scheming. I leaned forward, wrapped myself around

Babak, nuzzled his damp hair, breathed in the smell of him—
dirt and sweat and healing herbs and that sweet smell that was
Babak's own.

Pacorus rode up beside us, asked, with a glance, about
Babak.

I shrugged. "The same."

Some trick of starlight brought Pacorus's face into sharp
relief: his fine, straight nose; his dark-fringed eyes.

He was only half noble; we were his betters by far; and yet . . .

Again I wondered. Was it possible that Pacorus might have
known I was a girl all along, that he might see me as more
than just a friend? If so, and if he spoke of me to Melchior—
of Babak and me—and if Melchior agreed . . . and if Pacorus
then spoke with his father, and he agreed . . . Could I be content as the wife of a merchant's son, knowing that I had
sprung from the seed of kings?

Remember who you are, my grandmother would say.

But my grandmother was dead.

We stopped for the night at a small caravansary on the main
road from Jerusalem, not far beyond Bethlehem's walls. I lay
awake long after we had settled down for the night, setting a
hand on Babak's chest and feeling its steady rise and fall. It
seemed that he breathed in a more natural rhythm than
before—fewer jumps and starts. Once, he looked up at me,
clear eyed, and asked where we were. Balthazaar had said he
might get well on his own; I clung to that.

Just as the heaviness of sleep had begun to flood my body,
the door creaked open, and beyond the sudden flare of lamplight I made out Pacorus's face. I sat up quickly, half in hope,
half in dread.

"They wish to speak with you," he said. "The Magi. I'll
bide here with Babak."

I heard voices as I moved down the gallery—Gaspar's dry and
accusing, Melchior's an answering roar. Giv, standing by the

guard at the door, motioned me in. The talk ceased as the three Magi—seated on low benches and still arrayed in their finery—turned to face me.

Balthazaar gestured for me to seat myself on the carpet across from him. The air was thick with incense. Behind the Magi, on its silver tripod, the holy fire burned.

"We have been speaking of this latest dream of Babak's." Balthazaar flicked a glance at Melchior—an angry glance, I thought. "Melchior tells us it has to do with a king."

I nodded.

"Was this King Herod, the one we visited in Jerusalem?"

"Babak said, 'Melchior's king. With the palsy and the sores.'"

"I told you, it's Herod," Melchior said. "Did you see the sores on his neck, his arm?"

"And there was something about soldiers?" Balthazaar asked. "Herod's soldiers?"

"Babak said to me that they are bad. He said, 'They bring death with them.'"

Melchior arched his bushy brows at Gaspar as if to say, *You see?*

Gaspar frowned and turned to me. "Is that all your brother said? Was there more to this dream? Did it say who would be visited with death? The infant and his family? Or perhaps one of us?"

"There may have been more, but he didn't tell me. And I didn't want to ask because Babak . . . He's so ill, he—"

Balthazaar held up a hand to stop me. "Hush, child. No need to explain."

"What of Melchior's Bethlehem token?" Gaspar asked.

I said, "What token?" and at the same time Melchior protested, "There is no token!"

"You were bent over that baby far too long," Gaspar said. "What were you doing, I wonder?"

"I was gazing upon his countenance!" Melchior bellowed. "It's not every day you behold an infant whose birth was presaged in the stars and announced by angels. I wanted to fix him in my memory, to—"

"And I suppose there was no token before, with Herod, was there?" Gaspar said. "No purple tassel, purloined from the floor and pinned to the poor child's tunic?"

"You should thank me for that! I sought to know what Herod dreams of—what manner of man he is. If the boy hadn't dreamed for him—"

Gaspar cut him off. "And of course you had no thought of divining where lay your best chance for power—with the old king or the new!"

"But Melchior is right in this. . . ." Balthazaar waited until he had all ears. The fire popped and flared. "We must not return to Herod." Pensive, he put a finger to his lips. "'They bring death.'"

"It bodes not well for the infant and his parents," Gaspar said. "There cannot be two kings of the Jews at once, and the one is not a son to the other, nor even distant kin. A carpenter's son! This must be the death of which Babak speaks."

"If it had been left to you"—Melchior jabbed a beringed finger at Gaspar—"we would have hied ourselves straight back to Herod and risked our own necks! I tell you, *I* saved the infant's life by taking that tassel."

A gasp of protest escaped my lips.

"Perhaps," Balthazaar told him drily. "Though I think Babak merits some credit."

"To say nothing," Gaspar added, "of the Wise God, Ahura Mazda, from whom all good things flow."

Melchior flushed.

Gaspar turned to Balthazaar. "I think it best that we break up the caravan. That each of us three goes home a different way—but none through Jerusalem."

Balthazaar nodded. "I agree. And we must warn the infant's parents, without delay. Giv . . ."

Giv nodded, slipped out the door.

Melchior seemed about to protest—that Giv was *his* to

command, I thought—but he yawned instead, running his fingers through his unruly beard. "Well," he said, "I've done my part, though little enough credit I get for it. You can palaver the night away if you like, but I'm off to bed."

He began to heave himself to his feet, but Balthazaar said, "Wait. There's another child we've put at risk. Babak."

Melchior darted a guilty glance in my direction. "Herod cares nothing for him. Herod knows nothing about him."

"I do not speak of Herod."

Melchior sighed, lowered himself to his bench. Suddenly he looked tired, as if something that had been propping him up had been kicked away. "How was I to know what would befall him? Now there's nothing to be done."

"The least we can do for Babak," Balthazaar said, "is return him to his kin."

My heart leaped in my chest.

"Return him," Melchior began. "But—"

"I will do it if you are unwilling," Balthazaar said. "Giv says Babak's kin have gone to Palmyra." He turned to me. "Is this true?"

I swallowed, unable, for a moment, to speak. "I have heard so, my lord," I said at last. "And I believe it."

Balthazaar turned back to Melchior. "Entrust him—entrust them both—to me, and I'll see that it is done."

I walked slowly along the gallery to our quarters. The air was cool and spiced with the lingering aroma of incense. The nighttime sounds of the caravansary rose about me—the grumblings of camels, the murmurings of men, the melancholy strains of a lute. So familiar now.

"Palmyra!" I lofted the word softly into the air. "Balthazaar will take us to Palmyra!"

For so long I had yearned for this—passage to Palmyra. For so long I had stolen for this, scrimped for this, starved and lied and schemed for this.

Palmyra!

I breathed in deep, waiting for the joy to fill me, the joy I knew must come. But instead there were only questions, as if some dam had suddenly crumbled and now they were free to roar.

How could I be certain our kin had gone to Palmyra? Suren had told me this, but how had he known? Had he truly known, or had he just needed to believe?

Or was it I who had needed to believe beyond a doubt in Palmyra?

But how if our kin had fled somewhere else, to another city? Or, if they had gone to Palmyra, how if they hadn't stayed? How if they had scattered to many cities, many villages, many lands?

How if we arrived in Palmyra and searched the whole of the city—the rich districts and the poor districts, the seats of government and the marketplaces, the dim, dank crevices where beggars holed up at night—and found neither our father nor our mother nor Suren nor aunts nor uncles nor cousins?

How if Phraates' soldiers—

No.

How if Phraates' soldiers had—

No.

I stopped, gripping the gallery rail, and gazed out across the courtyard—beyond the far wall of the caravansary to where the stars wheeled above us, to where the Magi's star was setting in the west.

North and east lay Palmyra. Balthazaar would take us there. And we would find what we would find.

For the first time in many years I had nothing to plan for, nothing to bargain for, nothing to fight for.

And Pacorus . . .

What of Pacorus? What did I want from him?

✳

CHAPTER 49

THREE VISITORS

When I awoke, I was surprised to see sun streaming through the small window, illuminating the motes of dust that swam through the air, laying sheets of golden light on the wall, pricking out coppery flecks of straw embedded in the bricks. Dawn had come and gone. Sounds wafted up from the courtyard: soft murmurings and shufflings and scrapings, rustlings and cooings of doves. Clearly a goodly part of our company was taking this morning to rest. I yawned and turned toward Babak.

Melchior, crouching over him, snapped up his head to meet my gaze.

"What are you doing?" I said, hearing my voice rise in alarm. I stumbled to Babak, who was still asleep. I groped through his clothing, searching for whatever it was Melchior had put there. But I found nothing—neither in Babak's tunic nor in his cloak nor in his trousers nor in the bedding in which he had been wrapped. "What are you *doing?*" I demanded again.

I expected him to roar at me, to rant and bluster as he had the night before. A spark of ire kindled in his eyes, but he said not a word.

We stared at each other—I refused to look away—then he glanced down at Babak.

"*I* will take you to Palmyra," he said.

"You! But Balthazaar said—"

"He said if I didn't, he would. I will. I have pledged it. The boy . . ."

Melchior plucked a bit of straw from Babak's hair. The anger had gone from his eyes. For some reason I brought to mind the first time I had ever seen him, a vain peacock of a man, swaddled in silk and surrounded by servants who anticipated his every sneeze. Now, though the finery remained, there was something different about his face, something slack, uncertain.

"I will take you," he repeated. He rose wearily to his feet and shuffled to the door. He turned round then, hesitating. "Before," he said, "it was for me. Now it is"—he nodded toward Babak—"for him." And, before my tongue could stir itself to argue, or bargain, or ask precisely what he meant, he was out the door and gone.

Soon after Melchior left, the inn began to hum with footsteps and voices. Camels roared and donkeys brayed. Our caravan was breaking up, with each of the Magi setting off his own way. Pacorus came by with a pot of broth; Babak drank a little, half awake, then lapsed back into a deep sleep.

Pacorus could not stand still. He tapped one foot against the floor, paced back and forth, then stood beside me again, the restless foot thumping out its quick tattoo. And from that foot I knew there was something inside him, some news aquiver to get out—something he knew I would not wish to hear.

At last it came. Gaspar, Pacorus said, had offered to take him as an apprentice, despite his impure blood. They would go to the fortress near Sava, where Gaspar would school him in the portents of the sky, train him as a priest. Melchior had agreed to let him go. Pacorus's eyes burned with his dreams as he spoke of the trajectories of the stars, of the secrets of the heavens.

I smiled at him—I did!—though I knew the smile did not reach my eyes. It was a smile that reached only lip-deep, with kingdoms of disappointment behind it. I called to mind the night we had sailed across the face of the moon, on the great, wide stream of the Euphrates. I recalled the story I had secretly conjured from that moment—that one day I would tell him I was no boy, but a woman, and he would offer to take me as his wife. In this story, I gave up all my old dreams for him.

Now I saw there was no use in the telling. If he had been willing to read the secrets of my heart, he would have seen it long ago.

Koosha—he had seen me. But I had striven to push him from my mind, and now he seemed little more than the memory of a dream. Had he really appeared to us out of the darkness of that qanat? Had he sat with us by the fire and told us of his home?

And that stillness I had felt . . .

Tell your brother, he had said. *I have eyes to see.*

And so Pacorus and I said our good-byes, embracing as brothers. I came out on the gallery as he mounted his camel—with a lean grace that I had learned by heart and would know again if I saw it a thousand years hence—and watched him ride with Gaspar's archers out through the caravansary gates.

We had a third visitor that morning. Balthazaar knocked to announce himself, then came to sit cross-legged upon the carpet beside Babak. I waited for him to tell me why he had come, but he only moved his fingertips, in that way of his, across the wasted planes of Babak's face.

"I have many questions," I said at last.

He nodded, inviting them.

"Will Babak die?"

He seemed about to say something, drew it back within himself, then lay his long, knobby hands in his lap and rested the whole weight of his attention upon my face. "It is likely," he said. "Unless . . ."

I took in a deep breath, expelled it. "Unless what?"

"It is a sickness of the spirit that afflicts him. These

sicknesses . . . they *do* sometimes heal of themselves, for no reason that any can discern. He has not walked in his sleep for a day or two?"

I shook my head.

"That is a good sign. Is he ever lucid? Does he have moments when he speaks to you as he used to?"

"Not many. When he told of his dream of that king. And he was clear eyed for a moment this morning."

"Clear eyed? Lucid?"

I nodded. "And earlier he sat up and drank some broth. I did not have to force it down."

Balthazaar made a thoughtful *umm* in his throat. "Well, perhaps there will be more of those moments, and then . . . At worst, food and water will keep him with us for a while yet. Pray to the Wise God—that is my counsel. Though his plans for us may not be what we wish, prayer can lead us into his light."

It seemed a hollow comfort. Long ago I had prayed every day—prayed to the Wise God, prayed to my mother's gods— but the gods did not reply. *Return us to our mother, to our father, to our kin. Restore us to our rightful place of honor. Deliver us to Palmyra.* What was the use in praying if prayers were never answered?

And yet, from time to time of late, prayers just seemed to float up from within me.

"I thought *you* would take us to Palmyra," I said, "and now Melchior says he will instead. Will he? Can I trust him?"

"He has given his word on this to Gaspar and to me. I do not think he will break it."

"He broke it before," I said bitterly.

"True. But Melchior seems changed to me. Or no—not changed, precisely, but on the cusp of change. Unbalanced, teetering between his old ways and something new. No longer so certain of himself."

"He seemed certain enough last night. Arguing with Gaspar. Saying he had saved that baby's life!" Still, I had to admit, this morning he had been strangely subdued.

Balthazaar's eyes crinkled in a smile. "Sometimes, I have observed, we put on the greatest show of refusing to change . . . just as the changing has begun. In any case, I'm certain you can trust him to take you to Palmyra."

We sat for a moment in silence. I thought Balthazaar would rise to go, as he was a great and busy man and must have much to do to prepare for the long journey home. And yet it was a comfortable silence, sitting here with him, both of us attending to the rise and fall of Babak's breath.

"Did you . . ." I began.

He turned to me, waiting.

"Did you find what you sought? Is that baby . . . a king?"

"A king?" He furrowed his brow. "I don't know if he is or ever will be a king. Or at least a king such as the world acknowledges. But . . ." The furrows eased, and he smiled to himself. "There was something of the light about that child, something that filled this old man's heart. Yes, I found what I was seeking, but I don't yet comprehend the meaning of it."

From below, in the courtyard, came the roar of a camel and then a shouted command. Balthazaar looked about him and began to gather up his robes, as if the world had intruded upon us and he must go to meet it.

"Wait, my lord," I said. "One question more?"

He nodded.

"What happened in that house? Can you tell me? Or is it a matter only for priests?"

"No, not just for priests!" he said. "I think that may be part of what we are meant to understand. But what happened . . ." He shrugged, opening out his hands, palms up. "Well, we saw an infant and his parents, we heard the story of his birth. That is all. It does not seem much to tell, does it? It does not seem much to show for our long journey—and the price your brother has paid. But it was a remarkable story, with angels in it, and prophetic dreams." He looked down at Babak. "Dreams even more astonishing and perplexing than the ones we already knew of. Dreams that gave us to know that we had come to the right place. That the omens in the sky had not led us astray."

"But might it be," I ventured, "that he *is* a king—or will be when he is grown? Might it be that these people are not his rightful parents, that he was separated from his true kin? Might it be that they are in exile, and—"

"Do you set so much store by kings," Balthazaar interrupted gently, "knowing what you know of them? Kings have not been kind to you, nor to your brother."

"But my father—"

"Craved to be king. Sacrificed all for that."

I bowed my head, stung.

"You ought to have seen their faces when they looked upon those gifts we brought. They were perplexed. Almost afraid. Useless gifts! Except, perhaps, the gold. What would you have done, when you lived in Rhagae, if someone had given you caskets of holy frankincense and precious myrrh? You can't eat them, they won't shed light to see by or keep you warm—"

"I would have traded them for passage to Palmyra!"

Balthazaar threw his head back and laughed, a warm, comforting sound. "Well, perhaps they will be as clever as you. They will need passage; their old donkey won't take them far."

He looked at me, still smiling, nodding his head. "If you were mistaken, my child, in thinking we would find an earthly king, then so were we all. Those gifts, chosen to impress and gratify the highborn and powerful, were the badge of our error. So tell me: Why would the Wise God send so many signs in his heavenly lexicon to herald the birth of a lowly carpenter's son? What do you think?"

I shook my head.

"Surely you can hazard a guess?"

"No, I cannot!"

"I keep musing upon paradise and the way to attain it. Of the Prophet's admonition that greatness comes neither from wealth nor knowledge nor nobility of birth, but from our own good thoughts, good words, and good deeds. By these lights, he tells us, even a slave can cross to paradise, while many a king plunges into the abyss. The highborn and the lowly are as one.

"And yet I can't but wonder if any of us would have undertaken this journey had we known we would find no king, nor even the son of a great priest, but only a carpenter's baby in a tiny limestone dwelling in a backwater village of Judea."

Balthazaar sighed. "I confess I am mystified as to how to decipher God's alphabet writ across the heavens. But when I ask myself, What is the inner meaning of all of the outward signs we have witnessed? I wonder if the humbleness of this birth may be the very crux of the matter."

"I don't understand," I said.

He smiled sadly. "Nor do I, child. But I suspect that this birth has less to do with kingly power and priestly knowledge, and more to do *here*"—he placed an outspread hand upon his chest—"with the heart."

✴

CHAPTER 50

THE BABIES

Soon our time came to depart. I woke Babak, who seemed clear eyed again, awake enough to pull on his cloak and boots. As we climbed upon Ziba, I looked about for Giv but did not see him. Upon asking, I found that he had returned before dawn, and Melchior had dispatched him ahead to hire a desert guide who lived in Bethany. He would meet with us later, on the Jericho road. I looked about as well for any men Melchior had charged with guarding Babak and me. There had been none on the gallery this morning. And now again, in the caravan: no guards.

No call to guard against our escape, when they were taking us where we wanted to go.

Or perhaps it was that Melchior no longer needed Babak.

When we had traveled a short way on the road east from Bethlehem, Babak began to tug at one of his boots. "My toes pain me," he said.

I leaned to one side to look at him; his eyes were still alert. His gaze shifted; he pointed back over my shoulder. "Look," he said.

I turned round to see a great plume of dust in the distance, on the road that threaded among the hills toward Jerusalem. Amid the dust, a troop of red-cloaked, metal-helmed riders, coming this way.

Soldiers.

And it was upon me again, the old memory: the rumbling of the earth beneath the horses' hooves, the flash of sunlight on swords, the crying, the women crying . . .

I pulled Ziba to the side of the road and brought her to a halt. She cropped a tuft of dry grass as the caravan streamed past. My hands, I saw, were trembling. I tried to still them, my hands, but they had a will of their own; they began to infect my arms with their trembling; they began to infect my legs.

The soldiers. Coming fast, coming at full gallop. I stared at them, transfixed, as they disappeared behind a ridge.

"The babies," Babak said. He looked up at me, worried.

I hugged myself to stop the trembling, clenched my hands into fists. "The baby, you mean," I said. "His father and mother have been warned. Surely they're well away from here by now. Baby—not babies."

"No!" He was indignant. "*Babies*. I saw them in my dream."

"When? Did you dream again last night? Or—"

"No, before! When I dreamed of the soldiers before. They . . ." He swallowed, blinked.

Something cold came to rest on my heart. *They bring death with them.* "What happened to the babies?" I asked him.

He shook his head, turned his face from me.

"Babak! What did the soldiers do?"

"There was blood on their swords," he said. "The babies . . ."

Babies. Oh, Lord . . .

But why babies? Why not just the one?

Now the leading soldiers began to reappear from behind the distant hill. Sun glinted off their helmets, shot sharp spurs of light into my eyes. I looked round for the others in our caravan; nearly all had passed me by. "Wait!" I called. I urged Ziba forward. "Look! The soldiers—"

Heads turned round to look, and then a shout went out— "*Soldiers!*"—echoing from man to man to man, and then the neat file of camels began to bunch up, jiggle into a trot, and pull away ahead.

"Wait!" I cried again. But they did not wait. They surged down the road ahead of us, a tumult of jostling camels, bellowing men. Ziba, seeing that she was to be parted from the others, let out a mournful bawl and lunged forward. But no matter how she strained to keep up, she lagged farther and farther behind, until the gap was so wide I knew I could not overcome it to explain that the soldiers did not come for us.

The babies.

Ziba jogged to a halt, moaning long and loud at the loss of her companions. I, too, watched our caravan shrink and pale in the distance. *Palmyra.* There went Palmyra before us, with all my old hopes and dreams. I tried to call to mind the faces I had longed to find there—my father and my aunts and uncles. My mother . . .

But my memories, once knife-edged and clear, had come apart in trickles and runnels, had collapsed and dissolved and shifted in the winds of these past years, until the whole of the landscape was transformed. And the face that emerged in memory now was that of a kindly young woman in Bethlehem, with a baby in her arms.

✴

CHAPTER 51

SOLDIERS

By the time Babak and I reached Bethlehem—turning our backs on the others and retracing our path along the road— the soldiers had disappeared again behind the curve of a hill. I cried out, "Soldiers!" as we went jogging through the town gates; I pointed back in the direction from whence they came. A cluster of townsfolk, neither seeing what I pointed at nor comprehending my meaning, gaped at me as if I were mad. "*Soldiers!*" I called louder, knowing that wouldn't help, but what else could I do? Two men exchanged a wary glance. They advanced down the narrow street toward us; I drove Ziba right between them, forcing them to leap apart and press themselves against walls on either side of the street, scattering a group of boys playing catch-ball, startling a pack of chickens, which squawked and flapped and filled the air with a cloud of black-and-white feathers. I urged Ziba ahead, clutched Babak tight against me. I could feel from the alertness in his body that he was still awake. My hands had ceased with their shaking. It felt good to do something for once, not just sit helplessly by.

A lane split off to the right, winding steeply up. One lane looked just like another here, all hedged about with limestone walls and houses, yet this one seemed familiar. Ziba lurched around the corner and shuffled up the hill. People came to stand in doorways as we passed. A boy darted out toward us, but his mother snatched at him and dragged him back. "Soldiers!" I cried again. Surely someone here would understand the Persian tongue.

And now, just ahead, I saw the well I remembered, and the houses that backed into the steep hillside behind. Which one had the Magi visited? They looked so much alike, huddled all together. But there. Wasn't it the one just across from the well? And the other house, the one of the woman with the baby. Where had that been? I turned to look for it, and there she was, adjusting her mantle in her doorway, her hands dusty with ground meal, her baby on her hip.

I wheeled Ziba round, stopped before her. "You must . . ." I gestured toward her baby. I tried to think how to convey *hiding*, but couldn't. "Soldiers! They're coming. You must . . ."

I could see from her face that she was straining to comprehend me, but how could you explain such a thing? Even to someone who spoke your own language, you couldn't explain it.

Something caught her eye; she turned and looked behind me, and there was a man advancing quickly up the street, a knot of others trailing behind. The young woman called out to the leader; he hastened his step. "What is your business here?" he asked me. "What do you want?"

Persian. He spoke Persian.

"You must hide your babies," I said, "hide them all! That king of yours, that king you have in Jerusalem, he's sending soldiers to kill them. I saw them on the road; they're coming now."

The man knit his brow, puzzled.

"Hide your babies! My brother sees things in dreams; he has seen blood, he has seen death!"

I could tell that I had said too much, too fast. I took a deep breath. "You must take the babies away from here," I said, forcing myself to speak slowly. "You must hide them. Your baby"—I pointed to the kindly woman—"and the baby the Magi visited, if he's still here, and all the other little babies, every one in Bethlehem."

The man motioned for me to stop, then began to translate.

People had emerged from nearby houses to listen, men and women and children. I tried to read their faces, tried to see if they comprehended my meaning, or if they believed me. Some seemed doubtful, still others, afraid. The kindly woman said something, pointing in the direction of the house the Magi had visited, then the translator turned to me.

"They are gone, Joseph and his family. When the man from your caravan came looking to warn them, they had already left. But what cause would Herod have to kill this woman's son, or any of our children?" the man asked. "He might send to raise our taxes; he has done that before. He might murder the babes of the powerful; he has done that as well. But—"

All at once from below we heard a rumbling in the earth, a shout, and then a wild confusion of noise: a clangor of metal, a clattering of hooves on stone, bleatings of sheep and goats, children's screams, men's shouts, women's piercing wails.

Soldiers through the gates.

The translator flung me a wild look, a look that encompassed, it seemed, terror and urgency and gratitude. Then he and his group of followers fled back the way they had come. Others collected their children; some disappeared within their homes; a few, clutching babies, dashed into a nearby lane.

"Please," I said, leaning down and holding out my hands for the kindly woman's baby. Something wet on my cheeks. I swiped impatiently at my face, then held out my hands again. "Please."

She hesitated, searching my face with her eyes. Then she thrust her baby into my arms and pointed down the lane where the others had gone. She pantomimed opening something: a gate? Then she motioned farther out, toward a ridge of hills beyond the village.

I began to fumble with a saddlebag, thinking to fashion a cradle there from our cloaks and blankets. The woman signaled me to wait and disappeared inside. The sounds of hoofbeats welled up, suddenly louder. *Hurry!* Then here she was, holding out a wide loop of cloth, knotted at one end. A sling. I took it, pushed my head and one arm through the loop, and set the baby inside.

"Go, Ziba! Run!"

I drove her down the lane, between clusters of fleeing townsfolk, their mantles billowing out behind them, their sandals kicking up clouds of dust. We scattered a small flock of goats and then, with the goatherd's shrill imprecations still in my ears, careened through the rear gate. I turned Ziba off the road; we jolted down the terraced hill toward the ridge where the woman had pointed. The baby began to fuss and cry. There was a din all behind us—a terrible din. *Women screaming* . . . Glancing back, I saw, through the open gate, moving glints of silver, flashes of red.

But no one pursuing. Not yet.

We crossed a shallow gorge; the sounds of the village faded behind. Ahead, as the ridge drew near, I saw that it was pockmarked with caves.

Quiet now. In his sling, the baby gulped little hiccoughing breaths but no longer cried. Wind rustled in the leaves of an olive tree; a curlew cried hauntingly from a ledge.

We came to a place where a cluster of cave openings pitted the face of the cliff. I whooshed Ziba down and dismounted. Babak, still awake, slid down after. I scanned along the way back to Bethlehem, searching for soldiers. None—but they might yet come. Many people had seen us there; many people had marked us heading for the rear gate. If the soldiers caught sight of Ziba, they would know where to hunt for us. I slapped her rump. "Go!" I said. "Get along!" She bleated reproachfully, then began to forage along the slope, among the clumps of dry grass.

I clambered up the hillside toward the largest cave opening. Babak clutched my hand and, favoring one foot, stumbled along behind.

CHAPTER 52

✳

THIS PERFECT DARK

Darkness swallowed us up, cool, familiar. The baby fussed softly. I cradled him in one arm and tucked Babak's hand between my elbow and my side. I felt my way along the rough rock walls, deep into the cave. Soon, the walls shrank close about us, and soon again, I had to stoop and bend down and crawl. "Go before us," I said to Babak. He obeyed without question— crouching at first, soon dropping to hands and knees.

The baby was unwieldy, hanging down from my body. His head wanted to loll sideways and spill out of the sling; his little feet kicked and thrust against me. Once, his head nearly struck the floor of the cave, and many times I bumped my elbow, scraped my arm. But my body soon remembered what it was to move groping through the dark, through a close, knee-gouging passage while holding treasure in one hand— food, or a lamp, or some prize I had stolen and retrieved to the City of the Dead.

There was a ringing in my ears, a faint, tinny ringing— some dim echo of the terrible din in Bethlehem—and the dank, cool smell of stone and earth. The baby grew silent, grew heavier, his head large and solid in my cupped hand. My knuckles and palms and knees all sang with pain.

And now I felt Babak halt before me, felt him sit down. I settled myself beside him, laid the baby in my lap. Babak leaned against me. I nuzzled the moist, downy hair on the back of his neck. With my fingers I traced the dimensions of the small cavern around us: floor and walls and ceiling.

It pressed in close, enfolded us like a womb.

I waited.

I felt them breathing against me, Babak and the baby, each in his own rhythm. I could see nothing in this perfect dark, but oddly, I did not crave a lamp. My mind's eye blinked open, and bright images swam before it. Of Suren and Zoya. Of Giv and Pacorus. Of Melchior, Gaspar, Balthazaar. Of Koosha and his kin. Of stars wheeling slowly across the great arc of the nighttime sky.

What was it all for, the far, blazing omens of the night and all of this long journey? So that three old men, each chasing his own dream, could pay homage to the son of a carpenter?

Melchior—dreaming of power.

Gaspar—dreaming of knowledge.

And Balthazaar. What did he dream of?

I wonder if the humbleness of this birth may be the very crux of the matter, he had said. *It has more to do* here, *with the heart.*

It occurred to me now that one might know a man from his dreams. That dreams, like stars, might make up an alphabet, a pattern of signs through which we might read the pulses of his heart, the temper of his soul.

And I . . .

What of *my* dream?

I had sent Suren in pursuit of it, and now he was lost. I had bled out Babak's spirit to buy it. Clinging to my dream, I had held myself and my noble kindred above those who had shown me kindness. I'd shown kindness only to Babak. And now—because of me—he, too, was lost.

There had been nothing of humbleness about my dream. There was heart in it, true—but twisted by bitterness.

Still, who wouldn't be bitter, in my shoes!

I could feel the rise and fall of the baby's breathing against my legs. I could feel the rise and fall of Babak's breathing against my side. How strange that the whole of my grand dream had come down to this, the rise and fall of two small boys' breath.

And the babies . . .

Beside me, Babak began to hum. He rocked, back and forth. Rocked and hummed. Hummed and rocked.

"Oh, Babak," I whispered.

He shifted, moaned, threw an arm about me. I embraced him close, leaned back against the cave wall. My eyes drifted shut.

I dreamed.

Mother comes to me first, walking across the garden, her gown swaying, her silver bracelets jingling, flashing in the bright morning light of Susa. I can smell her now; the scent of jasmine fills me up with a long-forgotten joy. I see her face clearly, as if through sun-dappled water: her arched brows and curving lips, the dimple on one cheek. She smiles at me and a golden warmth envelops me and I remember how it feels to be loved. And now my father comes to stand beside her, handsome and proud, and here is Suren, too. Suren! I want to ask him: Where have you been? Did they find you? Did they hurt you? Why did you not come for us?

And now my grandmother appears—silver haired and lively eyed. She kisses each one upon the cheek . . . and this is how she tells me they are dead.

"Sister!"

I opened my eyes to darkness. Chilly darkness. Something heavy on my chest—the baby. Someone's hand moving across my face.

"Sister!"

Babak's voice.

"Sister, listen," he said. "I had such a dream!"

Dream. I, too, had dreamed, the first one I could recall since Susa. I reached up to my face, found Babak's hand there, covered it with my own. Tears prickled at the corners of my eyes, spilled down onto my cheeks.

"Sister, don't cry. It was a splendid dream. I was walking down from a mountain, with many people. There was a leper;

he stood at the side of the road. He came to me and asked me to help him. I touched him, touched his face, and—"

I stiffened. "Babak, I told you, never, ever touch—"

His hand slipped out of mine. "It was a dream, Sister! I touched him, and the sickness on his skin was gone. And when I woke . . . I was *awake*. Not dreaming anymore."

"Not dreaming, Babak? Truly awake?"

I groped to find his hand again—to find both of his hands. There. So small, his hands. He had something clutched in one fist, something that felt soft. I tugged on it. "What's this?"

"Oh," he said, sounding surprised. Blindly, I coaxed his hand open. I took out what was there; it felt like a crumpled piece of cloth. I unfolded it, tried to *see* it with my fingertips. Yes, a bit of—not wool, but linen. Soft and threadbare, perhaps from many washings.

"It was in my boot," he said. "Squishing my toes. I pulled it out."

A piece of cloth?

I recalled Melchior, in our room this morning. *What are you doing?* I'd asked.

I'd searched all through Babak's clothes, but . . .

It was in my boot.

What had Gaspar said to Melchior? *You were bent over that baby far too long. What were you doing, I wonder?*

"Whose is it?" I asked Babak now. "Whose cloth?"

"I don't know," he said.

"Was it a man? Was it . . . a child?"

"I don't know. This time, I don't. It could have been a man. Or a boy. It could have been a woman or a girl. I don't know."

And then I remembered something else. *Before*, Melchior had said, *it was for me. Now it is for him.*

For Babak? Was that what he had meant?

"Can we go now, Sister? I'm hungry."

The baby stirred against my chest. I had forgotten about him, forgotten . . .

The soldiers. The babies.

Tears were streaming from my eyes. I gave myself over to them, began to shake apart with sobs. Crying for those babies. Crying for my mother and my father. Crying for Suren, for what I'd done to him. Crying for Babak, truly awake at last? Crying for the sight of my mother's face—still fresh in memory—and the warmth of her love.

And now another crying. The baby in my lap. Alive.

Two cryings, braiding round each other.

At last, I took a deep, juddering breath, then another.

"Sister." Babak found my hand. "Sister, let's go."

I followed him, crawling first, then stooping, and finally standing straight, groping back along the cave walls toward the heartbreaking light of the world.

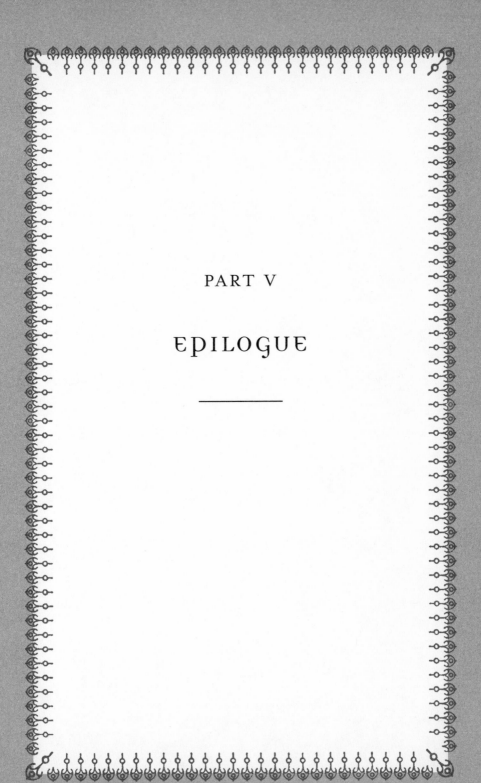

PART V

EPILOGUE

✳

CHAPTER 53

HOME

"Mitra! Mitra, come!"

Leah was calling me. I wiped the butter from my finger-tips, handed the pot to Babak. "Here, you finish with Ziba. I haven't yet swept the rooms."

I pulled a stool over so he could reach the mange high on the camel's shoulder. Babak stepped up and began slathering on the butter. "Is that better?" he asked. "Do you feel better now?"

Ziba groaned and snuffled in Babak's hair.

I watched Babak for a moment, let my eyes linger on the soft fullness of his face, the solidity of his body. It seemed he had grown a hand's length in just the past few months. Soon I would have to stitch a new band to the hem of his tunic.

"*Mitra!*"

"Coming!"

I slipped out the stable door and into the late-afternoon shadows that stretched across the courtyard of the caravansary. I wove among the travelers and their belongings—bundles and bales, crates of chickens, cooking pots, wine jugs, rolled-up carpets and beds. Leah stood at the top of the steps, waving the broom at me. "Sweep," she said. "A caravan comes."

Over the past months I had learned many words in their language. *Sweep* I knew well. And *caravan*. And *Mitra, come*. By now, my ears were nearly fluent in listening, but my tongue learned a good deal more slowly. *Thank you* I had learned early, for I had much cause to use it.

I took the broom from Leah; she relaxed her frown into a

fond smile and patted my cheek. "Hurry," she said—another word I had learned all too well.

As dust rose before my broom, I thought back to when we had first come here, to Bethany, this past autumn. Hannah—the kindly young woman in Bethlehem, the one whose baby we had taken to the cave—Hannah and her husband, Reuben, had brought us here when they left Bethlehem. They had had to leave. The sight of their live infant son had brought renewed grief to those who had lost theirs to Herod. It was too much to bear. Reuben had taken us to his brother Levi, who owned this caravansary, and to Leah, his wife.

Like their own two sons, Babak and I were expected to work—work hard—and received no pay beyond a room to stay in and food to eat. My waking hours were full of grinding grain and baking bread, of spinning thread and weaving cloth, of milking goats and drawing water. And sweeping! But Leah and Levi had treated us fairly and, over time, strong bonds of affection had grown among us. They even allowed me to take time from work to pray, and did not ask which god I prayed to. The Wise God, it was. It lent me comfort, praying.

Now, above the scratching of my broom, I heard the caravan coming through the gates and across the stones of the courtyard—the jingle of bells, the shouts of men, the groans of many camels. I wondered what this one would bring. Such far places the sojourners came from! India and Bactria, Egypt and Rome. I liked to watch them in their various garb, and to study the different shades of their skin and configurations of their faces. I liked to listen to the rhythms of exotic tongues.

But what I listened hardest for was the language of home. Such a comfort to the ear, the dear, familiar rhythms of Persia! And yet every time they caused a longing to rise in me, an aching in the heart.

I wished I could go to the gallery and look out, but the travelers would soon be wanting their rooms, and I was only halfway done with sweeping.

And so I was surprised when, not yet finished with the last

of the vacant rooms, I heard the jingle of Leah's ankle bracelet, saw her in the doorway. "Give me the broom, Mitra," she said. "Some sojourners are asking after you. Persians."

Persians? For me?

My mother's face leaped into my mind's eye, as clearly as if I had seen her only yesterday. And then my father's face, strong and grave. And Suren . . .

But no. I knew it could not be.

And then a frightening thought. *The Eyes and Ears of the king.*

Once, I had spoken to Levi about them, in case they should ever come to the inn. He did not think they would look for us here, nor recognize us if they found us. "But it is good you have told me," he had said. "There is need for vigilance."

"Did the travelers say who they are?" I asked Leah now.

"I know not. Levi said they were searching for you in Bethlehem, and someone told them to come here."

So Levi was with them. Good. Still . . . who might they be?

"Mitra? The broom?" Leah was holding out her hand to take it.

I blinked. "Oh," I said. "Here!"

I did not go directly to the stairs, but crept out on the gallery from a vacant room and peered down into the court-yard. Camels were kneeling as riders dismounted; men were unpacking, leading animals to the stables, fetching water. A group of men stood talking to Levi by the stairs. Persians, indeed; I could see it by the cut of their clothing. Women's garb here was not so very different from that of women in Persia, but I would never accustom myself to the men of this place, who kept their hair and beards short, and never wore trousers beneath their tunics, even when they rode!

But wait—the man who stood nearest to Levi . . .

Giv!

My feet sent me flying across the gallery and halfway down the stairs before I knew what I was doing. I slowed then, and straightened my headcloth, feeling suddenly shy as I walked down the remaining steps. "Giv?" I said.

They all turned, as a group: Levi, Giv, and three others. Giv's eyes widened; the whole of his ears and scalp seemed to shift. I let my eyes rest for a moment on his face, grown precious in memory: the high, jutting cheekbones; the slit in his nose; the deep furrows on either side of his habitual scowl. "Ramin," he said. "You are much changed."

I glanced down at my tunic and mantle—long, as women wear them. "I am Ramin no longer," I said. "Mitra is my name."

"Mitra." Giv made a small bow, as if introduced to me for the first time. "I did wonder. The name suits you." He hesitated. "And Babak?" he asked softly. "He is . . ."

"Well."

Giv drew together his eyebrows, as if he could not believe what I had said.

"Yes, truly he is whole and hale. You must come to him; he will be so glad to see you; he—"

"Mitra."

I turned to the one who had said it, a man not as tall as Giv. He was gazing at me intently, directly—most improperly!

"*Koosha!*"

I didn't realize I had said it aloud until he smiled, and I heard in my mind the echo of my voice.

"So I was afraid you wouldn't remember me, then," he said. "It's been long betweentimes, and you were a boy when last we met, as I recall."

I gaped at him. Having spoken without thought, I could not now think to speak.

One of the men sternly cleared his throat, and Koosha turned to him. "You recollect my father, Ardalan," he said to me. "And my uncle Kouros."

I nodded, shut my mouth. Now I recognized them as well. They, too, had been kind. Finding my voice at last, I asked after their journey; they said it had been long.

"But profitable," Koosha put in, smiling straight into my eyes.

Heat rose in my face. I looked away, but not before I saw Ardalan turn to glare at him.

"Come," Levi said amicably to the travelers in his heavily accented Persian. "Let us sit and talk together." Behind his back, he motioned me to go.

That night, wide awake and restless, I set a lamp beside Babak and sat watching him sleep.

A peaceful sleep.

Since the cave in Bethlehem he had had no dreams for others, no dreams of dreams that pointed to events to come. Sometimes I wondered if he missed it—the gift of prescient dreams. Dreams that powerful and wise men attended to. Dreams that made him a magical boy, unlike any other.

And sometimes it seemed that he did miss the gift. Twice, I had discovered, he had tried to make it come. Each time, he had stolen a sash from one of Levi's sons and slept with it next to his skin. Each time, he had been teased and had thought to find some way to tease back. But their dreams did not come to visit him.

I had scolded him severely when I found the sashes in our room, all the while thinking, *He would not have done this before. It would not have occurred to him.*

A large, pale moth now fluttered into the room. It made for the lamp flame, circling and bobbing. I shooed it away, jumped up, watched it fly back into the night. Then I paced back and forth, reflecting.

Babak was changed. No longer did the sight of a crippled bird cause him to sob inconsolably. Now he would pick it up and try to feed it. No longer did he seem to absorb the illnesses and injuries of others into himself. He was still a kindly boy—a thoughtful boy. There was a tenderness about him, but the boundaries between himself and others seemed firmer, more secure.

Yet he did have nightmares now—dreams of monsters, dreams of falling, dreams of burning fire. Leah had told me that all of her children had been visited by such dreams. Ordinary dreams.

Divining dreams were a grand and precious gift, like the gifts the Magi had brought to Bethlehem. But the freedom to dream ordinary dreams, dreams that were truly one's own— perhaps this was more precious still.

Footsteps on the stairs. I whirled round. It was Leah. "Levi wishes to speak with you," she said. "Go."

I ran.

Giv was there, sitting cross-legged on a woven mat beside Levi. Two lamps on bushels cast flickering shadows across the room. The men greeted me, then Levi nodded to Giv.

Giv wasted no time, but went straight to what he had to say. "When I saw that you and Babak were not in Melchior's caravan, I went back and searched for you along the road to Bethlehem and in Bethlehem itself. But I could not find you. So I returned with Melchior, journeyed up through Damascus and then Palmyra on the way back home. I searched for your kinsmen there." He hesitated. "I heard that they had moved on from Palmyra, and no one seemed to know where."

I swallowed, nodded. The fines houses and stately pillars of Palmyra had long ago faded from my imagination.

"Mitra," Giv said, and his voice was grave. "I did hear this: Your father, your mother, and your brother Suren are all dead. Killed by Phraates' men."

There was a strange, empty stillness inside me. "I know," I said.

Levi and Giv exchanged a glance.

"It was the king's Eyes and Ears who found Suren," Giv said. "Something he told them . . ." He cleared his throat.

I did not want to hear this, but I knew I must.

"Under torture, most like," he said gently. "*Something* must have sent them searching for Babak."

I bowed my head, a deep, familiar sadness dragging at me. I had known for some time what must have befallen Suren. I would always have to live with what I'd done to him.

Yet still . . .

It was also true, as Levi had said when I poured out my shameful story to him one night . . . It was also true that if I had done nothing, we all would have lived out the remainder of our lives in the City of the Dead.

"But these months past," Giv went on, "there have been rumors of fresh uprisings against Phraates. There are new enemies for the Eyes and Ears to ferret out, and I do not think they will spend much time searching for a boy of six years, last seen leaving Babylon, whose kinsmen are all dead or scattered."

So then, might we go back to Persia? The question leaped into my mind, but I didn't ask it aloud. It might seem ungrateful to Levi. Besides, we had no home there anymore, no kin.

"Melchior released me," Giv said.

I straightened, alert.

"You would hardly know him now," he continued. "He released most of his other servants as well. He prays to the Wise God without end and has given away the greater part of his possessions to the poor. Some say he has become feebleminded; others say bedeviled. And yet he seems not so to me. Surely he is not now such a vainglorious man as he once was. It might be that he is well on his way to becoming . . . wise.

"After he let me go, I journeyed toward Bethlehem to see again if I could find you. I happened upon Ardalan and his family in a caravansary just west of Ecbatana. And they, too, were on their way—to find you."

Koosha. It came to me with sudden certainty.

"To find me?" I repeated. I must have sounded simple.

"Yes. You," Giv said, "and Babak as well. It is the custom of the men of their tribe to find wives outside the village. This Koosha is a very resolute young man, and he has made his choice."

Koosha!

They all regarded me, seemed to wait for me to speak. I opened my mouth, but no words issued forth. I swallowed.

"Mitra." Levi spoke to me in his own tongue. His voice was gentle. "How do you find this Koosha?"

"I . . . I do not know him well," I said, switching back to Levi's language. "But . . ."

I recalled his patient way with Babak, and that night when he told of his village. And then later, how he had looked at me—had *seen* me. *You are entirely yourself,* he had said, *no matter how you hide.*

"But you do know Giv," Levi was saying. "Do you trust him?"

Giv was not my kinsman. But after all we had been through together . . . "Yes," I said.

"Giv speaks well of Koosha, and of his father and his uncle. Though . . ." Levi turned to Giv, addressed him in Persian. "How well do you know Koosha and his kin?"

"Not well," Giv admitted. "But I am a fair judge of character, and I deem they are good men. I am thinking perhaps I will travel with them for a while. They have said I would be welcome."

"Hmm." Levi rubbed at his beard, close cropped but beginning to curl. "Mitra." He spoke again in his own tongue. "Though we are fond of you and Babak, we would not hold you here against your will. And yet to send you off to live with strangers . . . it likes me not. And yet again, I have often thought you missed your own people, your own land. I have need of your help, Mitra, if I am to decide what is best for you. What say you?"

This had come upon me all in a rush; my mind kicked up hopes and fears as a caravan kicks up dust. "I would like," I said in Persian, "a day or so. To think."

Levi nodded. "This is a weighty matter. That seems wise."

I returned to our room. The day's events still roiled about in my mind; I could not sleep. I stole out onto the gallery, climbed the stairs to the roof. It was cool now, although summer was coming on, and the night air lacked the bite it had had of late. I lay on my back and gazed up at the stars, large and moist and bright.

I thought about our journey, born of dreams and stars. I remembered our home in Susa and our chamber in the City of the Dead. I thought about Palmyra, of the home I had yearned to find there.

But there was no home in Palmyra for us. Our kinsmen . . . All scattered, Giv had said. Or dead.

Only Babak and I were left.

Babak. For the thousandth time I wondered about that dream he'd had of the leper, about the cloth in the toe of his boot. Had Babak's illness healed of itself, as Balthazaar had said might happen? Or had it been the dream?

Whose dream?

The dream of an infant king? Or . . .

I sighed, rose, dusted myself off. I'd leave that to the wise men to answer. Let *them* decipher the mysteries of God's alphabet writ across the heavens! Babak was well—to me, that was what truly mattered.

And yet I had a decision to make.

I sighed again, and headed back down to my pallet.

In time, I slept.

And dreamed.

I am walking up a path toward a village in the mountains. A clear brook gurgles its way among the red mudbrick houses, and late-summer sunlight lies warm upon my shoulder. Around the edges of the village I see groves of almond and apricot and pomegranate trees; flat, round baskets of fruit lie drying on the rooftops. A breeze begins to stir, and the soughing of the willows near the brook, and of the trees in the grove that surrounds us, makes music lovelier than that of any lute. As I watch, the people of the village come out in twos and threes upon their terraces; they look down and smile at me. Friends. Beloved friends. And here is Koosha, walking down the village road toward me with Babak there beside him. Babak runs to me, takes my hand, and tugs me toward Koosha.

I stop for a moment, inhale a deep, sweet breath of mountain air, try to take in the whole of the scene before me.

It looks like nothing so much as home.

The story of the Magi's journey to Bethlehem has fascinated me ever since I was a child. These three exotic figures showed up once a year in our church Christmas pageant, wreathed in clouds of incense and wearing the best costumes in the show. There was something romantic and mysterious about them. Where did they come from? Were they wise men, kings, or both? How long had their journey taken? Did the star lead them the whole way? What did they expect to find? Each December the Magi materialized again out of the candlelit darkness . . . and disappeared all too soon.

In *Alphabet of Dreams* I have approached the Magi's story as a writer of fiction. I have tried to stay as true as possible to the story told in the Gospel according to Matthew, but to fill in with research and imagination the answers to some of my childhood questions.

As I wrote and thought about the story, many other questions occurred to me. I'll share some of them here, as well as others that might occur to readers.

Is the story of the journey of the Magi based upon well-known historical fact?
Of the books of the Bible chronicling Jesus's life, only two—Matthew and Luke—tell of Jesus's birth, and only one—Matthew—mentions the Magi. As far as I know, there are no other accounts of the Magi's journey to Bethlehem from anyone writing at or near the time of Jesus. But the historical record of such events during this time is sketchy, to say the least.

Matthew's story is a religious one, and people look at religious stories in different ways. Some accept them literally, on faith. Others believe that the Bible contains folklore, parable, and fiction as well as history.

Which of these is the story of the Magi? There seems to be no independent historical proof that the Magi's journey either did or didn't happen. To my mind, each reader is free to decide for himself.

And the massacre of the innocents? Did that really happen?
Although the ancient Jewish historian Flavius Josephus wrote much about the last years of Herod the Great, recounting many of his terrible deeds, he never told of this event. To my knowledge there is no other historical evidence of a massacre of children in Bethlehem, nor does it appear elsewhere in the New Testament.

Nevertheless, it seems to me that the massacre of the innocents is an integral part of Matthew's story of the Magi.

What about the other characters in the book? Which ones actually existed?
Only the kings—Phraates and Herod. There are allusions to actual kings of ancient Persia—Cyrus, Darius, and Mithradates. The rest, I made up.

What was the star of Bethlehem?
Some people believe it was a miraculous occurrence, unconnected with ordinary celestial events. Others suggest that it may have been something governed by the known laws of the universe: a comet, the aurora borealis, a nova or supernova explosion, the occultation of a planet or star by another body, or a conjunction—two planets coming so close together that they appear to the naked eye to be a single larger and brighter star.

I am neither an astronomer, an astrologer, a theologian, nor a historian. So I'm not qualified to choose knowledgeably among the many theories put forth and passionately defended by experts in these fields. Besides, to be honest, while I find the issue of identifying the precise nature of the star to be interesting, I don't think it's critical for my purposes here. I am more concerned with finding meaning, in human terms, in the story of the Magi's journey. And, of course, with its possibilities for fiction.

I liked the idea of a real celestial event, so I picked a theory that seemed fascinating, complex, and compatible with my ideas for the book. This theory, which has been around a long time, is set forth and further developed by P. A. H. Seymour in *The Birth of Christ: Exploding the Myth*.

Basically, according to Seymour, the star of Bethlehem was in fact a conjunction of two planets—Jupiter and Saturn—in 7 B.C. To the naked eye the two planets would have appeared as a single, bright star. Definitely bright enough to notice, but not terribly alarming or remarkable if you didn't know what you were looking for.

Jupiter's rising, says Seymour, was associated in ancient times with the birth of a king or leader. Saturn was considered to be the protector of the Jews. The conjunction took place in the constellation of Pisces, and Jerusalem, according to Seymour, was thought to be under the influence of Pisces.

So, taking this all together, we have: the birth of a Jewish king or leader, somewhere near Jerusalem. For most of their journey the Magi wouldn't literally have had to "follow the star." They could have followed where the "star" *indicated.*

What would have made this conjunction even more significant to the ancients, according to Seymour, was that it didn't happen just once. It was what's known as a triple conjunction; in other words, this same conjunction occurred three times within a single year. Seymour suggests that the Magi may actually have seen the first conjunction, which occurred on May 27. Then, with their considerable knowledge of mathematical astronomy, they may have been able to predict the other two: October 6 and December 1.

I liked this idea! So, in *Alphabet of Dreams* the Magi set out in early fall, their curiosity piqued, perhaps, by their having witnessed the first conjunction. As in Matthew's story, they miss the actual birth of Jesus—which Seymour claims, for reasons too complicated to go into here, took place on September 15. Matthew never makes clear exactly how late his Magi were; my Magi miss the birth by a number of weeks.

For much of the Magi's journey Jupiter and Saturn would have appeared to be very close to each other in the nighttime sky. In fact, for a great deal of that time the two planets would have been so near as to look, to the naked eye, like a single star.

Jim Todd, manager of the Murdock Planetarium at the Oregon Museum of Science and Industry, kindly gave me a computer disk with a schematic of ancient skies, based upon a computer modeling. From the vantage point of Jerusalem on September 15, 7 B.C., Jupiter and Saturn do indeed appear as a single star, the brightest object in the sky.

Incidentally, December 25 is never mentioned in the Bible as the date of Jesus's birth; nor is the year, nor even the time of year in which he was born. December 25 was not established as Jesus's official birthday until much later, perhaps the third century A.D.

Who might the Wise Men have been?
Matthew never says how many Wise Men there were, nor from whence they came, other than "from the east." Over the centuries much legend, speculation, and embroidery has attached itself to these mysterious figures. The second-century theologian Tertullian claimed the Magi were "almost kings," and, with the passing of several centuries, belief in their kingship became prevalent. According to J. Ross Wagner of the Princeton Theological Seminary, a contributing source of the tradition that the Wise

Men were kings was a "widespread ancient Christian reading of Isaiah 60:1–6 as a prophesy of the Messiah's birth." Although early accounts of the Wise Men's numbers ranged from as high as fourteen to as low as two, the third-century theologian Origen opined that there were three of them—presumably because of the three gifts mentioned by Matthew—and that number seems to have stuck. By the sixth century they had acquired names: Gaspar (or Caspar), Melchior, and Balthazaar. In the Middle Ages they were regarded as saints; supposedly their relics were removed to Cologne Cathedral in A.D. 1162. Alternatively, Marco Polo claimed they were buried in Saveh, Iran.

As to precisely where in "the east" they hailed from, some scholars and theologians have thought perhaps it was Arabia or the Syrian Desert, because gold and frankincense were associated with desert camel trains from Arabia. Others have assumed that the Wise Men must have been from Babylon, because the Babylonians, or Chaldeans, were well known for their expertise in astronomy and astrology. Still others, taking their cue from *magoi*—the word used for the Wise Men in the early, Greek version of Matthew's Gospel—make the case for a Persian origin.

Again, I am no scholar. But ever since writing *Shadow Spinner* I have been fascinated with Persian (Iranian) history. Also, the idea of a boy with the ability to dream for others came from a book by an Iranian scholar and friend—Abbas Milani's *Tales of Two Cities*. So I liked the idea of Persian *magoi*.

According to many historians, the *magoi*—or, as we spell the word in English today, "Magi,"—were probably members of an ancient Persian priestly caste. Although the original Magi were priests of an older, Indo-Iranian religion, over time they became identified with Zoroastrianism.

During the reign of the emperor Justinian, mosaics on the basilica at Bethlehem showed the Magi in Persian dress: trousers, belted tunics with full sleeves, and pointed caps. In A.D. 614 the Persian army overran Palestine, destroying many churches. But, evidently because of the mosaics depicting their countrymen, they spared the Bethlehem church.

In time the word "Magi" (singular: "Magus") became more broadly applied—not just to a Persian caste or Zoroastrians, but generally to people who were skilled in various kinds of secret lore and magic, including astrology and the reading of dreams. Indeed, the word "Magi" is at the root of our words "magic" and "magician." However, in this book I've kept to a narrower interpretation, that of Persian Zoroastrian priests.

288

For an excellent discussion of the Magi, the star, and other related matters, see *The Birth of the Messiah,* by Raymond E. Brown.

What religious beliefs might the Magi—and other characters—have held at that time?
There is some scholarly disagreement about the prevalence of actual Zoroastrianism in Persia's Parthian era. Most agree that, while Zoroastrianism was evolving, Persia seems to have had a mixture of religious beliefs and practices during the time of this story. In writing this book I've imagined that the Magi practiced a form of Parthian-era Zoroastrianism. But for the other characters religion is much less rigorous and pure, and mingles aspects of Zoroastrianism with local, Indo-Iranian, and/or Greek deities and practices.

According to scholar Mary Boyce, Zoroaster, in a departure from the old polytheistic Indo-Iranian tradition, proclaimed Ahura Mazda, the All Wise, to be "the one uncreated God . . . creator of all else that is good" and "from whom all other beneficent divine beings emanated." On the other hand was Angra Mainyu, "equally uncreated, but ignorant and wholly malign."

Zoroaster's ethical code requires good thoughts, good words, and good deeds. Paradise may be attained by women as well as men, servants as well as masters. Judgment occurs at the end of life and is determined by the sum of people's thoughts, words, and deeds.

Boyce says that in offering the hope of heaven to everyone—not just the upper classes—Zoroaster was breaking with the ancient tradition of his time and place, in which the priests and aristocrats got special treatment by God. In addition, Zoroaster threatened the mighty with the prospect of hell. His doctrines "were thus doubly calculated to outrage the privileged," says Boyce.

I am intrigued by Zoroaster's inclusiveness, because this story concerns the birth of Jesus, who also favored the humble and outraged the powers-that-be. Of course, this can be said as well of the great prophets of many religions!

What actual places might the Magi have visited?
I wanted to travel along a portion of the route the Magi might have taken, so late in 2002 I went with my sister Laura Clemens to Iran. (Iraq was not a possibility. The United States was moving toward an invasion of Iraq at the time. Our Iranian guide, when asked by my intrepid sister

if we might go there, assured us that we would be shot at the border.)

Here are a few notes on specific places mentioned in *Alphabet of Dreams*.

Rhagae. Located on the site of modern-day Rey, a suburb of Tehran, Rhagae was a flourishing city during the time in which this book takes place. Today there is an ongoing excavation in Cheshmeh Ali, a site with Parthian and other ruins, on the grounds of ancient Rhagae. There is no large complex of caves resembling the City of the Dead at this site at present, but Iranian archaeologist Jafar Mehr Kian says it's plausible that there may have been such caves two thousand years ago.

The marsh. Many thousands of years ago, an inland sea covered a large area to the south of Tehran. Today it's a vast salt desert. During Parthian times most of the lake was gone, but according to Mehr Kian, it's probable that there were large marshy areas in the vicinity. The geography of Iran during Parthian times was, he says, significantly wetter than today.

Sava, or modern Saveh. According to *The Travels of Marco Polo*, "In Persia is the city called Saveh, from which the three Magi set out when they came to worship Jesus Christ."

The fortress. The idea for this fortress came from Paul William Roberts's *In Search of the Birth of Jesus*. Roberts, having read about a castle of the "Fire Worshippers" in Polo's *Travels*, went to the area near Saveh and found a stunning ancient fortress with architectural elements suggestive of Zoroastrianism.

While my sister and I were in Saveh, we could not find anyone who knew of this fortress. However, its presence was later supported by Mehr Kian, who says that it's likely the site known in Iran as Kaleh Dasht.

Qanats. Traveling across the Iranian plateau, we saw what looked like giant anthills strung out across the desert. These are openings into qanats, underground irrigation systems. Qanats are constructed by digging a vertical well into a mountain spring, then creating a horizontal underground tunnel that transports the water into dryer areas. Vertical shafts are dug all along the course of the tunnel—like the shaft into which Babak escapes. There are hundreds of miles of qanats in Iran, many of them thousands of years old.

Ecbatana. Modern-day Hamadan. Although many of Ecbatana's ancient treasures reside in museums far from Iran, today visitors can still stroll through the site of the old palace and, elsewhere in the city, view Parthian-era stone sculptures.

Anahita's temple and Bisitun. Anahita's temple is located in modern Kangavar. We found mostly a field of broken stone columns there, hints of lost ancient splendor.

Near Bisitun I was surprised to see—far below the ancient bas-relief carvings of Persian kings high up on the side of a mountain—a sculpture of the Greek hero-god Hercules. Somehow, in the intermingling of Greek and Persian culture and religion after Alexander the Great, Hercules had become identified with an ancient Persian deity, a sort of patron saint for travelers.

The Village of the Red Mountain. Finally, in one of those fortuitous incidents that sometimes befall travelers, my seatmate on the plane into Tehran, an Iranian professor, insisted that we must see the ancient village of Abyaneh. Although this seemed to have nothing to do with the story of the Magi, I asked our guide if we might swing by there, and she agreed. I was charmed by Abyaneh—by the stream that gurgled through the village, by the ancient red mudbrick dwellings that nestled into the mountain-side, by the lovely carved doors, by the bright traditional clothing of the inhabitants. Abyaneh lodged in my imagination and emerged as Koosha's "Village of the Red Mountain," and as the answer that comes to Mitra in her final dream.

Matthew's Magi remain mysterious figures. While all certain knowledge of them has been veiled by the passage of millennia, human imagination has brought them vibrantly to life. I have enjoyed continuing in this tradition, and dreaming of the children who might have joined them on their journey.

Works Cited in Author's Note and Books for Further Reading

Bowersack, G. W., Peter Brown, and Oleg Graber. *Late Antiquity: A Guide to the Postclassical World.* Cambridge, MA: Harvard University Press, Belknap Press, 1999.

Boyce, Mary. *Zoroastrians: Their Religious Beliefs and Practices.* London: Routledge, 1979.

Brown, Raymond E. *The Birth of the Messiah: A Commentary on the Infancy Narratives in the Gospels of Matthew and Luke.* New York: Doubleday, 1993.

Bulliet, Richard. *The Camel and the Wheel.* New York: Columbia University Press, 1990.

Campbell, Joseph. *The Masks of God: Occidental Mythology.* New York: Penguin, 1976. First published 1962 by Viking.

Colledge, Malcom A. R. *The Parthians.* Ancient Peoples and Places 59. New York: Frederick A. Praeger, 1967.

Comay, Joan, and Ronald Browinrigg, eds. *Who's Who in the Bible.* New York: Bonanza, 1980.

Frye, Richard N. *The Heritage of Persia.* London: Cardinal, 1976.

Herodotus. *The History: Herodotus.* Translated by David Grene. Chicago: University of Chicago Press, 1987.

Hughes, David. *The Star of Bethlehem Mystery.* London: J. M. Dent, 1979.

Isidore, of Charax. *Parthian Stations.* Translated by Wilfred H. Schoff. Chicago: Ares, 1914.

Martin, Ernest L. *The Star That Astonished the World.* Portland, OR: ASK Publications, 1991.

Milani, Abbas. *Tales of Two Cities: A Persian Memoir.* Washington, DC: Mage, 1996.

Oates, Joan. *Babylon.* Rev. ed. New York: Thames and Hudson, 1986.

Polo, Marco. *The Travels of Marco Polo.* Translated by Ronald Latham. London: Penguin, 1958.

Roberts, Paul William. *In Search of the Birth of Jesus.* New York: Riverhead, 1995.

Sanders, E. P. *Judaism: Practice and Belief, 63 BCE-66 CE.* Philadelphia: Trinity Press International, 1992.

Seymour, P. A. H. *The Birth of Christ: Exploding the Myth.* London: Virgin Publishing, 1998.

Van Dyke, Henry. *The Story of the Other Wise Man.* Orleans, MA: Paraclete Press, 1984.

Yarshater, Ehsan, ed. *The Seleucid, Parthian, and Sasanian Periods.* Vol. 3, *The Cambridge History of Iran.* Cambridge, MA: Cambridge University Press, 1983.

✶ ACKNOWLEDGMENTS ✶

Many wise men and women came to my aid as I wrote this book! They deserve credit for what I got right; any mistakes I may have made are mine alone. My heartfelt gratitude goes to Hossein Ebrahimi (Elvand), founder of the House of Translation in Tehran, Iran, for his valuable and generous assistance. He vetted the manuscript twice; made insightful suggestions; answered many rounds of questions; provided me with relevant books, maps, and a CD-ROM; and consulted experts on my behalf. Thanks, too, to historian Saeed Vaziry and archaeologist Jafar Mehr Kian, who provided information through Mr. Ebrahimi.

I am once again indebted to Abbas Milani of Stanford University, who graciously vetted the manuscript, offered information, suggested references, and came up with brilliant insights. What's more, the idea of a child who dreams for others came from Dr. Milani's remarkable book *Tales of Two Cities*.

And many thanks to J. Ross Wagner of the Princeton Theological Seminary, who also vetted the manuscript and offered suggestions, citing passages from numerous scholarly texts and referring me to many Web sites for further information. I am so grateful to have received the benefit of his wisdom, expertise, and kindness.

I am grateful as well to my sister Laura Clemens for her support, encouragement, and courage on our journey to Iran. And I appreciate the knowledge and patience of our Iranian guide, Leili Shahabi Haghighi. My appreciation goes as well to my friend Zohre Darai Bullock, who gave me warm support and excellent suggestions, including Mitra's name.

I am very grateful to Ginee Seo for the painstaking care she took with the manuscript, her wise editorial guidance, and her penetrating insight. Many thanks go to my agent, Emilie Jacobson, for her patient and judicious shepherding of this project over many years, and to Dave Barbor for his hard work and faith in the book. Also, heartfelt thanks to my dear friends Margaret Bechard and

Ellen Howard for reading the manuscript and offering much-needed encouragement and inspired advice.

Much, much gratitude to my husband, Jerry, for steadfastly being there through all the challenges and for being a wonderful sounding board!

Jim Todd, Manager of the Murdock Planetarium at the Oregon Museum of Science and Industry, shared his knowledge, suggested references, and gave me a CD showing the positions of the stars over Bethlehem on the date in question. Eric Kimmel, ever supportive, entrusted me with precious books from his personal library. My aunt, Lois Dowey, kindly expended much energy and influence to come to my aid. Todd Feinman, reference librarian at the Lake Oswego Library, spent untold hours digging up invaluable information. Nancy Borman of Mary Woodward Elementary School lent me a fascinating glimpse into the world of five-year-olds. Jeffrey Arnold generously gave me the benefit of his wide knowledge and suggested many books and references. Writer Laura Greene directed me to valuable references as well. Julie Olson gave me insight into the experience of riding camels in the Middle East, and Cynthia Whitcomb offered a very unusual perspective on the setting of the novel. Amy Hultzman and Terry Moore shared their extensive knowledge of camels, led me on an adventure in the desert, and taught me how to ride the gentle giant, Clyde.

Last but not least, many thanks to the perpetrators of "donkey day": the organizers, Winifred Morris and Margaret Bechard; the intrepid pilot, Lee Boekelheide; the encouraging companion, Dorothy Morrison; the donkey owners, Claudia Layman and Veronica (Ronnie) Johnson; and the donkeys themselves, Cochatopa Ruby and Jenny.

Thank you, one and all!

DATE DUE		
JAN 1 7 2007		
FEB 2 8 2007		
JAN 7 2008		
SEP 1 4 2009		
SEP 0 4 2018		
JAN 1 8 2019		
GAYLORD		PRINTED IN U.S.A.